POSSESSED by SHADOWS

POSSESSED by SHADOWS

a novel by

Donigan Merritt

Other Press • New York

Copyright © 2005 Donigan Merritt

Production Editor: Mira S. Park

Book design by Kaoru Tamura

This book was set in 11 pt. Caslon 540 BT by Alpha Graphics of Pittsfield, NH.

10 9 8 7 6 5 4 3 2 1

Library of Congress Cataloging-in-Publication Data

    Merritt, Donigan.
    Possessed by shadows : a novel / by Donigan Merritt.
      p. cm.
    ISBN 1-59051-158-1 (hardcover : alk. paper) 1. Mountaineers—Fiction.
  2. Mountaineering—Fiction. 3. Loss(Psychology)—Fiction. I. Title.
    PS3613.E7765P67 2005
    813'.6—dc22

                           2004015812

But you now, dear girl, whom I loved like a flower whose name
I didn't know, you who so early were taken away:
I will once more call up your image and show it to them,
beautiful companion of the unsubduable cry.

Dancer whose body filled with your hesitant fate,
Pausing, as though your young flesh had been cast in bronze;
grieving and listening—. Then, from the high dominions,
unearthly music fell into your altered heart.

Already possessed by shadows, with illness near,
your blood flowed darkly; yet though for a moment suspicious,
it burst out into the natural pulses of spring.

Again and again interrupted by downfall and darkness,
earthly, it gleamed. Till, after a terrible pounding,
it entered the inconsolably open door.

The Sonnets to Orpheus
Rainer Maria Rilke

This is the day it began: November 15, 1988.

The sun appeared red through a thin haze. It was cool during the night and at dawn. The diffused sun, oblique and behind, stretching our washed-out shadows far along the ridge, began to feel warm. Around us dew condensed like primordial ooze. Molly went ahead with the rucksack and I had the ropes. She stopped for a lizard. It watched her and waited, not moving until she stepped by, then it scampered into the brush beside the narrow trail. A swift dived down the crag's steep face, and much higher a red-tailed hawk patrolled.

I remember detail because it is all so horribly true. I wish to be simply making it up for you, making a better story, although what could possibly be the point? I could tell you how our breaths still smelled of coffee, how a string dangling from the hem of her khaki shorts drew my attention to it time and time again, the raspy sound made by rocks under our boots . . . every trivial and ominous minute of that day.

We were at Tahquitz, in the mountains east of Los Angeles. There are hundreds of established climbing routes among its torn mountains and piles of granite boulders. We were hiking up to climb a route on a crag known as Vaginal Wall, a route called The Screaming Meanies. Many of these routes, probably most, because often they had been put up by teenage boys, had sexual names and were not very complimentary to women. Molly hated that.

The route actually began very high on the wall, ending up at the summit of the mountain ridge nearest the road. To reach it we would first have to climb a hand-width, zigzag split on a dihedral called Creep Crack. This ended at a bulging boulder with a flattened top which served as the belay anchor stand for The Screaming Meanies. So many rock shoes had shuffled around atop that boulder that it was as clean as the floor in a monk's cell. A pair of bolts with a rappel ring was attached to the wall, and from there you could either rappel down or use the ring to secure an anchor and continue up.

We went that way. Up.

Molly commented about the haze as she looked across the valley westward toward Los Angeles. She stepped into her harness and wiggled into the leg loops. Yesterday it rained, so by rights we should have had a clear day, but a wind from the desert side of the mountains accounted for both the steadily increasing warmth and the dust that hazed the view. She finished securing her harness and began shaking kinks from the rope, flaking it in big loops by her feet. I looked her over unobtrusively to make sure she had doubled back the harness belt. She didn't like to be reminded of things she thought of as obvious—she took it as criticism, as if she were too stupid to notice. But I know good climbers who have been killed or injured because they made a silly mistake, a mistake of familiarity. Once, when I was in the army, I jumped from the door of a C-119 holding the unattached static line in my hand. I had to come down on the reserve chute.

I put together a rack of various pieces of protection—hexes, cams, nuts, Friends—and clipped them to loops around my harness. We had climbed this route a few months ago and I knew what to take.

Molly stopped and took a bottle of aspirin from the pack and I asked if her head was hurting again. She said, "It comes and goes." She said she was all right with it. She was not prone to headaches, but lately, from time to time, she got them in the mornings. A few days ago she began feeling nauseous with the headaches, so we were wondering, full of hope, if maybe she was pregnant. She took a couple of aspirin and put the bottle away. She said, "Better living through chemistry."

The air was thin, washed out, drained of its character by the desert. I could see our red truck parked on the road far below, and now other cars were there. A motorcycle, the apparent size of a Monopoly game piece and sounding like a distant lawnmower, followed the winding road. Thick, high scrub brush obscured much of the main trail, so we couldn't see anyone else coming up, although now and then we could hear karabiners clinking together, occasional indistinct voices, and once a high-pitched pig squeal sort of laughter. Many climbers come here.

Molly spotted someone on Peter's Peter, a remarkably erect, free-standing phallic rock that marked the main trail's midway point. He moved well and we watched him get over the upper rib, known as the Foreskin Roll.

The Screaming Meanies is not so difficult. It's two pitches, about two full rope lengths, but you can't see much of the second pitch because the wall overhangs halfway above the belay anchor. It is wildly exposed, which is its thrill, since it's not really hard. If you're interested in the numbers, it's rated 5.8 on the Yosemite scale, but everyone grants that the crux move, that one move at the overhang, is 5.10.

"Shall we give it a go?" I said.

"Aye, aye, Captain," she mock-saluted.

I moved to the wall, karabiners clinking. In her journal, which you will be able to read here, Molly wrote that the pinging of metal against metal rendered to her images of a knight's armor. It is that kind of sound. She had already started a figure-eight knot before handing the working end of the rope to me. I fed the rope through my harness and finished the knot. Molly tugged on the sling that anchored her to the

3

belay ledge, then clipped it into the karabiner on her harness loop. I outweighed her by 25 kilos, but she was used to holding me.

The first move is easy, just a step up, like a rock ladder. That's the fool's step. Climbers have been tricked by the beginning, and later horrified when they got to the first pitch crux to find themselves clinging to the fragile edge of nothing with a vast emptiness yawning below. After three easy moves there's a lunge to a rock nub that's only big enough for about three fingertips, but you can get half of one foot into a deep pocket. After that you can put in the first piece of protection.

The route follows a four centimeter crack shaped like a comic book lightning bolt all the way up and across—a short traverse—to the beginning of the overhang. After that there is a long 75-degree slab of pockmarked granite. When I reached the end of the first pitch, I clipped into the anchor bolt and got ready to bring Molly up. Molly, some 35-meters below, looked like a doll, the rope umbilical, like twine dangling to tease a kitten. She told me there was a lot of slack in the rope so I took it up.

That November we had been climbing together for nine years, since we were married. Actually before that. We met at Joshua Tree in the winter of 1978 and married at the end of that summer, when Molly was 23 and I was 33. That day on The Screaming Meanies, Molly was 33 and the best female climber I have ever known. Only on routes that demanded pure strength could I outclimb her. We exemplified the profound difference between finesse and power. She moved like a squirrel through tree limbs, while I, who came to climbing later than she, moved more like a bear.

The belay ledge was about the width of my feet and only long enough for two people to stand side by side. Because we had started from a ledge called The Sidewalk, we called this belay station, The Curb. If there was another name we didn't know it.

At waist height were two bolts, and because there were enough opportunities to place removable protection, those were the only bolts from start to finish. They were only used for the belay anchors. On principle Molly and I did not climb routes that used bolts for protection. Molly picked this up from her father, who said that if you can't climb a particular route without drilling holes into the wall, don't climb that route. Some routes along this crag already looked like they had Frankenstein stitches running up them. There has to be some limits, I think, otherwise climbers might as well bring a jackhammer and cut steps into the wall.

Molly rigged the rucksack to the rope and I brought it up, then I tossed the rope back to her. I belayed her using a figure-eight descender and she came up pretty fast, only stopping to take out the protection I had placed coming up. I could lean out and watch her ascent. I said she was the best female climber I'd ever known, which isn't precisely true. There are better climbers, the young rock gymnasts who win contests and get their pictures in climbing magazines, who even in lycra cannot always be distinguished from boys. Molly could under no circumstances be mistaken for a boy. But maybe we don't want to count those magazine climbers, who treat rock climbing as a sport, something cool and a bit esoteric, like lacrosse. Being on rocks was the natural world for Molly. She climbed as an act of love. I climbed because I needed something from it. Her mountains were in her heart, mine in my head.

Metal to metal noises tumbled down from somewhere higher. Other climbers were probably on the summit ridge, and hikers as well. You could walk off the mountain on its back side; a popular trail went that way.

A few months ago after finishing this same route, Molly and I encountered two hikers coming up the foot path. "How did you get here?" one of the women asked. "We climbed up from over there," I answered, inclining my head toward the thin air over the cliff. "My God! But why?" she wondered. "You can walk right up here on the trail." I didn't have an answer for that. What sort of answer could there be to such a question? So I shrugged and Molly put her hand on my shoulder proprietarily.

I could see the top of Molly's head not far below, her straight sandy hair tied in a ponytail and a white sweatband circling her head like a halo. Pieces of retrieved gear danced out and back from the loops on her harness as she pushed herself off the rock to make the next move. The sling across her chest made her breasts pronounced in an attractive way.

To make it over the bulging lip at the end of the pitch it was necessary to hook one foot over the ledge and sort of heave yourself over by grabbing a rock horn on the ledge itself. I reminded Molly of this and she said, "Don't tell me how to climb." She was right. I wouldn't tell Picasso how to paint.

She maneuvered herself onto the ledge. As soon as she stood, I clipped her to the anchor. A bead of sweat tracked along the bridge of her nose and I watched it fall from the tip. I asked if she wanted the lead.

She flashed a smile and said, "I'd rather look up at your cute ass," which was her way of apologizing for snapping at me before. I did a hoochie-koochie dance and nearly lost my balance. Molly instinctively grabbed my arm and told me to stop showing off.

In a few minutes she was ready to belay me on the next pitch, which would take us out at the top of the summit ridge, from where we could walk off the back side of the mountain. The slab stretched above us like the side of a skyscraper and the sun was now bright and hot beyond the top. It was going to be hot walking down. But that wasn't the time to be thinking about going down, since a lot of up remained. I liked the pitch. It had great holds, good pockets for the toes. It was slightly off vertical, a bit less than 90 degrees in most places. Near the top, the wall fell away to a featureless slab, but at an angle that made friction climbing possible. Finally, one dangerous slick spot about three meters from the top.

I first heard them when I got to the slab. I suppose they were attracted to noises from below and had approached the ledge to look over. Sometimes people would try to see the climbers by looking down from the hiking trail, and I expected to see a screaming body come flying by. But usually all that came over the edge was debris knocked down by their feet, which is what happened.

I yelled up and told them to be careful. A shower of dirt and pebbles fell over me and I ordered them in no uncertain terms to get back.

"Sorry," a female voice answered.

Then the rock came over and flew by me. I saw it from the corner of my eye and turned to watch it sail into space. It was oblong, the size of a softball. I screamed "Rock!" as it disappeared beyond the bulging overhang about five meters below. Then the rope jerked and almost popped me off the wall. Seconds later I heard the rock crashing through the brush and shattering into pieces that pinged against rocks and clunked against trees. A whiff of flint, a gunpowder smell filled the air. Bits of grass and pebbles kept falling from the top. A woman asked if everything was okay and then a man said in an almost jovial tone, "Sorry about that."

"Just get the fuck away from the edge," I screamed.

Because of the overhang I couldn't see anything but air, and couldn't lean far back because I was barely hanging on by fingertips. I yelled down to ask Molly if she was all right. She didn't answer. I already knew she wasn't okay because the rope was slack and offered no resistance when I tugged on it. From this point I could only go up. I was less than five meters from the top and clearly I no longer had a belay. The best way to get to Molly was to finish the route and then rappel down to her.

The slab was dirty from debris and my heart pumped like a burdened engine as I felt my rock slippers losing their grip. I think only momentum and panic kept me on the wall and moving up. I had to lunge for the anchor chain. When I got to the top there was no one in sight. A gum wrapper fluttered in the breeze before flipping over the side and dancing on the updrafts on its long way back to the road.

Because I was so desperate to get the rope untied from my harness and rigged to the anchor ring, it seemed to take ten minutes. It was an odd and frustrating illusion—time speeding up as my body movements slowed down. I do remember that it was the fastest rappel of my life, my feet maybe tapped the wall three times in the 40 meters down to the belay ledge.

Molly hung from the thin ledge by the anchor sling. Her feet were on the ledge, but her eyes were closed, her arms dangled by her sides, and the anchor sling was all that supported her and kept her from having fallen more than 500 meters to the road below. The right side of her face and a lot of her T-shirt were covered in brilliant red blood. It was caked in her hair, turning rust-colored. I didn't know if she was dead or alive, but at that moment I realized that if she were dead, I couldn't survive it.

I touched her face. "Oh Jesus mother-fucking Christ! Molly! Can you hear me?" Above my hand blood oozed from her hair like molten lava through a crack in the earth. I screamed her name again, closer to her face. Her eyes opened, moved right and left and tried to focus.

"Molly! Say something! Do you understand me?"

She said my name, softly but distinctly, in a questioning tone. She stared at me like a stranger at the door.

I called for help. Molly tried to put her hand into the matted blood in her hair, but I wouldn't let her. She didn't seem to know what had happened. Watching her eyes focus was like watching someone awaken from a sound sleep with a hangover.

"Now *this* is a headache," she said.

I asked her to tell me what day it was, what month, and then got her to count backwards from some number, all of which she could do.

"Can you climb?" I asked.

She shook her head slowly and said, "Not right now. I'm very dizzy."

"How about belaying me?"

"I don't want you to depend on me, Tommy. Maybe in a few minutes, just give me some time to shake this off."

I didn't know if maybe she would bleed to death, or what kind of damage was done to her head. I couldn't just stand on the ledge and wait to see what might happen in a few minutes. I kissed her nose. She leaned her head into my shoulder and I could feel her sticky blood on my neck. I made her more secure by adding a second anchor sling to her harness. Then I got off the rope.

"I'm sorry, Tommy, but I really don't feel confident enough to give you a belay."

"I won't need it."

"Bullshit you won't!"

"I'll just get some help and be right back. You stay right where you are," I added, smiling.

"Don't, Tommy. I mean it. Yell for help again. Somebody will hear it."

I wasn't trying to be a hero. In fact, I just wasn't thinking all that clearly. I felt panic and only knew that Molly was bleeding and I had to get help for her. I had just climbed the route without slipping and knew I could do it again. I was so pumped with adrenaline that I moved over the rock like water flowing, and was to the zigzag crack before Molly knew I'd left the ledge. I heard her say, "Damn it to hell, Tommy!"

At the top I met two climbers coming up the trail in response to my cries for help. They were friends of ours; Phillip, an ex-pat Brit, had been the best man at our wedding, and a guy from the local climbing shop. As I explained what happened to Molly, two more climbers came up the back side. One of them said he had a phone in his car and took off down the trail. I told Phillip that I was going back down to get Molly.

"And do what?" Phillip asked.

"Bring her up."

"How might you do that?"

"On my back."

Scott, Phillip's climbing partner, said, "You're going to do a hundred and twenty feet of five-eight with Molly on your back? This ought to be good."

"Does anybody have a plan B?"

"Is it so bad we can't wait for a rescue team?"

"I don't know. But I do know she's lost a lot of blood already. Will one of you give me a belay?"

"Sure," Scott said.

"I'll abseil with you and lend a hand," Phillip offered. He asked the other climber, whose name I never asked, if he would belay.

Phillip and I descended on parallel ropes and he slowed a little to let me reach the small ledge first. There was barely enough room for all three of us to stand in a line.

"I could kill you," Molly said. Then she turned to Phillip and asked, "Where did you come from?"

"Heaven, me darling."

"Some angel! I got konked, Phil."

"Bloody damn fine job you did of it, too."

I handed Phillip a sling so he could clip into the anchor ring.

"Hi ho, let's go," Phillip said. It was something of a trademark comment of his.

"Go where?" Molly wondered.

"We'll use slings to clip her harness to my harness, and we'll take these two long ones and clip them around both of us," I began explaining to Phillip.

"Clip me to what for what?"

"We're going up," I told Molly.

"With me on your back? I don't think so."

I turned around and Phillip began securing her to my harness. Molly complained and we ignored her. But she helped Phillip get the long slings around both of us and I knew she trusted me to know what I was doing, no matter how strange it seemed. In a couple of minutes,

Phillip said, "She's on, Tommy boy," and I called up to Scott to let him know I was starting to climb.

"See you later," I told Phillip. "Thanks."

"So long, you two. I always did want to give this route a go."

We shook hands over Molly's shoulder and Phillip kissed Molly's hand. Then we started up. "Be still and you're the same as a backpack," I told her.

"Yeah, a hundred and twenty pound backpack. You are a real piece of work, Tom Valen."

It really wasn't so bad. I could climb, and had, at that level with a backpack. Molly never moved. Halfway up we heard the helicopter. When we came out on top, Scott said, "Sure wish I had a camera." The helicopter settled onto the mesa behind the summit.

"This is embarrassing," Molly said.

A few days later it was a brilliant day, cool in the shade and warm in the sun. Through a wide window in the hospital's waiting room, I could see the university campus to the west, stone buildings with red-tiled roofs shimmering in a cloudless sky that had the color and fragility of a robin's egg—air thin, washed out, without substance, hardly able to sustain life, resembling not so much air as glass or a distant mirror. I watched two old cars, a Buick and a Volkswagen, like a cow and its calf, graze thin lanes around the parking lot. There were psychedelic swirls painted on the VW; the Buick was black and clean, like a funeral wagon. Beyond the parking lot, bicycles consumed the pathways like locusts, and students marched to and fro in their various uniforms: backpacks and shoulder bags, shorts and torn jeans, tank tops and message T-shirts, shower thongs and mountain boots, sandals and bare feet. A young woman passed the window wearing a negligent blouse beneath which her breasts undulated like ocean swells.

I waited for Molly to return from an MRI. She surprised me from behind, catching me flagrantly watching the oceanic breasts flow by.

"It's a trip," Molly said.

I took her hand and asked about it.

"It's very strange. There are these magnets whirling around. You're on a slab and they slide you into it, like going inside a scuba tank. The walls are this close to your face." She put her hand a few centimeters from her nose. "It's not good for claustrophobia. I kept my eyes shut the whole time and thought about mountains. It makes a horrible noise . . ."

"I'll take your word for it. What's next?"

Suddenly Molly sat on the sofa, fell into it really, and put her hands over her face. I sat beside her with my arm around her shoulders.

"Molly, what is it?"

"I'm just really scared."

"What did they tell you?"

"They didn't tell me anything. But you know how they look, that way. They didn't need to say anything."

"I don't understand."

"I knew even before all these tests."

"Knew what?"

Molly straightened up and put her hands together in her lap. I put my hands over hers. I said something stupid: "Is this about being pregnant?"

Molly stiffened and stood abruptly. "It's not about adding a life, Tom. It's about subtracting one."

I refused to hear her.

The following morning was overcast along the coast, a marine fog forcing drivers to turn on their lights and use their windshield wipers. Coming up the road toward the university, the string of headlights reminded me of a Tyrolean ski resort's torch ceremony.

Molly had slept fitfully and kept me awake as well. We didn't talk about anything of consequence, as if our social gears had jumped into neutral. I sat up and read from four A.M., until I finally had to get up, shower and dress. Molly had finally fallen asleep by the time I left for the university. I remained in neutral through the first class and let the second one go half an hour early. I took a long walk back to my office, not thinking really, because I was actually trying not to think. Molly was not prone to exaggeration. If she said the word scared, that probably meant terrified. In my office there was a message to call her.

"Dr. Graber wants to see us later today. Can you do that?"

"Which one is Graber?"

"The oncologist."

"Oh. Okay."

It looked more like a lawyer's office, although the books lining one wall were medical and not legal. He liked African art, preferring sculpture and masks. The window behind his desk overlooked the white-coated roof of a nearby lower building. The ocean could be seen beyond. Molly had my hand. I looked at the air conditioner on the roof, refusing to pay attention. I could deny what I had not noticed.

"Let me show you a picture," Dr. Graber said as he placed an MRI image over a light board built into the top of his desk. Molly and I leaned forward. Dr. Graber used the snowcapped end of a Mount Blanc pen to point toward the center of what he said was Molly's brain. "It's this we're concerned about," he said, tapping the film click-click-click.

It didn't look like anything. Rather, it didn't look especially distinguishable from all the other odd swirls and smashed geometry. Maybe it was darker, maybe that's what gave it shape.

"What is it?"

"Well, Molly, we believe it's a tumor."

We remained in Dr. Graber's office for some time after that. I can't say much about it because it has never taken on the character of a real event for me, more like a distant dream. I remember watching Molly stare at the MRI as if she could find the wrong name printed on its label. Dr. Graber said it, the tumor, shouldn't be there, and I said he was a master of understatement. He confirmed that other doctors had seen the picture, as well as the results of the other tests she'd taken, and that, in combination with her history of morning headaches coupled with nausea, had produced a consensus that she had a type of cancer known as glioblastoma.

I said, "You can fix this." It wasn't a question.

"That's difficult . . . we are at the earliest stages here, but I can assure you that we will do everything possible for Molly."

Molly kept staring at the picture of the inside of her brain, at the discoloration that now had a name. Dr. Graber asked her if she wanted to know anything right now, and she said in an unusually plain voice, "Am I going to die? From this thing, I mean."

"Glioblastoma is a very serious kind of tumor, especially in this part of the brain. I don't think you want me to lie . . ."

No, I wanted him to change the truth.

"We cannot remove a tumor from that part of the brain. It's near the auditory cortex. You're probably already experiencing some aphasia —that's difficulty speaking, finding the word you want, and mixing words up. Probably vertigo."

"Did you answer my question somewhere in there?"

"I have to tell you that there are no reported survivors of glioblastoma after five years, with or without treatment."

I could not look at her, I remember. I knew that if I looked at her I would come apart. I looked at the MRI. I looked for the error that must have been made. Molly kept asking questions in that odd, strained voice.

"You're saying it can't be treated? Drugs? Radiation?"

Dr. Graber shook his head.

"Will it hurt?" Her voice became weaker and I felt her hand slide into mine.

Dr. Graber handed her a tissue and I saw that now there were tears streaming down her cheeks. I wanted to run away, I wanted to hide, I wanted to die, I wished I had never been born and never met this woman who just took my hand, I wanted to do anything to make this go away.

"We can do something about that," Dr. Graber answered.

"Do I have five years?"

"Nothing is really certain."

"Which means you don't think I do."

"I'm afraid not. Maybe one year, eighteen months at the outside. But that's only an educated guess, Molly. You know, it's ironically fortunate that you were hit by the rock, because otherwise we might not have discovered this until it had already progressed to an advanced, quickly debilitating stage. This way you have a good deal more time to enjoy a relatively healthy life."

"Relatively speaking is the only way a year can be called a good deal of time," Molly said. Then she turned to me and asked me to take her home.

I don't know if I ever spoke during this. Probably I did. I remember Dr. Graber scheduling an appointment with another specialist to get a second opinion. We would get three more of these terrible opinions. I remember going out of his office and seeing a woman in the waiting lounge whose clearly bald head was covered by a nice scarf, and Molly saying, "Guess I won't have to go through that," and I thinking that I would happily spend the rest of my life loving her bald and with lots of nice scarves just to have those years. And I remember that when we got into the car I suddenly opened the door and vomited on the floor of the parking garage.

Molly wrote a sort of autobiography, working on it just about every day for many months. When she stopped, the last few pages were gibberish. She didn't show any of it to me and asked me not to read it until she was gone. She wrote in a big spiral notebook and on the first page wrote, "Possessed by Shadows." The title comes from a verse in Rilke's "The Sonnets to Orpheus."

I kept her notebook in a bag and carried it back to California without reading it. When things went bad in California and I lost my job at the university, I carried it back to Slovakia, where my friend Štefan arranged for me to work for the mountain rescue service in the Tatras. Another year passed before I read it, and a long time after that before I typed it into a laptop. Molly never said if she intended this memoir to be private, and at first I thought some of it would embarrass her. On the other hand, it was obviously not written as an extended private letter to me, nor do I think she kept a diary for its own sake. I might be wrong about this, but now I believe that Molly wanted to break the silence of a private life, to establish her presence in the world, to say—"I am." I take this course because of the last thing she wrote before most of it became scribbled gibberish. She copied a few lines from the Rilke poem:

> And if the earthly no longer knows your name,
> Whisper to the silent earth: I'm flowing.
> To the flashing water say: I am.

This book exists as the context for her memoir, and my story of how we lived that last year.

Tom Valen
Starý Smokovec, Slovakia
November 2000

Tom

This is about my wife. Who died. And about her husband, who is trying to die but cannot. Winter started and it was cold in the High Tatras. I came back from the mountaineer's symbolic cemetery in the early dark, in snow, following the service road down to find my way. I was the last to leave. I don't know how many hours passed after Štefan said good-bye to me and went down. Then I didn't know about them. She had been right when she speculated that I never knew.

I was 44 years old that night in November of 1989, alone and surrounded by cold and darkness. Almost everything important that I know about myself began then, there. I am trying not to forget any of it. But I was drunk by the time I wrote the first words, and the forgetting had already taken hold.

None of it was the way I thought it would be: the mysterious tests, the doctors, each one appropriately sad and bent on disinformation. Both Molly and I went through the entire textbook cycle of responses— panic, anger, denial, bargaining, despair, and even, I suppose, a kind of acceptance. But, you see, I had always believed that I would die before Molly, so this vicious turn confused me and made me seem to be reacting coldly about it. Molly, always more volatile and emotional than I, went through panic and fear in a matter of days, exhausting herself in an adrenaline rush. She never was really angry. That was my way. I held onto the anger for months, although it turned out ultimately to be an unsustainable emotion. Molly forced me to fall back from its hot flames, although I have always hoarded its embers, and still do.

We did not make spiritual bargains, not after the sort of lives we led. We made no religious deals, which would have only added foolishness to our last year together. It was despair, with its costs all delayed, that stalked our every moment. Molly was not the kind of person who would let herself be tortured by visions of a future in which she was not present. I couldn't stop doing it.

Molly told me that, in spite of herself, she had fantasized a dream world of continuity, where she would continue as if in one stream from one place to some other place, and that she would recognize everything from an irrational vantage point. She would only make a kind of transition, not explainable because it is inherently irrational, in which she would continue to have "some sort" of experience, and in that way not have utterly ceased to exist. It is a comforting and probably necessary situation that consciousness cannot deny itself.

We lived most of that year in a fog, but this is how I remember it now.

Until Christmas, our days were filled with medicine and its ultimately futile wonders. We filled the rest of our time with the cloying noises of domestic life. I hated the significance of everything.

We put up a Christmas tree. I placed her gifts beneath it, but Molly hid mine, as usual, knowing I would peek. She would produce them from her secret hiding place on Christmas morning. It was a small tree, circled by miniature white blinking lights that from the street resembled a cluster of distant stars. All the houses around had them; Molly called them the Christmas Constellations.

Molly asked me to dry the dishes for her. "I'm late and need to get dressed," she explained.

"Dressed for what?"

"I'm going to the office for a few hours."

"It's Christmas Eve."

"I know that, Tommy. But the paper still comes out in three days and I have a column to finish."

"Why?"

"Why? What do you suppose I should do instead? Shall we sit around watching TV?"

"I just don't . . ." I have no idea what I wanted to say or what the problem was. Maybe I just wanted to tell her not to die, and then she could go to her office and then we could do normal things.

"Don't make me crazy," she said.

"That's not what I'm trying to do."

"I know. But that's what you *are* doing."

"What do *you* want me to do?"

"Kiss me and dry the dishes . . . and don't cut yourself like you did last time."

As she left the kitchen, she paused, glanced back and said, "I want to go climbing Saturday."

"Are you sure?"

"Look, they aren't going to take that away from me."

We went out that Christmas Eve and ate sushi at the Japanese fish house we could walk to on a quiet street to the harbor. Then we saw a few friends in the neighborhood, popping into their various Christmas parties. Molly tired early and we didn't stay long at any of them. When we got home, Molly asked me to read the draft for her column—she worked as a feature writer and columnist for an alternative paper. I laid in bed and read it while she took a shower. This is it:

I have cancer in my brain and will eventually, sooner rather than later, die from it. Once I was asked if I was afraid of anything—climbers are asked such questions from time to time. I recall saying that I was afraid of death and senselessness, which is, of course, redundant. Maybe some people believe that we climb due to a kind of subconscious suicide wish, but I don't know a single climber for whom that would be true. We are as passionate about living as the next person.

Do you know how hard it is to be dying in Southern California? Land of the prettiness cults. Land of eternal health, perpetual youth, and astounding beauty. People don't like you very much around here if you're dying. It's like being fat or ugly. It's just not allowed here. I'm sure there are signs prohibiting death and anything connected with it.

Have you seen the TV commercial for one of the California HMO health plans? We're shown limitless, palm-flecked beaches filled with playful young and beautiful people, bouncing girls in volleyball games, hard boys playing beach football, and for a bit of balance, we even find a pair of handsome, "Calvin Klein"-clad seniors power walking along the torrey pine cliffs. Into this heavenly vision enter Joe and Betty Tourist. We see them standing at the edge of the beach, prohibited from entering the beauty zone by an apparent force field of good health, dressed like Ma and Pa Kettle in Waikiki. Mrs. Tourist drinks a malt. Mr. Tourist clutches a grease-laden burger. Before them is spread the tableau of health.

Joe turns to Betty and says, "Sure ain't Nebraska."

Well, Joe, fact is, it's not anywhere. This notion of life is no more real than the silicone we pump ourselves up with or the fibers we weave through what's left of our hair.

It is good to think of health and to be reminded that we have some responsibility for maintaining it. But that doesn't make it bad to remember that we are all dying, and no amount of plastic and fat vacuuming, no amount of yogurt and jogging, will change that. By forgetting that we will die, we may forget how to live. I wish we were better able to deal with dying in this country. Living ought to be more than trying to look pretty as we trek from one mystery to the next.

Make a place for us, we who are dying among you, because we are your pathfinders. Without us, you are pointless.

When Molly came from the shower, a towel wrapped around her wet hair and another around her waist, I was still on the bed with the pages beside me. The window behind the bed was open and the smell of night-blooming jasmine filled the room like the scent of a grandmother's breasts. Behind it came the salt air of the sea, which was only a few blocks away. Molly unwrapped her hair first and her waist and pitched the two towels toward the laundry hamper, then took one of my T-shirts and pulled it on. A damp spot appeared where she had not completely dried her chest. Her soft beauty stunned me. Sometimes I was used to it and simply didn't notice so directly. But now and then, I don't know why one time and not another, I was electrified by my love for her.

"What did you think?" she asked, piling into the bed next to me and picking up the two sheets of paper.

"It was perfectly stated," I answered.

"Don't get carried away," she teased.

I turned over, my back to her. Sometimes I just couldn't bear to look into her eyes. She draped one arm over my shoulder and said, "Oh Tom." She scooted closer, put her breasts into my back, and whispered, "I love you."

"I love you, too."

"Let's do it now."

"I don't think I can."

"Hey, it's Christmas Eve. Besides, I won't break, you know."

She used her hand and made me hard in spite of myself.

In the morning we exchanged gifts. I had wanted to get for her everything she had ever expressed any desire for, but realized that it would be worse than getting her nothing. Molly insisted that our lives go on pretty much as they always had, which was patently impossible. So I gave her an auto-locking karabiner and a John Irving novel. She gave me the same karabiner, a bottle of Glenmorangie whisky, and a collection of Rilke poems she'd had specially bound in red leather. We gave each other a new climbing rope.

It was over in ten minutes. We cleaned up the debris, Molly made another pot of coffee, and we sat outside on the patio to finish breakfast and read the paper. Later we had a walk and the village neighborhood we lived in was virtually empty; it seemed to belong to us. Lurking between us was the feeling that we seemed to be flittering away what was likely to be our last Christmas together. Molly's last, period.

We went climbing the day after Christmas. It's what Molly wanted, and I did not tell her that the dizziness worried me.

It was still dark when I got up. Molly stirred, then turned over. I left the bedroom quietly and went to the large closet below the stairs where we kept all our climbing gear. A strand of linked-together karabiners clanked loudly when I pulled them from the bag and I thought the noise would awaken Molly. But I didn't hear her get up and the thought crossed my mind that I could find her dead. The vision made me nauseous.

When everything was ready, I went back to the bedroom and touched her shoulder to wake her.

"I'm up," she said suddenly and rolled herself over to the side of the bed. She had only started doing that recently—awakening explosively, as if surprised.

"You'll need sweats," I told her. "It's cool today."

"Where are we going?"

"Woodson."

She went into the bathroom and sat on the toilet. I could see her reflected in the mirror, elbows on her thighs, chin cupped in her hands. She looked like a little girl and I turned away, left the room.

When she came into the kitchen, I had just finished putting together a lunch. She poured a cup of coffee and peeked into the paper bag. "Busy little beaver," she said. She was just so goddamn cheerful.

My old canvas rucksack was on the floor by the coiled rope. It was covered with patches from climbing places. I'd started the habit before Molly and I met, and it was easy now to see which ones I'd sewn on, sloppily, and which Molly had, perfectly. Some of mine were half off. The rope had the colors of a coral snake. It was the new one.

"We won't do anything really hard," I said stupidly.

"Don't baby me!" she snapped.

The sun appeared and we drove straight into it. One town blending indistinguishably into another made it appear to be one monstrous, continuous city. After half an hour we left the highway and headed north through farms and ranches surrounded by boulder strewn hills, some a thousand meters high. Dormant orchards sliced across the nearer hillsides. Now there were more trailer homes than houses, with yards large enough to raise animals. Some places were for sale. Because this was Southern California, soon enough there would be houses with red-tiled roofs all over these hills. For now it was still clean, there wasn't a cloud in the sky, the air smelled strongly of horse shit and eucalyptus.

After driving for an hour, we reached a pullout beside the highway where there were already parked about a dozen cars and trucks. A mountain littered with granite boulders rose above us. The massive rocks looked like they'd been tossed across the slope in some playful giant's game. Some of the best rocks were at the top, below a group of microwave towers, along a service road. Others required serious bush-whacking to reach.

The air continued to hold the damp morning chill of late December in Southern California, but in the sun we felt hot and sweated from the exertion. The grade was steep. Molly was uncharacteristically breathless. I had thought of doing a long route called Tush in the Bush, but it was quite near the top and still a long hike up. I asked Molly if she'd rather look for something where we were, but she said, "To the top!" and plunged her fist into the air. As if to prove her stamina, she whistled a few bars of "Onward Christian Soldiers," but stopped quickly, out of breath. Then she was nauseous. I turned away when she stepped into the brush beside the service road to throw up. She preferred privacy. When it was finished, she just rolled her eyes and said let's go.

Now I saw everywhere what I had hardly noticed during the past few months, before we knew: How easily Molly got tired, how often she complained of headaches, and the mistakes she made with words.

We could see other climbers along the way. We passed a man and woman bouldering near the road. The woman, Japanese, wore lycra running tights and a halter top and had an exceptional tan. She had one foot hooked in a crack above her head and was hanging by one arm. The muscles in her back looked carved from dark wood, polished to a high gloss. Her spotter, wearing identical tights and a long-sleeve T-shirt, stood below with his arms held out.

In the distance we could see a climber on a rope halfway up the side of a 15-meter boulder. Farther ahead, two climbers sat like perched falcons atop a boulder as high as a pair of buses on end.

We followed a switchback and came across Philip and his girlfriend setting up for Robbins' Crack. He saw us come around the bend and waved us over.

"What's her name?" I whispered to Molly.

"Oh, I know it," Molly insisted so forcefully that I was sorry I asked.

"Hey guys," Phillip called out.

I could see in her face—her name is Annie and she would the next year become Phillip's wife—that Annie must have read Molly's column.

"What're you blokes about this fine A.M.?" Phillip asked.

"Something higher up," I said.

"We're doing Robbins."

"*He's* doing Robbins," Annie corrected. "I'm the good old belay slave."

Molly came over to Phillip and took his hand. She said, "I never got a chance to thank you, Phillip."

"For what? All I did was watch Spider-Man here climb a five-nine with you on his back. He's a bloody hell show-off, that husband of yours."

"He is that . . ."

"Hey!"

". . . but you know what I mean. So, thanks."

"Looks like you're healing up nicely, though." Phillip had a look at the place where Molly's hair had not yet filled in over the ragged scar.

"I'm sorry," Annie blurted out, stepping forward and taking Molly's hands in hers. "I just can't stand here ignoring it. I read your column, Molly. I'm so very, very sorry." Then she turned to Phillip and added, "Molly wrote about having cancer. I didn't tell you."

"Cancer?" Phillip stared at Molly, as if seeking a sign.

"It wasn't easy to write," Molly said. "I'm glad you saw it."

"And you were so right on about California," Annie, with a perfect body, said.

"God, Molly dear, I sure hope everything turns out all right for you," Phillip blurted out. "Of course it will."

"We're all hoping for that," I said.

Then we all stood silent as bricks until I said at last, "I guess we'll go find a rock to scamper around on."

Annie impulsively hugged Molly, then we waved and started back up the road. Maybe before this we would have joined them and climbed together, but Molly was right when she wrote that sickness, especially cancer, changes everything.

"I hate this," Molly said when we were away.

"Hate what?"

"What I've become."

"You haven't become anything. You're Molly."

"There's a word for it . . . I know there's a word."

"What word? For what?"

"If I knew would I ask?"

"I'm sorry."

"Oh, damn it! Stop being sorry every ten seconds."

"OK."

We walked silently for another five minutes, then turned off the service road onto a beaten path through waist-high brush. We could see the rock we were heading for, like a monstrous loaf of sparkling silver bread cleaved down the middle by a giant's knife. A remarkably even crack with an average width of seven or eight centimeters severed the boulder completely from top to bottom, through and through. In sunlight, spiderwebs glistened deep inside and a prism played over the strands. From the ground the crack ran up 15 meters to the rounded top. The boulder lay partially on its side; the steepness of the rock near the top was only 50 or 60 degrees. There were good hand jams, so in spite of its angle, the climb was rated five-eight. From a distance it held an uncanny resemblance to its name: Tush in the Bush.

"Banshee," Molly said, as if she'd won a contest. "It's banshee. That's the word I wanted. I'm becoming a banshee."

"Oh, come on, Molly."

"Why not? Isn't that what I've become, a spirit warning people they are going to die?"

All I could do was give her a look that said I wanted her to stop talking that way. I sat on a rock and opened the rucksack to get out a water bottle, and also fished out an apple. The sun was warm on us and we were overdressed. Molly said she wanted the lead. I crunched the apple and watched her. She pulled out various pieces of protection as she looked over the crack again. She took two number three Friends, a number eight and a number nine hexcentric, rigging them with short runners and karabiners. Then she arranged them along the harness loops. I got up and pulled on my harness and hung a belay ring from it. Molly sat on the rock to put on her climbing shoes and I flaked out the rope. Above us a buzzard worked rising warm air currents, and from somewhere in the bush came the familiar clink of karabiners, as common a sound to climbing areas as horns honking in city traffic.

Molly stood near the rock and touched it with her hands. It looked like she was praying, but actually she only warmed her hands and re-called the corn kernel texture of the rough granite. She slapped chalk over her hands before sliding her right hand into the crack and making a fist. Then she climbed, the rope trailing behind her like a vestigial tail.

"You look like King Kong climbing the skyscraper," I called up to her.

"Is that supposed to be a compliment," Molly answered as she placed the first Friend, clipped the rope, moved up, "or a nasty reference to my butt?"

"I love your butt," I said.

"Me, too," cried an anonymous voice from somewhere behind us.

I laughed and Molly yelled down, "Don't make me laugh up here."

That was the first time we had been climbing since the accident. I don't know what I expected: Revelation? Epiphany? *The Sound of Music?* It felt good to be climbing with my wife again, that's all. It felt like life had always felt. That's what was so strange about it, the absurd normality. Climbing, one thinks of nothing but climbing, that's the purity of it, the salvation of it.

"Wish I'd brought a halter top," Molly said. "It's damn hot up here."

The sun was hot on our shoulders. For some reason I remembered the time, a sparkling hot day at Joshua Tree, we went bouldering in the nude after sunset. It was Molly's nice idea.

I watched her top out and disappear from view. There were two bolts drilled into the top where she could anchor herself to bring me up. Molly first climbed this rock more than 20 years ago, with her father belaying and calling out instructions, until finally Molly shouted: "Let me do it, Daddy!"

From the top the view came in a 280° arc to the horizon. Far to the east rose much higher mountains, looking west and down revealed the highway where we'd parked. The pullout was now almost filled with cars, pickup trucks, jeeps and motorcycles. Trees and boulders blocked our line of sight to the service road, and the distant, smog-shrouded coastline was a thin silver smudge. There were no clouds. Sometimes there were muffled voices nearby.

"This is a classic crack climb," I said on top.

"You mean it's too easy for you."

"No, I don't. I mean it's fun."

I kissed her quickly, touched her hair, and asked how she felt. She said she was all right and wanted to climb something else. I suggested Feets of Steel, another good crack climb.

"Let's rap down," she said, preparing a rappel anchor.

"It's either that or jump," I joked.

"No, I'll save that for when it counts," she said.

I wasn't paying much attention to her, intent then on checking the rappel setup, and it was not until we were down that it occurred to me what she could have meant by that remark. I didn't say anything because maybe I was wrong and anyway it would only make her angry.

We climbed all day. Molly got sick once more. Some of the rewards of climbing are related to the difficulty, just as increasing the quotient of danger enhances the joy of survival. But just being in the mountains, or outside on a nice day is reward enough. It's an odd mix: danger and tranquility.

At the end of the day we sat in the shade beneath the last boulder and drank beer. We were tired and lazy. Molly lay back against the rock while I coiled the rope, using my neck to form the loops. In the middle of nothing, Molly said, "Can you get leave from the university?"

"Leave?"

"Sabbatical, I suppose."

"I'm up for it in two years."

"Two years?"

"Why do you ask?"

"Could you get it earlier?"

"I don't know. I'll find out. Why?"

"Tommy, we've been dancing around this thing and I want to stop now, face it."

I put down the coiled rope. Molly rested her hand on my leg.

"I want to go away," she said. "Together."

"All right." I couldn't look at her face. I knew where this was going.

"I don't want to just sit here waiting to die."

"It's not *waiting to die*, Molly. There are many things we can do, things we can try. I don't plan to simply give up."

"You're putting up a wall in front of reality."

"I don't know what reality is . . ."

"And I don't want to do philosophy, either. The reality is, Tom, that while, yes, we are all going to die sooner or later, I'm to be among the sooner."

She put her hand over my mouth to keep me from interrupting.

"I know we've talked about options ad infinitum, but what we never talk about is the fact that I am going to die this year or the next."

"I am not capable of accepting that you will die from this."

"Or anything else."

"Or anything else, yes."

"I love you very much, Tommy."

"And I love you."

"Which doesn't change anything. There is a tumor in my brain, it is growing, it is malignant, it can't be removed and it can't be treated. Now maybe there will be some miraculous spontaneous remission, maybe it's just a mistake and the damn thing is a calcium deposit, maybe there's a god who will take pity on me and spare me to prove his occasional benevolence. Or maybe I'll just die from it. Horrible things to say in a beautiful place. What I'm saying is . . . it isn't easy . . . after I'm gone you'll have a life to live, bills to pay, a world waiting, so I know how much I'm asking."

"Molly."

"Just give me another minute. I am leaving behind nothing of me in the world, nothing that will endure beyond me, no children, no work, no evidence of my presence in the world. I only have you. I don't mean *only* to sound deficient. Only you is more than enough for me. But what remains of me is in you, and only there.

"What I'm saying is, if you can leave for a while, until it's over, without losing your job, I would like to spend this time being with you."

"It's done," I said.

I was crying then, because maybe it was only then that I accepted the reality of Molly's dying. It was the saddest moment since we left the doctor's office after getting the diagnosis. She lay both hands on my thigh.

"I want to go away," she said.

"All right."

"We might be able to lease the house."

"I'm sure."

"I never realized how much we are prisoners of our stuff."

"We don't have to be. It's just stuff."

"A decade of saving and accumulating."

I shrugged.

"I don't want to make a pilgrimage from one friend to the next, each sad face a continual reminder. I don't want to spend months wallowing in pity."

"We'll do whatever you want."

"This isn't fair to you."

"Jesus, Molly!"

"I mean this will exhaust our savings and afterwards you'll basically have to start all over."

"Nothing could be less important to me."

"Once on top of a mountain in Switzerland, you said you would always take care of me."

"Our honeymoon."

"I believed you. I still do. I always will."

"Where do you want to go?"

"To the mountains. Climbing, of course, as long as I can."

"I don't know about altitude bringing on . . ."

"I was thinking of the Tatras. They aren't high enough to induce edema."

"Then that's what we'll do."

Now I know that she needed to see more than the Tatras again, that she needed to see Štefan. I have come to terms with that.

Molly

The first thing I remember is the sound of metal against metal—karabiners, hammers and pitons—the sounds of my father. All my life I would fall in love with climbers, often stupidly, because of the way they sounded. I thought they were all good knights, bold and true; nothing that made such a sound could be bad. And when I found out that some of them were bad, I knew it was because they wore the silver armor of my father under false pretenses, a pose of charlatanry. I have not been able to decide if I was meant to be a damsel or a knight; I have desired both from time to time.

I was born atop a mesa in the golden hills of Southern California; born at home, so urgent to be alive and free of the womb that I crowned minutes after my mother realized that she was in serious labor. They named me Molly Louise Cook. Louise was my mother's name and Molly the name of my grandmother on my father's side. From our mesa-top house when the coast wasn't fog-bound and the air was clear, I could see the shining silver water of the Pacific Ocean, from the mesas well into Mexico all the way up past the big white cross on Mt. Soledad, above La Jolla. At night, many-colored lights sparkled like gems spread out over the dark descending earth—my crown jewels. Ours was the highest house on that mesa, and all the higher mesas were to the south and east, so I grew up used to panoramic vistas, and when I am low or in a forest or inside a building, I am claustrophobic and have feelings of terrible, but unfocused dread.

I have always loved being in nature, especially walking in the dry, rocky hills with my father, walking ridge lines where I can see to the horizon in any direction, and the higher we climb, the better. I was so often behind my father that now, whenever I am hiking, I feel soothed by the small pieces of memory that allow me to imagine my father's back, his canvas Boy Scout rucksack, his cap with its bill often turned up, the bristle of his crew cut sandy hair, his long legs with their ridges of prominent veins rising from battered Red Wing boots.

I look like my father, I am his height and not far below his heaviest weight—he was a skinny man and I am a big girl. I have his long fingers and thick, heavily veined forearms, his hair the color of sand in the California low desert, his green eyes, his small feet. I also hope that I have his character and honesty, although I must quickly admit that I don't have his mind: his clear, rational, scientific, logical and linear brilliance. My mind simply flies all over the place, tethered to nothing. But my father's most important gift to me is the self-confidence bred in mountains, the pastime that has dominated my life. He made me a climber.

From my mother I received imagination, the gift of words and dreams. In the evenings of my childhood, while my father graded papers, or more likely, constructed climbing equipment in his garage workshop, Mother read to me. We never had a television set. My father said that it was easy to spot people who watched too much TV. "They look a bit heavy afoot," he said, "slow movers, because their heads are so full of junk." (Later I would have a TV set, but I always felt heavy, bloated, after watching it, picturing myself as a fat little

Buddha with a silly grin on my face.) So Mother read to me in the evenings after she had finished cleaning up the kitchen and her husband had disappeared to his bedroom office or the garage. She left the kitchen radio turned on—she liked show tunes, big band jazz, and crooners like Bing Crosby—while she read to her only child. When I was small, Mother called me Pixie. I sat in her lap with the book folded open so I could help turn the pages. When I was older and larger I moved down to the floor where sometimes I sat cross-legged, sometimes leaned back on my elbows with my legs stretched out in a vee, or sometimes lay on my stomach with my head cradled in folded arms. Mother sat in an overstuffed armchair that was always covered with a thin tan rug. She propped her stocking feet on an ottoman and read by the light of a floor lamp with an ashtray surrounding the pole. She used cigarettes to enforce dramatic pauses into the stories. She sipped tea from a china cup on a saucer. I grew up craving the telling of stories, fascinated by storytellers. I wanted to be one, but instead I married one.

Mother didn't climb and she hated camping. Climbing was her husband's hobby. She said, "Some men go bowling, some play with cars, your father climbs up and down rocks. At least it keeps him out of trouble." I thought that she didn't understand him at all. I knew that climbing wasn't his hobby, it was his *country*, his *homeland*, the very sustenance of his soul. Because I was allowed to go with him and find my own sustenance there, I was forever alienated from my mother, who was a foreigner in the xenophobic society of rock climbers.

My father taught mathematics at La Mesa High School. He was not a patient man and didn't like teaching very much, although he loved mathematics, playing with numbers, which he called the only rational god. He also called climbing the activity that leads to god. When I asked how he ended up a teacher, he answered, "By default." Most of his decisions were "made" that way. He had a one-track mind, and that track led directly into the mountains. It was not necessary for me to understand him. I simply loved him.

Frank Cook was an angular man who always wore khaki slacks, dark socks, brown loafers, and polo shirts with pockets for his cigarettes. In winter, which isn't much to speak of in Southern California, he added a jacket; an old green army field jacket for leisure and a forest green tweed sport coat for work. He wore a crew cut every day of his life. He carried a fat Zippo lighter with a Marine Corps logo in his right front pants pocket. He liked that lighter, I'm sure, because it clinked open with a sound similar to the snap of a karabiner gate.

I do not remember exactly the first time he took me climbing. He said I was two. He said it was natural for children to climb to the highest place around, and if you never ordered a child to get down, if you never frightened them, they would not develop a fear of heights. I am not afraid of high places, but I respect them. In fact, I crave high places.

I went climbing with my father to the virtual exclusion of all other activities. Mother registered me for piano classes, but my pathetic protests brought them to a halt after two lessons. Then she bought a dress and enrolled me in a dance class, but the dress hung unworn and I cried to avoid going. Then my father convinced me that dancing would help to develop balance and style on the rocks, so I started attending and even wore the required dress. He was right. But I danced like an athlete, not the young lady my mother hoped for. I danced alone when I could, when the teacher didn't force me to pretend that I was dancing with some gangly, useless boy.

Father and I went on hundreds of climbing trips; some for only a few hours, some lasting an entire two-week holiday. These trips run together in my mind as one long, glorious adventure in the mountains. Day trips were frequent because there were so many fine climbing rocks within an hour or two from our house. When we ventured farther and longer, it was to Joshua Tree, Tahquitz, Castle Rock and Red Rocks, where we would camp out over a weekend. We spent three consecutive summer holidays in Yosemite, where, my father said, god would live if he needed to be in one place. My father was well-known, I could say famous, among Southern California, Arizona and Nevada climbers. With his friends from the Lizards Climbing Club, he set up many routes and had many first ascents. You can find the name of Frank Cook in a dozen climbers' guidebooks. You can also find routes he named after his daughter: Molly's Dream, Molly's Smile, Molly's Face, Molly's First, Molly's Torment, and Molly's Buttress—a name that gave my friends the giggles.

It was a perfect life. I cannot imagine anything better than my childhood, that blissful period before I became a teenager.

The universe does not allow perfection; it simply has no place in the scheme of things. There are gremlins of chaos and disorder loose among us. I have one riding on my shoulder all the time, and I call it Antithesis. It goes everywhere with me, usually patient and silent, but a malevolent presence, like a vulture on a rock. Then, when my life begins to tend toward perfection, when I am suddenly sure that nothing could be better than whatever it is I have, at that moment Antithesis leans close to my ear and in a warm, breathy, sensually compelling voice, whispers: "Hey! Let's fuck this up!"

My mother's parents killed themselves. I have never seen pictures of them and they were never spoken of in our house. It was as if they never were, as if my mother had appeared on the planet through osmosis. I was still a teenager when my father told me that my grandparents had committed suicide. He hoped that giving me that information would heal the bitter wounds my mother and I inflicted on each other.

I don't know where I heard or read this, but isn't it true that when it's time for them to live an independent life a mother wolf will take her cubs somewhere into the wild and attack them until they are afraid of her? Then she runs away so they can't find her? Whether or not this is true, it's a useful metaphor. Maybe there is some biological necessity leading a mother to shove her children into the world and out of the den. My mother started trying to get rid of me when I was sixteen.

She never trusted me, and I gave her sufficient cause. She snooped in drawers and cabinets, under my bed, smelled my clothes for suspicious odors, phoned my friends to check when I was supposed to be there; so I became flagrant in torturing her. What she saw as the ruin of her only child was for me just a character, a role I had chosen for that time. What I did not realize was that once you've gone to so much effort becoming some character—you've memorized all your lines, perfected all your postures, gestures, movements—it never leaves, and you will carry throughout your life the accumulated weight of all those mingled lives and their ever-widening circle of influences, good and bad.

I decided—it is my habit to decide something then cling to it tenaciously—that the Freudian theory of repression is wrong. Freud supposed that we have any number of repressed memories which create and sustain repressed feelings and desires, and it is by way of repression that we hide painful or dangerous memories from the light of consciousness. Lurking in the dark subconscious, these repressed memories play havoc with our emotional well-being—the things that go bump in the mind. Freud invented psychoanalysis to coax repressed memories into the light of consciousness, to identify these ghostly events and thereby cure their nasty effects. But I believe that in fact the converse is more likely the case: Traumatic or painful memories are quite sturdy and durable and extremely difficult to repress. Any threat to emotional well-being would more than likely arise from the inability to repress terrible memories, so maybe the task of psychoanalysis ought to be about helping us to forget, not inducing us to remember.

It is what I cannot forget rather than what I cannot recall that shapes me. I do not understand how I can be influenced by what I am not conscious of, what I obviously do not know in any conscious way. The blame for whatever I am does not come from what I do not know or do not remember, but from what I cannot forget, from knowing too much. There are no ghosts in the attic. They all stand in the bright light of day.

Like the day, when I was 16, that Mother found my diary.

I began keeping a diary when I was about seven, maybe eight. I didn't save any of them, and the world is better for it. In the diaries of my teenage years I practiced the use and sound of the most foul and offensive language, words that were then new to me and had a tremendous impact when I used them, even secretly. You know the words and they don't need to be repeated here, for their power has not diminished over the years, and being offensive for no purpose ought to remain a characteristic of youth.

My bedroom was at the rear of the house; a small, square room overlooking the yard, mostly scrub brush and ice plant cactus, to the crumbling dirt cliff that dropped away to houses built into the hillsides below. It was an old house. My father's father built it in the 1920s. Then it had high ceilings, but sometime later a dropped false ceiling was installed. This abortion had white, mica-flecked acoustical tiles fitting loosely in a metal grid frame, and it would lead to my doom. On the other hand, with even the smallest light the mica chips sparkled like a near galaxy.

I kept the diary in the ceiling. In the corner nearest the backyard I could stand on a chair and lift out one of the tiles. At that corner a pair of 2×12 joists came together and I could lay my diary—along with a marijuana stash—across them.

I came in from school and saw my mother sitting on the end of the bed with my diary in her lap, her hands laying across the open spiral-bound notebook like in one of those wedding photographs where the couple clasps hands over a Bible. At that moment I realized my mother now knew that the smell on my clothes she probably thought came from cigarettes was actually from marijuana, that I often lied to her about where I went, that I often, against strict orders, went down to Mexico dancing with friends, and that I was very definitely no longer a virgin. She also knew I recorded dreams.

Mother looked up when I came in. Her face was as red and swollen as if she'd been slapped. In a voice urgent with venomous disgust, she said, "You've never told me the truth about anything, have you."

I began screaming at her: "How could you steal my private things!"

As if I'd not spoken, she moved her hands from the diary, her tone unchanged, and continued, "But I want you to tell me the truth now."

I made a move to retrieve the diary, but she raised her hand to stop me. "That's my personal and private property," I said, my strength fading quickly. I felt horrible, sick to my stomach with both righteous rage and deserving fear.

She screamed my name, then stood and closed the diary with her finger inside to mark a place. She held the notebook to one side and away from her body, as if it held slithering serpents. She looked me in the eyes and said, "Molly, did you have sex with your father?"

I never had sex with my father. There was not and never had been even a remotely sexual component in our relationship. I had no ability to connect my father with anything sexual. I couldn't even really conjure an image of my parents making love.

Except once, in a dream. One stupid dream I stupidly recorded in that stupid diary more than a year earlier, when I was fifteen. I dreamed that Father came into my bedroom and . . . what? It was a dream vaguely recalled, filled with nebulous images, irrational and confusing scenes. Had I not been in the habit of trying to remember dreams and record them, I doubt that I would have remembered it, and had Mother not found the diary, I'm sure even that record of it would have gone in dissipated time to its rightful place—the brain's trash bin.

I wrote this:

Daddy came into my room and got into my bed. I'm sure it was my bed, but sometimes it seemed like we were outside under a starry, starry sky. He said some stuff, like you know that he would always be my daddy and he loved me most in the world. I felt weird, you know, but not bad exactly. Just weird. I saw he was undressed and I was too, not in my sleeping shirt. I could actually see his cock—I had crossed out cock and wrote penis, then crossed that out and wrote sex—and like instantly we were doing it. I was there, but also outside watching, like in a movie when people do it behind a gauzy curtain. I don't remember anything else or any real details, which is probably good, I think.

That's what Mother read.

I bolted toward her and jerked the notebook from her hand, then stepped back into an indignant, defiant pose. I thought she was going to walk out, but as she approached, she slapped me hard enough to knock me to the floor. When I tried to scoot away, she followed, kicking my legs and feet. I screamed over and over, "I hate you I hate you I hate you I hate you."

Suddenly she knelt, no, sank to the floor on her knees, settling into the lump of herself like wax put near a flame. I was so utterly saddened that I leaned over and put my arms around her. I had never seen my mother cry, but this wasn't crying; she wailed, and great long muscle spasms ran through her back and shook her shoulders. She held her hands over her ears and rocked back and forth in my arms.

That I had produced this, and so unintentionally, was not believable. "It was just a stupid dream," I repeated. But she didn't listen.

For the rest of our lives we lived like occasionally polite strangers who by happenstance were stuck together in a train compartment. Mother had, except functionally, ceased to be a mother to me. She no longer questioned any of my activities, nor spied on me, nor asked where I was going or what I was doing. She took no interest in my school work, never insisted that I take on my usual household chores, and hardly ever spoke to me beyond necessities. To punish her, I became pretty much a slut.

Yeah. Right.

I was desperately hurt by what I thought was a massive overreaction to a dream. After all, it was just a dream.

But what my mother did that I could never forgive her for was taking my father away from me. Never again did we go alone on overnight camping trips, nor have our summer holidays together. We never attempted to make the reason visible; it lived in a dark corner of our lives like a malevolent family spirit, a gremlin.

Tom

We went first to Paris and stayed at our favorite hotel, Le Hôme Fleuri, on Rue Daguerre between the Montparnasse cemetery and Avenue du Maine; Sartre and de Beauvoir lived around the corner at the Mistral and were buried in the cemetery across the street. There's a laundry nearby, and a good restaurant serving food from Reunion Island. Rue Daguerre runs into the Place Denfert-Rochereau near the entrance to the Catacombs, and there's a good pizza restaurant with tables outside. It was for us a sort of personal neighborhood and we had stayed there four times, once for a month.

The first time was 1981, when we came up from doing Alpine routes near Chamonix and wanted to be in a city for a while. It was winter, Christmas week. Because there were no leaves on the trees and because the air was so crisp, the lights had seemed brighter and more concentrated. There was a little snow. Not enough to make it pretty.

Now everything was muted. There was no sun for three days, and more often than not the air filled with a sharply falling gray rain. The colors of Paris washed along the sidewalks and down the slow river the way a fascinated child dribbles paint from his fingertips. The river looked thick enough to walk across. We liked cafés by the river where we could sit and watch marine traffic, but the rain forced us inside and the cafés were filled with smoke and food smells, anonymous chatter, and we couldn't see the river. Finally we just decided to ignore the weather. Paris was built to walk through. We took the Metro and rode to unknown destinations, getting off because the stop had an improbable or incomprehensible name, then arose into whatever neighborhood lay above. We were always tourists. Every time.

Molly wore a dark green beret from which her long, sand-colored hair hung in moisture-curled ringlets. Hard to believe it was so far into June, but there were bright new leaves on the trees, flowers everywhere.

I had not told Molly the truth about leaving the university because it seemed pointless and would only depress her. I said, the truth, that it wasn't possible to get a sabbatical early, but that the Dean had generously offered me a one-year leave with pay. At least she pretended to believe me. My leave was without pay and I cashed out my IRA retirement account to pad our savings, as if my pay continued. Molly would not have gone otherwise. I don't know if she ever figured this out.

We had no immediate plans, just Paris, then east. We left California seven days after I turned in grades. They didn't know the reason, I suppose, but my students rejoiced when I cancelled the final exams and gave everyone a perfect score for the exam they hadn't taken. They considered it a gift; I knew it was because I had stopped caring, which is the opposite of a gift.

We wrote postcards and prowled the largest mountaineering store in Paris. Molly bought a day pack that by coincidence matched her parka. We tested climbing shoes on the two-story artificial wall in the shop. I saw Molly write the word treen on a postcard when she meant train, and raisin instead of rain. These were not mistakes she would normally make, even writing in haste. I let it go. It didn't matter. Sometimes it was hard to walk in the neighborhoods because they abounded with life, and while previously we had enjoyed wandering around in Parisian cemeteries, this time we stayed away.

We went to Fountainbleau on the train, intending to go bouldering, but a heavy mist made the rocks too wet. Instead we toured the chateau. We walked through the square and people flowed around us like gray ghosts. We went to a wine bar and I got into a potentially violent argument with another American, which is not in my character. I suppose that subconsciously I wanted to hurt someone, and he was misfortunate enough to have been a typical American bore in the wrong place at the wrong time. His offense was a loud voice in an otherwise quiet bar, and I remarked something to the effect that it's jerks like this who give Americans abroad such a bad name. Molly stopped it by urging me to take her back to the hotel.

We liked the hotel mainly because of its location and price, cheap enough for us to afford long stays. Breakfast was good and the staff almost familial. But the rooms were small, about twice the size of the walk-in closet in our California house. A floor-to-ceiling French window was its best feature, and we slid the small writing desk beside it.

The last night we were to stay in Paris, we didn't go out. I glanced through a guidebook while Molly sat in the straight-back chair by the desk and looked out at the street, two stories below. I asked if she wanted to go to Chamonix.

"Do you?"

I wanted to say that none of this was up to me, but I said, "There won't be much good climbing for another month or two. Everything's melting and falling down."

"I guess not, then, unless you want to."

"Not really. We'd just spend our time ducking paragliders and standing in line for a decent route. Of course, there are other places, quieter, with good climbs. More south. We could go to Spain."

"I like France, Tommy. But I thought I'd feel differently."

"Sure, I understand. Not Spain?"

She shook her head, still staring out the window. At least it wasn't raining and the street was alive with people.

"Switzerland? Interlaken?"

"Maybe."

Now I could see that her headache, which began in the wine bar and intensified as a result of the tension from the argument, was much worse. She sat by the window with her elbows on the tiny desk and her chin in her cupped hands, the tips of her fingers massaging her temples. I had already asked her ten times if she was all right, and there was nothing I could do.

"The weather sucks," she said.

"But it seems to be getting better."

"Maybe."

"Would it help if you lay down?"

She turned and seemed to start to speak, but said nothing, and finally stood and walked slowly, deliberately to the bed and lay on her side, curled like a fetus. I lay close to her and rubbed the back of her neck. She vomited on a towel I brought and placed beside her face. I washed it in the shower.

She had shown few signs of illness through much of the spring, while we packed up the house and put our things in storage. She was nauseated so frequently that we hardly took much notice of it. I could see it coming and knew when to produce a towel for her or help her to the toilet at the same time she knew. We had been waiting for the other symptoms but for months she only had headaches and nausea. There were times she couldn't remember even a simple word, and sometimes she made slightly incongruous statements, but I also did that sometimes, and I wasn't dying. I think we had begun to hope for more time.

Later, after Molly fell into a sound sleep, I dressed and went out. It was just after midnight and I could see a few stars among flying clouds, and a sliver of moonlight popped out once. I didn't want to leave Molly alone for long, but I felt the need to walk off a nascent panic attack. My heart thudded and I felt light-headed from hyperventilating. When I sat still, I got dizzy and my skin tingled.

I walked south on Du Maine where there were many hookers and odd characters, passed the St. Pierre church, went under the railroad bridge on the Rue d'Alesia, and passed the psychological hospital. Then I was lost. I knew I had gone as far as the Parc Montsouris, but I had apparently made too many turns to simply turn around and go back. Wandering around just made me more lost, but after almost an hour I found myself in the small neighborhood where Henry Miller once borrowed a studio and knew how to get back to a main street.

What would happen, I wondered, if Molly woke up in the middle of the night and found me gone? It was stupid to have gone out like I did. Not even taking a map. I was gone well over an hour when once more I found myself at the Place Victor Basch in front of the St. Pierre church. The moon was gone again and a faint mist touched my face. I looked at the church, as if I wanted to go inside, which was a ridiculous idea. But I did sit on the steps beneath the eaves and out of the mist. The doors were probably locked anyway. A drug deal took place on the opposite corner. I wanted a cigarette, although I quit smoking something like a dozen years before. How, I wondered, did all the lines of my life come together here and now? How was I going to survive Molly leaving me? I had known a lot of women, and maybe I was in love before, but probably not, because there had never been a woman like Molly. Why her and not another, I cannot say. What would happen when she died, I could not imagine.

I have always believed that the line between reason and senselessness is extraordinarily fragile and desperately tenuous. I have entertained enough incongruous—I could say insane—thoughts in my life that I understand how razor sharp, how thin the dividing line is. It is the loss of control that most frightens me, that some event I had not determined and could not manage would knock me over the line and I would not be able to recover. I studied philosophy, I realize now, solely as an attempt to understand and then maybe control the mysterious exegesis of fate. I see in the faces of my few serious students that they are looking for the same thing.

I have failed to find a god I could believe in. From the tragic Catholicism of Unamuno and the trembling leap of Kierkegaard to the deductions of Descartes and the practical realities of James, I have still not been able to find salvation from the condemnation of reason. The only gods I can find were obviously created from human need, having no other existence or purpose. This fact saddens me. It was this sadness that had me sitting on the steps of the St. Pierre church like a penitent.

Molly was still asleep when I got back to the room, but I was thoroughly awake. I sat in the chair by the window and looked out. The buildings across the street were dark. I could see one lighted window in the building on the corner where a dark-skinned, turban-clad technician often fabricated teeth well into the night. There was an accordion shop and I once had an urge to go in and buy one, although I could not play. But I would take lessons and serenade Molly with French songs while we picnicked by the Seine, like a scene from a movie.

I don't know how long I must have been thinking about this, but I decided, like Pascal, to try cutting a deal. The only thing that could be hurt was my ego, my sense of personal stupidity. A cheap enough price.

I overcame the embarrassment and clasped my hands, vaguely prayer-like, in front of me—who can judge the value of ritual, regardless how inane? Looking out the window, more or less toward the sky, I whispered this: "If you exist, if you happen to actually exist in any comprehensible, rational way, I would like to make a deal with you. I can only assume, given the ridiculous senselessness of horror in the world, the fact that it is so random, that you must be at least a cosmic sort of godfather, bestowing life and wealth, death and despair, in very nearly arbitrary ways. If that is your character, then I appeal to you to spare my wife this certain and terrible death sentence that you and only you could have pronounced on her. In return, you may do with me whatever pleases you. If that is not enough, if you will spare Molly, I will produce converts to your cause in as great a number as I am capable. I am a teacher of young people, they are impressionable, and I can get a lot of them to join your side. I will become your chief proselytizer. I will bring you worshippers, since that is what you seem to desire. I will even believe in you. I am quite serious about this. Test me, abuse me like Job, torture me to see how serious I am. I will believe. But first you have to spare Molly. You have to take the cancer out of her and give her perfect health. You come through for me and I'll come through for you."

Then I got up, undressed, and went to bed, smothered by silence.

We left from Gare de l'Est for Vienna on the second of July without having seen Paris in the sun, pulled east by memories of mountains, villages with narrow streets, quiet cafés, of Czechoslovakia and the High Tatras, where there waited perfect climbs and good friends.

We left Paris in the rain, which streaked the windows of the train compartment like sticky snail tracks. A dog nosed through trash on the sidewalk. There were flowers in window boxes along the balconies of high-rise apartments, and wilted laundry sometimes. The tops of high buildings were lost in mist. Paris disappeared quickly as the train reached speed. Oddly, the rain was blue, as if a precursor to an eventual view of the sky.

There was a man in the compartment sitting near the door. Molly and I had opposing window seats. He put his face into a German newspaper and only looked up from time to time, apparently to see the rain. I thought he would get off in Bern, a burgher, and was right.

There was a girl, probably a student, reading a French translation of volume one of Freud's collected works. She had blond hair and a plain face, bitten nails, but good clothes and an expensive leather rucksack. She sat next to Molly, across from me, and flirted with me rather flagrantly. Another time I would have enjoyed teasing her, but this distressed Molly and I ignored the girl as much as possible. She got off in Nancy.

After Nancy, Molly took out the spiral notebook in which she kept diary entries, but she only wrote one or two lines before putting the notebook on the shelf below the window. I bought two cans of French beer from the vendor's cart and asked Molly what she wrote.

"A note about the scenery," she said.

I thought she wrote about the girl. I know how she could be sometimes. She fought against jealousy and often lost. I think then she was worried about women who might come on to me. Afterwards. When we were first married she confessed that she could hardly bear the image of me with another woman, kissing her, holding her, coming inside her. She said such a picture made her sick to her stomach and she simply would not let herself think about it. A few months ago we talked about the possibility that there might be another woman someday, although I told her that I, also, could not imagine it. She said she wanted me to fall in love again, and be happy when she was gone, but I knew it was a lie. She wanted it to be impossible for me to even look at another woman. It was for a very long time.

At Bern we changed for Zurich. From Zurich everything was familiar. The snow line was still quite low. Now sunshine, the first since St. Anton, darted among the trees and flashed from the braces of hang gliders dipping toward the valley and racing the eastbound train. Rivers ran with spring melt, a kind of medicinal green, and roared below the underpasses. The mountain tops were still hidden in clouds and sometimes there were the cable tracks of chair lifts. We watched cars on the highway beside the train, headlights flashing as the swift passed the slow, their tires spitting up a filthy spray, their lights dimmed by grime, rainbows coming and going across the glass beneath hesitating windshield wipers.

After a while she fell asleep against her backpack, her hair mussed, and I watched her sleeping like a little girl.

Vienna Sudbahnhof was filled with Turks, Serbs, Hungarians, and various Africans selling pornographic magazines and picking pockets. They had ominous stares, eyes with emptiness behind them. Women who would kill you or cook for you with the same expression. Children alone without fear. Gypsies expressing themselves.

We took time to get something to eat at the Rosenkavalier, the station café, where the waiters wore tuxedos and carried white napkins over their bent arms and treated us with amused deference, like abdicated royalty.

The late afternoon train to Bratislava ran only three cars, and they were mostly empty. We stood on the platform and watched a small group of teenagers with school bags board the last car, so we got aboard the middle one. The last two were Austrian, the first a grime-streaked Czechoslovak car. Soon kids were roaming the aisles making as much noise as they could.

The train pulled out precisely on time, heading south and east for the border between Austria and Czechoslovakia. We had a compartment to ourselves and stood side by side at the window watching when we crossed the Danube—which is not blue and moves nothing like Strauss's music. Where do you suppose, Molly contemplated, Strauss got his ideas?

The setting sun was pale and rugged as a moon. The air cool but not cold and the compartment overheated. We could hear laughter from the compartment behind, then a girl screamed and other girls giggled. Boys hooted, and soon four or five of them bolted the compartment and assaulted the aisles. In a few minutes the ticket agent arrived. The first was Austrian and offered us a "Grüss Gott" as he examined then punched our tickets, which were good for the portion to Marchegg, the last stop before crossing the border.

I opened the window after he left and we stood by it, the fresh air helping to waken us. We passed through farmland. A family of deer stood watching the train from the edge of a wind break. A nonchalant farmer rode a red tractor, from behind which rose no dust. There were tall storage silos with signs in fancy German script. Then we entered Marchegg.

Three men in suits and two women dressed like secretaries got off. The school kids departed like abandoning a ship. Czechoslovak customs officers with their bellies stretched stood by the track smoking and talking with Austrian border guards who carried Glock automatics in holsters as small as those used for piton hammers. They boarded the train finally and we pulled out. The border was close, five or ten minutes more, and in spite of reason the train seemed darker, quieter, tense.

The guards came, two in military uniforms, one with an automatic rifle, and a third man in a black suit, white shirt and black narrow tie, wearing Wayfarer sunglasses like an anorexic Blues Brother. We handed over our passports and they disappeared into the corridor with the Blues Brother from the secret police. We reached the railroad bridge over the Morava River and passed behind the Iron Curtain. From the window we could see a high fence topped with razor wire, guards with machine guns, dogs, red and white border markers. It would have felt more appropriate to have made the crossing in the dead of night, a foggy night, with searchlights, barking dogs, sparks snapping atop the electrified wires.

Molly whispered to me, "Welcome back to the Disneyland of Communism."

Our passports were returned, we were ordered to change money at the next stop, Devínska Nová Ves, to cover each day in our visas. The soldiers were still poking around in our bags, and one of them enjoyed playing with the climbing gear. "*Horolozec*," he said, the word for mountaineer.

Once we crossed at Petržalka in a rental car, the guards had made us wait, stamping our feet and slapping our hands in the cold

December air while they tore the car apart. We were smuggling two books—an Ivan Klima and a Milan Kundera. We had replaced their dust jackets with covers from two bodice busting romances. We did not think that for smuggling a couple of books we'd be sent to the Gulag, or whatever they had in Czechoslovakia, but we didn't want to disappoint our friends, who had asked for them. They didn't remove the dust covers although a guard thumbed through the books. It was obvious that he couldn't read English.

This time, on the train, it was easy, and maybe because of all the climbing gear, we were left alone for the last few minutes as the train crawled through the Bratislava suburbs to the main station.

Molly

There is a photograph of me and my father taken at Joshua Tree when I was 16 years old, two weeks after Mother read the diary. We are facing the camera. I look younger than 16, but the date was written on the back, so I know. It is an ordinary picture, there must be millions of its kind in photo albums everywhere: an outing, a father and daughter, uncomfortably posed, a nice day somewhere, sometime. Behind us is a gigantic boulder called King Otto's Castle. There is a cave the size of a room at its base, and we used to try to get to Joshua Tree early enough to make our campsite in the cave's shade, before someone beat us to it. You can see the cave in the picture, but someone else's tent is dimly visible inside. This was only a day trip for us, the first of what would always be day trips in our future. It was early enough in spring for it not to be too hot. I am wearing ridiculous blue and white polka-dotted pedal pushers and white sandals. My rock shoes are tied by their laces to a loop on my harness, where they dangle like bags of coins, and I am wearing an old blue T-shirt with a rip in the right armpit so large that if I raised my arm you could see most of my breast through the hole. I thought it was quite a brave hole. I am wearing a Baltimore Orioles baseball cap and my hair is stuffed under it. We are facing the sun and are both squinting, our eyes just slits. My father is wearing a Marine Corps fatigue cap with the bill turned up. A Goldline rope is coiled over his right shoulder. His harness and shoes are in a heap in the dirt by his feet. By today's standards our equipment looks primitive and dangerous. The monolith of King Otto's Castle is white hot in the sun. There is blood caked on both my father's knees because I had dropped him half an hour earlier. I was belaying with a Munter Hitch and not paying enough attention. A Munter Hitch is simply a twist of the rope around a karabiner and only as secure as the attention paid to it by the belayer. He slipped and I didn't catch him until he had slid down the rock face for at least 20 feet. He didn't say anything at all after finishing the climb. I sat on a rock crying, waiting for him to walk off the back side. He only said it was time to go home and we started gathering our gear. I wasn't only crying because I'd dropped him, or from embarrassment. I knew then that my life was now divided between before and after. I missed before. We packed up and someone, I don't remember now who, took the picture. I kept it to remember what I looked like on the day I discovered loneliness.

I chose not to say anything to Father about the diary, although I feared that Mother had. It was certainly not coincidental that I was only invited on extended climbing trips when there were others along. We never went alone again. I was too embarrassed to say anything, and accepted the conditions of fate.

I began to leave my family that last good summer, when I was 16, to find my way alone in the forest of wolves, and I began learning to climb alone.

I wanted to be popular and did not like solitude—it seemed to be assigned to me rather than chosen. As an only child I developed few social skills and had a tendency toward privacy, but that doesn't mean I didn't want to have friends. I just chased popularity in stupid and awkward ways. I tried sports, but only enjoyed the solitary events, like cross-country running, which was also good for climbing stamina. I joined the Literature Club my junior year, but quit soon enough, realizing that my idea of literature wasn't a popular one. I don't remember all the things I tried, but when I just couldn't stand being lonely anymore, I found companions in the most direct way—sex. Of course, the only "friends" this produced were male.

It was surprising that boys wanted to have sex with me. I wasn't pretty as a teenager, and certainly not sexy. I had an athletic body, legs like a boy, no butt to speak of, and my chest didn't grow consequentially until I was 16 years old. Yes, I know that a teenage boy will have sex with anything, including such amazing objects as watermelons, mud and vacuum cleaners. I suppose I was at least a step up from those things. I did, at least, try to limit my sexual partners to boys who would go climbing with me. I needed a belayer to replace my father.

At the end of the '60s and through the '70s the population of climbers in America was small. It was such a compact community that within various specific geographic areas it was likely that every single climber would be known to one another. In 1971, I knew fewer than 20 people who were climbers in the technical sense. I was the only female climber among them. One Saturday in the spring of 1972, I was climbing at Mission Gorge near San Diego with four boys from two different San Diego high schools, and within the previous six months I had slept with each of them. That day I realized that they took me with them, not because I was a good climber—I was in fact a better climber than any of them, but because I could probably be induced at day's end to mess around. Not with all of them at once, of course, but with one of them. I was virtually a mascot. But this was not about sex, which I always kind of liked, except when it was boring; it was about not being treated seriously as a climber. So, in 1972, I began a year of sexual abstinence. I simply wouldn't sleep with anyone who couldn't out-climb me.

I took up bouldering because I could do it alone. Except for a few day trips with my father, all the climbing I did in those days was

55

free-soloing, which means climbing alone without a rope or any means of protection from falls. Bouldering is a rock dance using the simplest means, and I have bouldered nude, that is, with only rock shoes to protect my feet against the sharp crystals in the monzonite granite, in order to find out just how cleanly one could climb. It is highly stylized. You are never far from the ground so you are free to move without the umbilical of a rope. It is a solo game. For almost two years, because my father no longer took me on his longer excursions, and our day trips were rare, it was the only kind of climbing I did.

Not far from my house, near Santee, a field of granite boulders lay strewn across the desert mesa between two highways. In summer the sun heated the rocks to a point where to touch them would produce a blister, but it was a wonderful place in winter and early spring. I could ride there on my bicycle in about 40 minutes.

Some kids from nearby high schools—the "bad" kids—went to the Santee rocks at night to drink beer, smoke dope, fight and make out. We had one-handed climbing contests in the dark to see who could climb the highest, the fastest with a beer in one hand. I won more times than I lost. Only a few of us were capable of climbing the most difficult boulder problems, and we formed a sort of elite club. Although it was informal, we did have a name: The Santee Geckos. One of the guys suggested the name because he said geckos are lizards and good climbers, and because their call sounds like "fuck you." We named the highest boulder, Gecko Rock, and the hardest route we named, of course, Fuck You. Maybe four or five of us could climb it. The top was some 30 feet from the ground, a pretty long fall if you made a mistake. One classmate broke his ankle and hip falling from it. But he was drunk. After that the sheriff's office hung no trespassing signs on the fence along the road, which everyone ignored.

In those days Santee Rocks was not thought of much as a place for climbers. It was just a good, private area for a wild party. During the daylight hours, I owned it.

I stopped being lonely on a hot day during the spring break of my senior year of high school. I had awakened before dawn in order to get to Santee before the rising sun heated the rocks. After hiding my bike in the brush, I headed for any interesting rock. I heard her first, a grunting sound coming from the east side of Gold's Gem. I didn't want to surprise her, maybe cause her to fall, so I stopped and waited a couple of minutes until I thought she had made the top. The best route on the east side of Gold's Gem was called Gem Crack Corn And I Don't Care, and that had to be where she was.

Shielding my eyes against the sun, I looked at the top and saw her looking down. "Hi," she said. I said, "Hi." She was standing on the slightly sloping top of the boulder, hands on her hips. "I go down if you want come up," she said. Her voice was old, husky, and accented in a way I had never heard. I just knew it wasn't Spanish.

"I'm just going over there," I answered, pointing toward Potato Face. She waved, I waved back, then I left.

It wasn't common then to see a climber at Santee. It would become more popular in another 10 years, mimicking the growth of climbing in general. Occasionally I would come across a climber or two, guys I knew from high school, but I had never seen a woman climbing at Santee. Seeing her on top of such a hard boulder problem was like seeing a fish go by on a bicycle.

I sat down on a tabletop rock next to Potato Face and took off my sandals, then fished a water bottle from the pack for a drink. The air was still cool, but in the sun there was no problem feeling how hot it would be soon enough. Wearing only a T-shirt and shorts, there were chill bumps on my arms and thighs. I could see her down-climbing the easy west side of Gold's Gem, which was about 100 feet away, and she was extraordinarily good. Her toes found rock nubbins without looking down, and she was also stylish, graceful. Because she was silhouetted by the sun when I first saw her, I stared now to see what she looked like. She looked strong. I wondered if she was a tourist, maybe from Europe. But in Santee? Curiosity interfered with my concentration and I was slow getting started. I put on my shoes, clipped the chalk bag to one of the belt loops on my shorts, and stood looking at Potato Face while warming the flexors and muscles in my forearms by clenching and releasing my fists.

The route was called Potato Skins, and was next to French Fries. Potato Face looked like a giant unpeeled potato, and all the routes had appropriate names, including Mashed Potatoes, Cream Potatoes, and Curly-Q's. Potato Face had a rounded top on which someone had placed a pair of pitons in a crack. They were old, rusted, but useable. Even my father didn't know who placed them. He said they had always been there, which means before his time. Potato Face was 27 feet high and apparently some people only climbed it using a top rope for protection. Potato Skins was an 80-degree face climb with negligible holds, and it was hard.

My palms were sweaty and I loaded them up with chalk, which Father got in bulk from the school gym. A small cloud rose when I slapped my hands together. A fly tormented me for a moment, then left. I tried to concentrate on the moves, but every little thing distracted me. I couldn't stop thinking about seeing a woman downclimbing Gold's Gem.

At knee height a narrow ledge ran along that side of the rock, and I put my left foot on it, then reached up for the first hold, which would only take the first digits of three fingers. I was aware of the sun on my back and the smell of aloe and sand and chalk. The most difficult moves were at the bottom, so it was okay to solo. The rock fell off after about 15 feet and there were more substantial holds. I have fallen from Potato Skins more times than I have climbed it.

I came off the third move, landing awkwardly on my heels and sitting down hard on my butt in the, thankfully, soft sand. I said *shit* and slapped the dirt.

"You not concentrate, I think," came a voice from behind me.

The woman from Gold's Gem stood watching, hands on her hips again. She wore cutoff blue jeans—cut so short the pockets protruded, and a sort of halter top made from a blue- and white-checkered bandana that hardly contained an astonishing pair of breasts, the kind that make boys bite their index finger and use words like hooters. Her legs were short and muscular and she was barefooted, holding her rock shoes—ancient French Eb's—by their laces. She had the oddest rust-colored shade of red hair I had ever seen and it was cut to frame her face like an oval picture frame. She was deeply tanned, not very pretty, rather old—from my perspective then, old meant over 30, and it turns out she was nearly 40. Climbers tend to be long and thin. She was built like a mountaineer, not a rock climber. She looked like an aging ragamuffin.

"You're damn right," I said, getting up and brushing off my sore butt.

"Hi," she offered her free hand to me. "I am Alexandra, but am call Saša." We shook hands.

"I'm Molly. You're the first girl . . . woman climber I've ever seen here."

"Same for me. You are first."

"You always come in the morning this early?"

"Must before work. You?"

"Me? Before school. Sometimes at night."

"Climb in dark?"

"Sure. Sometimes."

"Also me. But dark in morning, not night."

"If I can ask, where are you from?"

"Czechoslovakia. You know it?"

"Well . . . it's a country in Europe. A Communist one, right?"

"You are true. My country is in central part of Europe and I am from Czech part. From Prague."

"You are the first person I've ever actually met from Europe. Are you on vacation?" I wanted to ask if she was a Communist, too. She would have been the first real live one I'd ever seen.

She shook her head. "Now I live here. From 1968, I live here. You know 1968?"

I didn't understand what she was asking. I shrugged noncommittally.

"Is not so good story. Climbing is more interesting, you agree?"

"Let's climb this," I challenged her to the rock I had just fallen from. I followed Saša, mimicked her moves, and in a few minutes we were sitting side by side on the small, pointed top. I told her she climbed Potato Skins beautifully.

"Potato skins? Like skin from potato?"

"Exactly."

"Is good name. You give this name?"

"Nah. I don't know where the name comes from. My father told me."

"Your father is also climber?"

"Definitely. A very good one."

"My father is also climber. Wery good, also."

"Here? Or in . . . ?"

"Czechoslovakia. Vas climber. He is died."

"I'm sorry."

"He died from 1968 and I come here."

"That route," I pointed behind and changed the subject, "is called French Fries, and the one coming up this seam is Mashed Potatoes."

She laughed in a husky, beautiful way. "I like these names."

"My father and his friends named most of these routes. We named some, me and my friends from school. For example, the route you were on when I came up is called Gem Cracked Corn And I Don't Care. Gem is spelled g-e-m. You see, the rock is called Gold's Gem. It's a place to work out, you know, like for athletes. Only it's spelled g-y-m . . . never mind."

"I also give names to rocks. The one I am on when you came, I call it *kalíšek na vajce*. This name means cup where you put egg to eat.

And this one we just climb, I call it, *kalhotky*. This word means in English panties."

"Panties? You mean like *panties*?" I snapped the waistband of my own.

She nodded and we both laughed.

"First time I climb here is summer and is hot. I wear only panties."

"No shoes?"

"Yes, shoes also."

I tried to pronounce her word for panties and told her it was a strange word. She said panties sounded strange to her. I could not imagine a woman climber nearly the age of my mother who climbed in her panties.

I wanted so much for Saša to be my best friend that I felt a rush of panic from the fear of saying or doing something wrong. For another 45 minutes we climbed together, spotting for each other, which allowed us to try more difficult moves than if alone. We climbed Baby Face, which she called *šlehačka*—it means whipped cream—which is one of the most difficult routes at Santee. Saša did not make it look easy, but neither did she fall. I managed to climb it by copying her moves. At eight o'clock she said she had to leave. I asked where she worked and she said she was a gardener for a company that serviced hotel accounts. She said she hoped we would climb together again, and said *ciao* when she waved goodbye.

I didn't understand the feelings that meeting produced in me at the time. What it felt like was falling in love. I craved Saša's friendship.

Tom

In 1985, I published a book of essays called *The Impulse to Self-Destruct—The Communist Ontology*, a socio-political rendering of more esoteric and academic ideas regarding phenomenological ontology I had tried to develop in a doctoral dissertation. Because as a mountaineer I had met and befriended a number of Czechoslovakian climbers, and had traveled often in that part of Europe, I began converting academic speculations into reports on the philosophical underpinnings of life in totalitarian societies. That underpinning seemed to me to be hopelessness. A central feature of life in totalitarian social systems is to be without hope. Hope is not the same as desire. Hope is, among other things, an idea, while desire is an action, even a sort of lifestyle. Hope belongs to the province of dreams; we may hope for something that does not yet exist, hope is the embodiment of dreams. Desire is a confrontation with the real, where we may have success or failure. Hope is a force for creation. Desire is the impetus for acquisition, or the failure to acquire and possess. Hope is ontological, desire is phenomenological.

Now, in the summer of 1988, as Molly and I came into Bratislava's main train station, arriving in the moist and strangely cool evening air of early July, we had abandoned all our impotent desires, replacing them with a passionate and boundless hope; desiring nothing, hoping for everything. We could not choose what was happening to us, but we could choose how we felt about it, and what we believed. In the dark and drab bowels of the train station, we seemed to glow with this sense of freedom, although surrounded by the degradations of infinite hopelessness, like the common man lives in a totalitarian state.

Outside there were only whores, drunks, pickpockets, police, gypsics, the denizens of every late-night train station in this part of Europe. We were the only foreign passengers getting off the train. An electric trolley bus with smudged windows moved toward a platform and we ran to get aboard. The architecture of the station was hidden behind corrugated tin construction walls, some torn, and astonishingly without graffiti. There was mud everywhere, but the only trash consisted of useless scraps of paper; the bottle and can scavengers had picked over the sidewalk and platform as clean as bones in the jungle.

We dragged our packs off the trolley at the Mostová stop and walked around to the Hotel Carlton. The United States Consulate was nearby. The Carlton was once the best hotel in town, and one of the oldest in Central Europe. Now it was probably the worst. The newer hotels were for foreign businessmen and priced for them. In the Carlton's dark lobby you could imagine spies, although mostly there were just whores wearing too much makeup, their bodies swollen from starch and sugar. Everything was sour. I had stayed here before and it wasn't quite this bad. I thought it needed to be torn down, and in fact it closed two years later.

"It's too much for this place," I told Molly after the desk clerk told us the price of a double room, for which we had reservations.

"Let's just get some sleep and deal with it tomorrow," Molly said. She was getting sick.

The second floor room was dark with only a single light bulb hanging from a fixture in the ceiling. There were plastic flowers in fat vases in the hallway, which smelled like smoke and mold. There were two narrow beds with frames covered in blond plastic simulated wood. There was a stuffed chair, a cigarette-burned dresser and a veneered armoire. The single picture on the wall was of a snowcapped peak, Kriváň, the Slovak national symbol, and seemed to have been cut from a calendar or magazine. Our window overlooked Hviezdoslavovo Square, a long, skinny park named for the Slovak poet and linguist whose statue—the poet seated with pen and book—dominated the center. Across the park was a Hungarian restaurant and at the other end, the baroque Slovak National Theater.

I unpacked a few necessities and Molly said she wanted a bath, but changed her mind after seeing the tub. It was mercifully quiet, except for the clattering of trams going by from time to time. Faintly we heard music, which seemed to be coming across the park from the Hungarian restaurant. I pushed the beds together and we lay down to rest.

"It wasn't this bad before," I said.

"Ten years ago."

I had only stayed here once, ten years ago, and Molly had never been here.

"Right. But things change so slowly here, I thought . . ."

"We can look for something else tomorrow."

"It is much easier crossing the border by train than car, don't you think?"

"The girl on the train was hot for you."

"What girl?"

"The little French one pretending to read Freud."

"I didn't think so."

"Maybe we should just go to the mountains and forget staying in the city."

"We can do that."

"But I want to see Štefan."

"Tomorrow, first thing."

"But maybe he's in the mountains."

"We'll go by his office in the morning."

"I'm happy to be here, Tom. In spite of this depressing dump."

"Me, too."

I ate breakfast in the hotel café, standing at the bar with coffee, bread, cheese and jam, surrounded by workmen gazing at tissue-thin newspapers, wearing the same baggy blue denim pants, cheap shoes. Two men in shiny suits sat by a window, smoking and gesturing expansively, speaking Russian. Ageless women in smocks and floppy slippers that slapped the linoleum floor like the pop of snapped wet towels brought food and coffee to the tables. The smell of bacon lay heavily over everything.

Molly still slept. This difference was always between us: she liked nights, I mornings. It rained during the night. The cold front had followed us from Paris, and it was still drizzling in the morning. It was cool enough for long sleeves or a light jacket. In the United States, it was Independence Day.

I checked a map in the hotel lobby, thinking we might walk to Štefan's office. Štefan Borák was president of the Slovak Mountaineer's Club and his office was in one of the sports universities at the edge of the city. It looked to be seven or eight kilometers and I didn't know how Molly would feel. I decided not to push her; we'd take a tram as far as the *tržnica*, the central market, and walk from there. After arranging with the clerk to get some laundry done, I went to get Molly up.

"How do you feel?" I asked, after touching her shoulder to wake her.

"Okay," she answered.

But I knew better from the way she stood, slow and unbalanced. I had already noticed changes in her depth perception—stepping higher than necessary at a curb, cautious on stairs—and worried that she might already be losing her vision.

"Bad headache?"

"I'm going to take something."

"Hungry?"

"Yes, but I might as well wait . . ."

She didn't have to wait. She rushed to the bathroom and knelt by the toilet. It was just dry heaves, she hadn't eaten last night, but they lasted a long time. Afterwards she said she'd like some juice.

"It's not the real stuff," I told her.

"We're back in the land of the ubiquitous orange-ish drink, huh?"

"Exactly. But the coffee, it's Turkish, is very good."

"I'll just wash my face."

"I'm just going to take these clothes down to be cleaned. I'll meet you in the café, okay?"

She nodded, went back into the bathroom and closed the door. I thought she was trying very hard to be happy in this derelict hotel, when I knew all she wanted was to be in the mountains.

Outside the air smelled of grease, cooking grease days-old caught in a brass trap. An old man and an old woman wearing dull orange smocks and felt boots that were damp and dirty from the drizzle-bedecked and filthy streets, passed the front door of the hotel, each carrying a bucket and mop. They turned the corner heading toward the Philharmonic and disappeared before I could see what they were intending to mop. A man stood in a telephone booth, his cardboard briefcase holding open the door, a glowing sticker on the side of the case advertised BMW cars. At the magazine kiosk, a small group of people crowded together buying newspapers and cigarettes. A packed tram passed. A woman sang an operatic aria from an open window on the side of the Slovak National Theater at the end of the park, and her voice came and went as passing buses, trams and trucks over-whelmed her pure, controlled singing.

A man in a Škoda taxi beckoned to us, asking in German if we wanted a taxi, which we did not. We had decided not to get on the packed tram and walked across the park toward the old town, deciding to try for a tram on another street. The drizzle stopped and there were clear indications the sun might appear. It was cool still, but also humid. We walked up Michalská Street toward the old town's one remaining gate and stopped to look in the window of the Tatran book store.

"Nothing changes here," Molly commented. "It's like a time warp."

"So Heraclitus was wrong, everything isn't constantly in flux. It just seems to be."

"Isn't communism about stability, keeping the trains running on time?"

"That's fascism."

"Same difference."

We were last in Bratislava five years before and the same useless things were in the shop windows. People lined up on the street outside the same way, in the same numbers, waiting to be passed a shopping basket so they could go inside to paw over the same things for the same prices, each person clutching a plastic *perhaps* bag expectantly. Maybe someday something they actually wanted to buy might appear in one of the stores.

Even on sunny days darkness dominated. Nothing was clean. Shop windows carried decades of grime disguising their vacuousness. Cobblestone alleyways near pubs reeked of vomit and grease, the cafés of coffee and grease, the air of mold, bad cigarettes and grease. People walked with their heads down and their arms laden with plastic bags as they scrounged from store to store to stand in infinite lines for anything they could buy. A city and people unconscious, life in limbo. Hopeless.

Molly put her arm through mine and we walked on to find another tram; often she lay her head on my shoulder, and we walked like lovers. The drizzle stopped. We got on a half-full tram and headed out of the old town.

"This is it," Molly said as we approached a stop after riding for about 10 minutes.

"You recognize it?"

"The smell. This is it."

The air smelled of rotten eggs. The Dimitrovka chemical plant was only a couple of stops further on. She was right. We got off and I recognized the building. There were about a dozen young people in various colors of velour outfits waiting at the stop; old women in black carrying bags stood apart. We dodged a truck and a candy-colored Škoda car as we crossed the street and tried to find a way to the building that didn't involve tramping through a muddy athletic field.

We had no idea if Štefan was even there. I had tried to call but couldn't get through; no busy signal, no nothing. Even the desk clerk failed and just shrugged his shoulders, sort of smiled.

There were guards and potbellied men in jogging suits smoking near the entrance. Students sat around a broken fountain. Everyone stared at us, in our western clothes and shoes. "They think we've come to steal their sports secrets," Molly whispered as we pushed open the vault-like doors.

Because I could speak a little Slovak, we were able to get the guards to understand that we wanted to see Štefan Borák, president of the Slovak Mountaineer's Union. One of them devoured our passports while the other got on the phone. Finally we were told a number and pointed toward one of the small elevators at the back of the lobby, where more men in jogging suits stood in clumps, smoking, some with coffee. Molly's chest seemed to be even more interesting to them than our shoes.

The hallway on the fifth floor was bare except for some small, crinkled notices stuck up with tacks and a couple of official travel posters of Bulgaria and Yugoslavia. There was one orange plastic chair with an overflowing ashtray standing next to it. We could hear muffled voices from behind doors that had panels of obscured glass. At the end of the hall we came to a door with a postcard-size sign reading: *Slovenský horolezecký spolok—prezident, Štefan Borák.*

I knocked. A woman opened the door and had no idea what to make of us. Then Štefan leaned around to see who it was.

"Tomaš! *Ježis Mária*! Molly! So it is *you*! You are the Americans."

Štefan Borák sat on the corner of a desk piled with papers, one pile held down by an old Leeper piton, his hand resting atop a metallic Soviet typewriter, leaning over to see around the woman who still stood gaping at us through the open door. There were two other men in the room, and one of them was built like a tank. Štefan jumped up and gave us both great bear hugs. He smelled of harsh Sparta cigarettes and industrial soap.

In 1988, Štefan Borák was almost 50 years old. His thick black hair and ragged, long black beard had very little white in it. He wore thick horn-rimmed glasses that made his eyes seem too large. He kept a second pair for reading in his shirt pocket. He was slightly taller than Molly and a dozen centimeters shorter than I. When Molly first met him, she said he had the sturdy face and athletic body of a mountain man, but the eyes of a priest. I had known him for almost 15 years then. We met at base camp below Nanga Parbat in Pakistan, with separate teams, preparing to climb the ninth highest mountain in the world.

"I cannot believe," Štefan said, squeezing Molly's shoulder with one arm and gripping my hand tightly in his friendly hand. "Is big surprise for me."

The other two men stood and the woman went back to her chair, but continued watching us like thieves. In Slovak, Štefan said he would introduce us, then back to English, added, "All here speak some little English. But Eva not. Later I explain her." Eva smiled when she heard her name. Štefan positioned himself between us and put his arms around both our shoulders. "This is Tomaš. My good friend. Is climber from America. Is also *filozof* from university." Then, excitedly kissing Molly on the cheek, continued. "And this beautiful woman is wife Molly; better climber than husband, true?"

I said yes and Molly said no at the same time. The men laughed and, a second later, Eva, certainly mystified, also laughed.

"Is also journalist," Štefan added.

"We are interrupting," I said. The other two men were nervous, not knowing whether to sit, stand or leave. "We can come back later."

Štefan shrugged a sort of apology and I could see that indeed we had interrupted something. "Only some small meeting for school. I must." He looked at his old Russian watch and tapped its face with a forefinger. "Maybe 15 more minutes. You can wait?"

"Sure," I said. "We came here to see you."

"I will show you place for wait. Not far."

We said good-bye, politely shook each one's hand, accepted blurted apologies in awkward English and went with Štefan into the hallway. He took us to the orange chair by the ashtray and realized there was only one place to sit. "Please to wait," he said, then went into one of the offices, returning with a metal chair. He tried to excuse his English, saying he almost never had a chance to use it. He hugged Molly again and shook my hand at the same time, then hurried back to his office.

"He looks very good," Molly said. "Why doesn't he get old?"

Molly

I fell in love with Saša. She was the first person I loved, besides my parents, of course. None of the boys I slept with. I never felt romantically attached to them. I just liked the physical contact, the way it felt, and, naturally, having climbing partners. The next person I would fall in love with is my husband, Tom. I suppose it could be said that I am bisexual, because I do in fact have strong urges toward men and at the same time am attracted to women, but it is somehow two completely different things, these attractions. My attraction to women is not so much sexual as emotional. This isn't worth pursuing. I just want to say that I was very much in love with Saša, and I am even more in love with Tom.

Saša was gay. She had sex with men from time to time in the past, but in all ways preferred the company of women, including climbers. She said that all women were at least bisexual, which I believe is pretty much not true, although it made her happy to believe it. She said that women were sexual creatures and men were sexual predators; women *were* sex, so that made them prey. Saša did not say she was gay, she said she was omni-sexual. "I like some nice cock," she would say. "I like to squeeze them like a little sausage." She talked very dirty when she was drinking, and she had a problem with alcohol, although it never got in the way of her climbing. But that's what we talked about most of the time: sex and climbing. Saša replaced my father as climbing partner and my mother as creative stimulus; she replaced my dubious and intermittent boyfriends as companion and playmate. Throughout 1973 and '74, we spent most of our free time together.

Ironically, my father took an immediate liking to Saša, and sometimes he went climbing with us, particularly when we went to Mt. Woodson on Sundays. Frank Cook and Saša became fast friends, and there were times I was jealous of what they knew, of the times their shared history left me out. Saša was closer to my father's age than to mine, and they were intellectually compatible—highly educated, rational, scientific. My father understood what happened to her in 1968, in Prague, but they had to explain it to me.

For a long time we went to Mt. Woodson together every Sunday. At the summit there is a telephone relay station and an old, broken-down fire watchtower. At the end of the day the three of us would sit on the concrete slab of the old watchtower and eat some bread and fruit and drink warm cans of Budweiser that Father hauled all day in his pack. Saša always laughed about the Buds and said they weren't the real thing. In the distance you can hear highway traffic, although you can't actually see it. When it isn't too smoggy, you can see a long way across the valley toward the coast: granite boulders, scrub pine and wild flowers, hundreds of acres in orchards, horse farms, golden mountains and irrigated green valleys.

Our first time together at Woodson we all did Robbins' Crack, which was established by Royal Robbins, once my father's climbing partner, and who these days sells faux climbing clothes with his name on the label. We climbed it for time, and my father showed off, beating us both by more than three minutes. Then we went higher and did Cook's Corner, a 42-foot dihedral my father established in 1959 on a rock called Lost In The Wild West. It was a grand day. We finished on top of the mountain with lunch and warm beers, which would become a habit. That day was in late spring, hot and dry; rocks like slate in the sun.

I went into the bushes to pee. I could see Saša and my father sitting on the edge of the concrete slab below the old tower. Saša sat with her knees bent and her arms clasped around them, her metallic red hair shining. She wore black lycra bicycle shorts and a cheap, stretched-out T-shirt, and I could see the lower ridge of her spine descending into the waistband of her shorts. She was always tanned because she worked and played outside. The skin of her face was becoming leathery and her hands were almost ugly with their scars, embedded dirt and cracked nails. She had a large, slightly hooked nose and her teeth weren't very good. She shaved her legs but not under her arms. I thought she was beautiful. Father called it "presence."

Anyway, I watched them as I pulled down my pants and squatted gingerly among the rough desert bushes. My father was clearly impressed with Saša, even to the point where he seemed to be flirting with her sometimes. I couldn't hear what they were saying. Father took a can of beer from his rucksack, pulled off the tab, which he slipped over his smallest finger, and handed the can to Saša. My father liked Budweiser, but Saša remained adamant that it was a stolen name, that the only real Budweiser was Czech. She said American beer tastes like water for washing dishes, so one was as bad as another. Her favorite drink was brandy. Soon the flies found me and I hurried back.

They were talking about her country. I sat next to Saša and fished a beer from my father's bag. He frowned but didn't say anything. I wasn't old enough to drink legally. Father said to Saša, "I feel as if we should apologize to you, however insufficient a gesture."

Since I had missed the beginning of the conversation, I couldn't imagine what we were apologizing for.

Saša shook her head. "No," she said. She looked pensive, sad and I wondered what I had missed.

"We are not the brave saviors of the world we think we are," Father continued. "We are too in love with ourselves to threaten our luxury with bravery or morality. Fact is, most of us would have happily stayed out of World War II and just let Europe immolate itself . . ."

"What is immolate?" she asked. I didn't know, either.

"To kill yourself by fire."

"This is good word. I remember it."

"The point is, we traded you to a bully for a little peace and quiet for ourselves. Ironically, nobody got much peace or quiet."

"Who's the bully?" I asked, a bit jealous for feeling left out.

"Your papa say about Stalin, I think."

"Yes, Stalin, and others. We traded you off. I cannot tell you why we failed to support the Hungarians in '56, nor why we so cowardly failed your country in '68. All I can tell you is that it makes me ashamed. That's all."

"Is not responsibility for you."

"Whose responsibility is it, if not all of us?"

"Mine. Is my country . . ."

"Our world."

"Ah, but my country. And it is I who run away to this . . . ah, sanctuary. Mine is real shame. Something necessary was to be done, and I do nothing. Only run away."

"I don't accept that," Father said.

Saša continued. "I remember American soldiers in short, brown . . . vhat is it? Is not coat, exactly. Vhat is vurd for such short coat like this?" She ran her index finger around the front of her waist.

"Jacket," Father answered.

"Ah, jacket."

"We called them Eisenhowers after one of our presidents who was a general in that war—he wore such a jacket."

"I know Eisenhower. Is famous man. I remember soldiers in Eisenhower's jacket come to my family willage on west Prague vhere we hide during war because my father is partisan soldier. Vhen soldiers come, ve are smiling because they are Americans to liberate us, not Soviet. Maybe one of these men vas you?"

"Not me. I was on the other side of the world."

"But you vere soldier?"

"Yes, but in the Pacific."

Saša nodded, then said, "So, but we get Russians anyway."

This we had talked about. She told me what happened in Prague in 1968, about her father, who was an anti-Communist dissident, a writer of nature and mountaineering books, who was beaten and stabbed to death in a street near their flat, in what authorities called a robbery. It was odd, Saša said, that these "robbers" stole only her father's tongue.

After that, her mother lost her job as an actress in the state theater and went to live with her sister in a village near the German border. Saša, who was only one year away from completing her internship as a neurologist, rode in a meat truck to the confluence of the Morava and Danube rivers just north of Bratislava and swam the fast currents into Austria.

That was my first guided excursion into the world outside the bucolic hills of Southern California.

We were quiet for a while, drinking beer, given to our own thoughts. I wondered if my father had a crush on Saša, and what I would think about it if he did. He was very attentive to her, full of praise about her climbing ability, and sympathetic to her past. They seemed to share secrets. The questions of that day were not to be answered by him, then or ever. He would not live much longer. In fact, he was already sick that day, and he died four months later, September 1974. I had just started college. He had lung cancer. He smoked Lucky Strikes since he was 14 years old. Boils appeared on his neck, and some swelling. He went to the doctor. He was dead a month later, 54 years old.

When he was in the hospital, I tried to tell him what Mother had seen in my diary, and how wrong it had been, and why so many things had changed after that, but I was afraid to let him see how useless and ridiculous it had made our last years together.

He was lucid until the few days before he died, when the morphine doses were so high that he was more or less comatose. I visited every day. His room was filled with flowers. When I came in to visit, Mother, who virtually lived in his room, got up and went out. It broke my heart to see how deeply she loved my father and how much she needed him. Once, after she left, Father handed me the card from a gorgeous bunch of wild flowers near his bed.

"Who's it from?" I asked.

"Read the card," he said. "You've always been like that, Molly. You can have the answer in your hand, and still ask the question."

It was a handmade card, the edge of the paper burned to age it. In a beautiful calligraphic hand were the words, *You are my hero!* It was signed, Saša.

I began to cry. I walked to the window and stood with my back to him. I think that was the moment I accepted the fact of his disappearance from the world.

"It's not that great a card," Father said.

I dried my eyes and turned around. "You are a hero," I said.

"It's nice you girls think so. Saša is a good friend to you, Molly. You can learn from her."

"I know. I am her friend, too."

"You are awfully pretty for a rock jock."

I went to his bed and leaned over to kiss his cheek. I will always associate the feel of a scratchy cheek with my father, the smell of Avon aftershave, the odor of smoke on his breath. But when I leaned close to him, I could smell something else, something it was impossible to bear, for which I had no name. Now I know it was decay. I smell it oozing from my own body.

I picked up his hand. An IV tube ran from a tape patch near his wrist, so I didn't lift it, only held it on the bed. "Daddy," I began, "there is something maybe I should tell you. About Mom. About me and Mom."

He stopped me, said my name.

"I want you to understand . . ."

"Honey, there's nothing you can tell me about you or your mom that I don't already know, or that isn't too late to matter."

"Don't say it like that. It's never too late."

He didn't say anything else, which I took as permission to continue. It seemed that he was just going to let me get it over with.

"One time I did a horrible thing, something I feel guilty about."

"You have nothing to feel guilty about, Molly. Guilt is not a good emotion. Promise me you'll avoid it in the future."

"But you don't understand . . ."

"Yes, I do."

"But you don't know what I'm trying to tell you."

"Yes, I do."

"You don't understand . . ."

"I understand that you should let go of this, honey. It's not your fault and I want you to stop feeling guilty right now. Anyway, it is I who should feel guilt, I who let you down."

"Of course you didn't! If you'd just listen to me for a minute."

"Okay, go ahead if you need to, tell me about the diary."

He spoke flatly, as if his words had no importance.

"You know?"

He nodded.

"She told you?"

He nodded again. "So, you see, there's nothing really to say."

I squeezed his hand too tightly and he had to reach over with his other hand to pry my fingers off. I apologized. The pain closed his eyes and forced him to take a deep breath. "I wish you'd sit down," he said, his eyes still closed. I sat on the edge of the bed, trying to avoid the tubes. He asked me to hold his hand again, and he stroked my fingers with his thumb.

"When your mother was a child, she was abused by her father."

I covered my mouth to stifle a cry. In that instant, years of confusion were wiped away, but I did not feel instantly better.

"Your grandmother killed herself when she found out."

"My God, Daddy."

"Then your grandfather hanged himself."

"Oh God."

"I have always hoped there would never come a time you would need to hear this."

"But it would have explained so much."

"Your mother couldn't have lived with your knowing. Do you understand me, Molly? She could not have lived if you knew. I thought it was important to protect her, even if she was wrong, and to do that I had to let you suffer."

I could only nod my head, I was crying again.

"Do you understand, Molly?"

"Yes. I understand. I'll never tell her. I won't say anything."

"Your mother has always lived with this. It's sort of like carrying the symptoms of a fatal disease and waiting for them to get bad enough to kill her. She was afraid of what people would say if they knew, what you would think of her, that maybe you would not be able to love her, even that I. . . . She thought she had done something terribly wrong, and I suppose that deep inside she believes it was something she did that caused her parents to die. She must believe no one knows."

"But you know."

"She doesn't know I do."

"Then how?"

"She was a minor, thirteen years old, when it happened. She was sent to live with her aunt and uncle. He, your Uncle Ned, told me after Lou became pregnant with you."

"Mom doesn't know you know?"

"Listen to me, Molly. Lou doesn't think *anybody* knows. It has to stay that way. Do you truly understand?"

I nodded, let go of his hand and stood. I walked back to the window and pretended to look out. I had to think about all this. Like gears meshing, I began to understand the interrelationship of dozens of disparate events, including her reaction to my diary. "But then, that means she really *believed* that I—"

"She believed what she read in your diary to be true."

"How could you let her! It had to be horrible for you."

"What it was for me isn't the point. I've made more than enough mistakes, and time has run out, I can't repair them now."

I turned back to the window, crossed my arms over my chest and looked down. A stubby palm tree struggled to live in a small wooden box. My eyes were so focused I thought I could see ants on the box. I was both frightened and embarrassed, and could not look at him. I couldn't even respond to the implied desire in his voice. The desire for redemption. A desire I have come to know.

"In some way, I think, Molly, she needed to believe it. I think it made her feel less alone, less . . . chosen. This probably makes no sense, I can't really explain it, but ironically it was kind of a bond between you that was even stronger than her erratic and untrustworthy feelings of motherhood. She wanted always to be a good mother to you, and she tried so hard in the beginning. She just didn't have the skills."

"She was a good mother," I protested.

"Yes. I suppose we can only try to be good enough."

"How long have you known?"

"The diary? She told me the night she read it."

"Oh God, I ruined everything."

"Turn around, Molly."

"I don't want to yet."

"Molly!"

I turned slowly, but avoided his eyes. Instead, my gaze fell on the lovely wild flowers Saša brought.

"I'm tired, honey."

I looked at him finally and could see his exhaustion. I wanted to hug him, but all those tubes and bottles made it impossible.

"Don't dwell on this, Molly. Just let it go. You did nothing wrong. Nothing."

He closed his eyes. He closed them so suddenly that I thought he might have passed away at that very moment. Without opening his eyes, softly he said, "I'm going to sleep now."

"I'm sorry, Daddy. I'll come back tomorrow morning. I love you."

"I love you, too, rock jock."

Six days later he died in a coma.

But the summer before, although secretly cancer was quickly devouring him even then, he was very much alive and involved with the world. As Saša, Father and I walked down the service road to the base of Woodson where we had left the car, he and Saša continued talking about the failures of people to take care of each other. Saša talked about her father and his life in the mountains. We stood on the roadside by the car for another half hour, still talking. When Father went off to relieve himself in the bushes before we started back to the city, Saša turned to me and said, "I like your father wery much."

"He is my hero," I said.

"Then he vill be also my hero. Ve need heroes, Molly, or ve do not survive absurdity."

Tom

Štefan Borák was always a climber. It is his only occupation, and outside of wine, his only pastime. He has stood on the summit of Everest, one of only three Slovaks, and they were together. One of them died coming down. He saved my life on Nanga Parbat. I have never made friends easily; I'm not a very social person. Štefan was, he is, my best friend.

We waited for him less than 15 minutes, then together we walked to a café filled with smoke and the morbid smells of fried food. We just beat a large lunch crowd and got a table by the front windows. The windows were opaque with greasy dust, and people passing were only shapes and movement, like the constant traffic was only noise. We ordered the standard Slovak café lunch: fried white cheese, grilled potatoes, a salad of cabbage, carrots and pickles, and amber beer served in big fat glasses.

We had not warned him we were coming to Bratislava and he seemed to be inspecting us as he searched for answers, but he just asked where we wanted to climb. "Everywhere," Molly answered.

"You are here for August?" he asked.

"Our plans are indefinite," I said, and realized he didn't know the word. "Until our visas expire anyway."

"Is good. Then you are here for *tradičný horolozecky týždeň*."

"We hope so," Molly said,

We had talked about staying for Traditional Mountaineer's Week in the Tatras, when just about every climber in Czechoslovakia got together for a few meetings and a lot of drinking and climbing. I think Molly saw it as a goal. To participate in the traditional mountaineer's week.

"I am on meeting next week. Starý Smokovec. You go with me?"

"Sure," I answered.

"But tonight you come for Anna's kitchen."

"Maybe you should ask Anna before bringing guests for dinner," Molly said.

"Guests? What is guests? Guests is like friends? I think no. You will come. Yes?"

"Of course. I look forward to seeing her," Molly said.

"Is done," Štefan proclaimed. "You remember to find my flat?"

We said we did, and finished quickly. Štefan had to leave. We separated on the sidewalk in front of the café and hopped on a tram back to the city center. We didn't realize it was the wrong tram until it went into the tunnel beneath Bratislava castle and we headed for the concrete mazes of the northwest suburbs. We got off at the next stop and ran across the highway to the Danube River embankment.

"We can walk back," I told Molly. "It isn't far. If you're all right."

"I'd like to walk."

I took her hand. It was turning into a beautiful afternoon. There was sun now. Morning clouds rolled off to the east. Bratislava Castle sat atop the hill on our left, the Danube on the right. We removed our windbreakers and stuffed them into the day pack I carried. It was going to be hot. Maybe summer was coming back. The wind blew Molly's hair into her face.

An old bent man walked a small white dog. Another man sat on a bench and ate something he picked from a paper sack with his fingers; a bottle of socialist imitation Coke, called Kofola, sat next to him. Coming toward us, a *babička* pushed twin babies end to end in a carriage. Sea gulls, 2000 kilometers from the sea, lined the retaining wall like an impatient audience to the strollers, squawking as each passed. There were a few statues to Slovak heroes and plaques commemorating valiant, empty historical moments. Ahead rose the flying saucer structure of SNP Bridge.

The Danube flowed quickly past Bratislava on its way into Hungary, not so far away. The turgid brown water was foamy from residual early summer rains. A tug pushing a barge struggled against the current, an Austrian flag marking the wind across its stern.

"Let's go to Woodson tomorrow," Molly said.

"I'm sorry?" I should have realized that she had made a mistake, but I was preoccupied by the scenery.

"What did I say?"

"About going to Woodson. Did you mean Pajštún?"

"Yes."

"Great idea. I vote for it."

I could see how much it bothered Molly to keep making place name mistakes, even if I thought it was understandable. It was only a slip of the tongue.

"Tom, do I tell you too much that I love you?"

"Never."

"I do love you. Very much."

"I hope you get it all back, and with extras."

"I always have."

"Oh God, the sun feels so great."

"This is going to be hard for you. After I'm gone."

"What is?"

"You left your job, we're spending into savings. You'll have to start all over from zero."

"That is completely irrelevant to me. We've had this discussion."

"You have to think about these things, even if you don't like it."

"I do think about it. Sometimes I seem to think of little else. But it's hard to talk about it. I understand your curiosity. I would feel the same way."

"Curiosity? About what you will do after I'm gone?"

"*If* . . . and I want to emphasize that, if you should die before I do, I will mourn. I will be impossibly sad. That is what will happen."

"Don't be impossibly sad, Tom. Tomaš. I love the sound of your name in Slovak."

I stopped and turned her by the shoulders to face me. I could see the castle rising behind her face, like a monstrous four-poster; could hear the river, the gulls. Then I looked into her eyes, which were damp, and said, "I can't help it, and I'm sorry if it bothers you, but darling, I am already impossibly sad and I can't see the end of it. Just let me have it, okay?"

"But it's me who's dying," she blurted out, and the tears came.

Molly

After my father died, I moved out of the house and into a dorm. His will left the house to Mother, all his climbing gear to me, and the insurance money was split between us. I discovered that he had been taking out government bonds in my name since I was born, and now they were worth what to me seemed a small fortune. I had a scholarship in English, and with the other money there was enough to pay for my degree and living expenses without having to work, and there was enough for my first car, a red Toyota Tercel. I moved out of the house and into the dorm at the end of the first semester. I called my mother that weekend to say hello and tell her that I was settled; the university was only an hour drive from La Mesa. We did not speak again until June. We had become capable of saying many things while saying nothing.

I liked college well enough, especially the freshman English composition course. The comp class was easy because it was just writing, and I have always been good at that. I also liked history because it seemed to be trying to find an explanation for the hows and whys of human existence, thus maybe I might find my own. But the daughter of a mathematics teacher would have flunked algebra had it not been for Saša.

It seemed that Saša was enjoying my university life more than I was. I saw Saša more often than ever before, nearly every day. When it happened that she was working a job near the university, we met in the Student Center for lunch. She liked to go to the library in the evening while I studied. She would roam the shelves like a treasure hunter without a map. I wouldn't see her for an hour, then she would lean over my shoulder to see what I was reading or writing and say, "Good, good." When the library closed we would go to an espresso shop near campus and have coffee and ice cream. We climbed somewhere every weekend.

The university had a climbing club and I joined after attending one meeting. There were the usual groupies and show-offs, but there were also some good climbers, men I had seen at crags and on mountains all over Southern California. The guy who would write the definitive guidebook to Southern California climbing a few years later was in the club. There were men in the club who had already climbed Denali. That school year, 1974–75, there were almost thirty members. Four, including me, were women—well, there were actually seven, but I didn't count three of them; they were just rock groupies.

My membership in the university climbing club lasted two more meetings and one rock climbing outing and one boyfriend. I quit after finding out that only university students could belong, and that excluded Saša. I had already told Saša about the club, so I had to come up with some excuse for quitting or her feelings would have been hurt. I told her that there were no real climbers in the bunch and that it was just an excuse to go camping and get drunk in the mountains. Saša said it sounded like the perfect club and laughed, but I figured that Saša probably knew why I no longer wanted so much to be a member.

I dated a lot. It was just about the easiest thing in the world to do, which was a surprising discovery. I think I accidentally became prettier as I got older. Certainly my breasts grew large enough to be the focus of a lot of attention. Sometimes I felt like snapping my fingers to get a boy to look at my face and not my chest. Before college, I found dating to be problematic, which was mostly my fault, because for a time I was *easy*, but it was not the kind of reputation I wanted. Although I liked sex well enough, I hated the attitude that went with it. During my senior year of high school, I hardly dated at all. I didn't go to a one of the senior dances or to the prom. I really don't think there was much to miss. I was extremely focused on climbing.

The first boyfriend I had in college—his name was Daniel Martin, like the Fowles book—once told me: "Climbing is what you have to avoid having a life." Danny was a climber, I met him because of the climbing club, but it was for him a sport. I mean only a sport; he was just a rock gymnast. He was an excellent sport climber but he didn't know very much about rocks and mountains. I didn't sleep with him for almost a month, and we broke up about a month after our first tryst in his dorm room. Saša hated him, anyway.

But I wondered if it were true? That I did not "have a life"?

I asked Saša. It was midnight in early spring and, although the air was cool, we were sitting at one of the sidewalk tables outside an espresso shop. My book bag lay on an empty chair, with Saša's heavy coat across it. She often wore more clothes than necessary; we were in Southern California, after all. She had on a dingy white Irish fisherman's sweater and jeans. I had on shorts and a cotton sweatshirt. Vivaldi played from outside speakers, and I hate Vivaldi's classical Muzak. We were the only people left outside, but the tables were filled inside.

"Danny says that climbing is what I do instead of having a life," I said.

"Vhat means, 'having life'?"

"I don't know. It just means living, I suppose. You know—living."

"Danny is stupid."

I laughed. "I know, he's your favorite."

"Favorite boob," she said. She liked boob. Lots of things and lots of people were boobs. "So, climbing is not part of living?"

"I think that's what he meant. It should be *part* of it, not the whole thing."

"He is boob. Is this not living?" Saša held her arms wide to encompass the scene around them. "Vhat about this?" She pulled my book bag from beneath my coat and put it on the table, rattling the espresso cups. "You are student." She reached into the bag and fished around until she found the notebook in which I kept a journal for English composition class. "You are artist."

"In my dreams," I said, taking the notebook and putting it back, then replacing the book bag under the coat. There were some things I had written about Saša that I did not want her to see. I had shown Saša some of my character sketches, but not the one of Saša herself.

"You are living, Molly," Saša said finally. She got up and went across the street to buy a pint bottle of schnapps, which she proceeded to pour into her coffee. I took a little, too.

We said good night after that and I walked back to the dorm. Janet, my roommate, was in bed with her boyfriend, so I got undressed in the hallway bathroom and slipped into bed without waking them. I couldn't sleep for an hour, wondering if I had a life.

Danny Martin's question pursued me, dogged my steps like a shadow. It was probably just the age, teenage angst, a girl positioned on the stark edge of womanhood, peering into an unknown where lay hidden who-knows-what perils. I had lost my father and essentially lost my mother, so I felt a distinct sense of orphan-ness. I unloaded a lot of this on Saša. But she hardly expressed appropriate sympathy. She told me not to complain so much. Sometimes she called me a wuss, which was a female boob. She pronounced it *vuss*. I don't think she had any idea where those idioms came from, but it wouldn't have mattered if she did.

That year I seemed to be finding Saša drunk as often as not, unless we were climbing. She would not drink when we climbed, only afterwards. Once I asked Saša why she never drank when we were climbing, since I might have a beer sometimes, and frequently I smoked a joint before climbing easier routes. Saša just said it was from her training. Training was a word she used in relation to her father.

One Friday night just before midnight she phoned me from the city jail. She had been arrested on a charge of public drunkenness and indecent exposure and needed bail, or she would have to spend the weekend in a cell. She needed $500 and I had to write a check. She was pretty much shit-faced and I had to hold her arm as we walked down the street to where I'd left the car. All the while she was muttering, "I give you money, I give you money."

I poured Saša into the car and she immediately fell across the seat. I had never seen her even half so drunk. I gave up trying to prop Saša in the passenger seat and instead laid her across the back seat. "In my country person is no arresting for simple go to toilet," Saša complained. "Where did you go to the toilet?" I asked, bending Saša's legs so she would fit. "In my country people are arresting by our vonderful police for vhat come from head, not vhat come from . . ." She gave up trying to think of the English word and gestured in an exaggerated manner at her crotch, spitting out a word that sounded like *peaches*. I could only guess that she had taken a leak somewhere in public, which she did all the time anyway, even sober, with very little concern to who might be present.

I took her home and we stood on the steps to her apartment building for a long time before she found her key. She lived in a basement two-room apartment furnished in eclectic minimalist. There was a futon on which the covers were always messed up, a wooden crate next to it that held some books and a clip-on reading lamp. A laundry basket sat on the other side of the bed and it was usually overflowing. There was also a chair from the dining table and a pair of old hiking boots sat on it. The windows were small and high up. There were bamboo roll-up shades over them. On a bookcase made from bricks and boards there were, among the books, five pieces of very fine sculpture. Once Saša had a lover who was a sculptress. Above her bed was a travel poster from a Czechoslovak travel agency showing the baroque buildings lining Prague's old town square. A walk-in closet was filled with climbing gear, which was appreciably more organized than her clothes, books and kitchen supplies. In the other room, which contained a tiny kitchenette, there was a round glass dining table with three chairs, two canvas lawn chairs, a pair of potted dwarf palm trees in spectacular health, a Salvation Army sofa and another bricks and board bookcase. On the walls were tacked up posters of mountain pictures and a Cézanne flowers print.

I guided Saša to the bedroom and dropped her on the futon, where she immediately rolled onto her side and lay her head on both hands. I asked if she wanted to get undressed or sleep in her clothes. Saša said she was sorry three or four times. I said I had to go, but Saša sat up quickly and swung her legs off the bed. "Molly," she cried, then lunged toward the bathroom. I could see her only from the waist down, where she knelt at the toilet and threw up. I went into the kitchen and got a glass of water and soaked a dishcloth in cold water. Returning, I found Saša curled up by the toilet.

"Do you want some water?" I asked, helping her get up. "Are you finished in here?"

"Is not so good," she said, but took herself back to the futon and sat on the end with her head in her hands.

"Can you drink a little of this?" I asked, offering the water. She took a couple of sips then handed the glass back. I rolled the wet dishcloth and put it around the back of Saša's neck. She smelled sour and sweaty. She began taking off her clothes.

"Do you need help?" I asked.

In reply she lay back on the bed and held her legs out so that I could take off her sport shoes. Her socks were thick, dingy white, and there was a hole in each heel. I reached up and undid the snap on her jeans, pulled down the zipper, then tugged them over her hips and off. I dropped the socks and jeans on top of the full clothes basket, then lifted her arms and pulled the sweatshirt over her head. The hair under her arms always surprised me. I envied her the freedom to avoid shaving there, but simply could not make myself copy her. I asked Saša what she wanted to sleep in and she looked around as if lost. It was not so cold, so I lay her down again and left her in bra and panties. Then I rolled one side of the comforter over her and pulled away the dishcloth. Her eyes were closed.

"I'm going now," I said.

Saša opened her eyes and held out her hand. I took her hand and sat on the edge of the futon.

"Molly . . . ?"

"Yes?"

"Today is birthday of my father."

"Oh. I'm sorry, Saša."

"Sixty-five years," she continued. "Is still good age, good time for some man."

"Yes, it is." I thought it sounded very old.

"But he have only fifty-nine."

I took a moment to count, then said, "My father only had fifty-four." Suddenly I was very sad and angry that Saša reminded me of this.

"Do you know I sleep with him?" Saša said.

"With whom? Your father?"

"No, you goose. *Your* father."

"*My* father?"

I let go of her hand and turned to face her.

"You did not know."

"No, I did not . . . well, maybe, I guess I wondered. Really?" I didn't know how to express the way I felt then. I had to force from my mind an emerging image of my father with Saša, naked. "Once?" I asked.

"No. More. This surprise you?"

"No . . . yes . . . of course."

"I am drunk. I say too much."

"Were you in love with him?"

"No."

"Then why?"

"He vant it. Is not so much to do."

"Saša, you are crazy!"

"True. Saša is crazy woman."

I looked at her. She was talking with her eyes closed, almost as if she were talking in her sleep.

"I vant you to know your father have some happiness before he dies."

I felt an impulse to defend my mother, to say that my parents had been happy together, but I didn't know if it were true. "So I should say, 'thank you,' is that it?"

Saša rolled away from me and off the futon. She ran to the bathroom in a crouch. I left before she came out. I hated Saša at that moment but didn't want her to know.

Because I did not hate Saša. I loved her. She was my best friend. In any serious sense, she was my only friend. Except for being passionate about climbing and having a certain lack of social graces, we did not have much in common. Our ages were twenty years apart. Saša was a well-educated European from a Communist country. I was an adequately educated American teenager from the mecca of capitalism. Saša seemed always to be in pursuit of sex and I always trying to keep sex from overtaking me. Saša liked to grow things and I only wanted to consume the things grown. I had enough money and Saša was always broke. Saša was an alcoholic and I only tolerated liquor, in those days preferring marijuana. I was well-organized and Saša was a slob. On and on.

Saša appeared at my dorm room door three days later with ten 50-dollar bills and an apology. She made up an obvious cock-and-bull story when I asked where she got 500 dollars in cash. She didn't mention what she had said about my father and neither did I, although Saša apologized specifically for saying stupid things. She wanted to know if I could go climbing with her. Since it was 7:45 on a Tuesday morning and I had class in an hour and 15 minutes, it didn't seem very likely.

"Don't you have to go to work?"

"I have new job."

"New job? Where?"

"Night job."

"Night job doing what?"

"You look at new cocktail vaitress."

Saša stuck out her chest and simulated looping her thumbs beneath non-existent suspenders.

"Cocktail waitress? Are you kidding me?" I didn't want to say that for Saša to work in a bar was like hiring a fox to guard your chickens.

"But is good job. Much pay. And big tips!"

I held 500 dollars cash in my hands and wondered how she got it. She had come in but the door was still open behind her and we were standing in the middle of the room. Janet, my roommate, who always looked especially pudgy and punch-drunk in the mornings, got out of bed and staggered sleepily off to the toilet. The room smelled like sleep, incense, Janet's cigarette butts, sour clothes in the laundry basket, books, and now Saša's odd, plumeria bath oil. I was wearing one of my father's T-shirt and brief panties. I sat down on the corner of the bed and picked up my jeans from the floor, wishing Janet would hurry because I had to pee.

"Where is this job?"

"Some place by airport. You don't know it."

"Is it like a bar?"

"Yes, like bar. Nightclub, maybe."

"What's the name of it?"

"French name."

"Saša, are you trying not to tell me that you took a job at Les Girls?"

Janet stuck her head around the bathroom door and said, "You're working at Les Girls? Wow!"

"I only bring drinks to table. I am not dancer."

"Well, you've got the body for it."

"I think that is compliment?"

"Of course it's a compliment. But, Jesus, Saša! Les Girls is a hang-out for sleazebags, for guys with long eyeballs and drooling tongues."

"You have been there?" Saša asked in a huff.

"No I haven't been there." I stood and jerked up my jeans, then tugged on the zipper.

"I have," Janet said, coming out of the bathroom at last. "It's actually sort of elegant in a black and chrome art deco sort of way. The girls are pretty, but man, are they raunchy."

"Vhat is raunchy?" Saša asked.

"You know," Janet answered, as I headed for the toilet. "They come right up to the tables and dance with their pussies in some guy's face, or knock him around with their tits."

"That's a pretty raunchy way of putting it," I commented on Janet's vocabulary.

"Raunchy," Saša repeated, filing away her new word. "I think is American problem to think is something wrong with man and woman do such things together. Is not so bad in Europe."

"I'm not saying there's anything wrong with it," I said loudly from the bathroom.

"Anyway, I am not dancer."

"I hear the money's good," Janet said. "Do you wait tables topless?"

I flushed the toilet and came out in time to hear the end of Saša's answer.

". . . in two days what gardener make in three weeks."

I looked at the 500 dollars laying on my desk.

"No shit?" Janet said. "What the hell am I going to college for?"

"*Do* you wait tables topless?" I asked.

Saša shrugged, which I took for a yes, and she said, "I am going to Voodson."

"I have to go to class. What about this afternoon . . . but no, you have a night job now."

"Saturday," Saša said, going to the door.

"Early?"

"Vhen you vant."

"I'll pick you up about eight or eight-thirty."

"Is good."

Saša and Janet waved good-bye to one another and I closed the door behind her when she left.

"When did you go to Les Girls?" I asked Janet, who was starting to get dressed.

"Jack took me. You didn't know him, he was before Rick. It's really a hoot, you know. It's worth the price of the watered-down drinks to watch the old guys drooling over their shirts like babies. Besides, some of the girls are really exceptional dancers. Don't be such a prude, Molly."

"Jesus Christ! I'm not a prude."

"You couldn't prove it by me. You don't even look when Rick and I are doing it hardly ten feet from you."

"What would I want to look at? I've seen people screwing. I'd rather do it than watch it."

"You know what I mean."

"Anyway, how do you know I don't look?"

"Do you?"

"I'll let you guess."

"You don't," she said authoritatively, and she was right. I didn't watch, although it was impossible not to catch a glimpse now and then. I didn't want to watch them rooting around each other. What's wrong with that? Anyway, I thought it was inconsiderate and rude to sleep with your boyfriend when your roommate was in the room. Wasn't I gone plenty often enough?

Janet stood at the closet door and sifted through her dresses, skirts and blouses. I asked if I could get in for a moment and Janet stood aside. I pulled out my climbing pack and rope.

"What are you doing?" she asked.

"Going climbing."

"You're going to cut classes?"

"It's not the first time and it won't be the last."

"You're an addict, Molly."

An addict? Is that the same as not having a life? I wondered while sitting on the bed to change into my climbing clothes for Mt. Woodson. Saša knew that I had classes every morning. She knew that I seldom missed any, and so we did our climbing in the afternoons and week-ends. She had not come by this morning to invite me climbing. She wanted to talk to me, and I had brushed her off.

"Toodle-oo, hot stuff," Janet said, grabbing her book bag and head-ing out the door.

I was not far behind Saša when I got to Woodson. I parked next to the old Datsun gardening truck and walked quickly up the service road, looking at each boulder, until I saw Saša sitting on top of Morning Glory, with her arms crossed around her bent legs.

"I know you," Saša called down.

It was a low boulder, 18 feet to the top, and three sides were shaped like a child's toy wooden block; the back dropped off like a ramp and the front had an overhanging bulge five feet high. Saša stood and started to walk down the sloping back side.

"Wait," I called out, stopping her, "and I'll come up."

I took off my jogging shoes and put on the thin socks I wore with bouldering slippers. Saša whistled a flagrantly impatient tune. I took the B-2 problem on the front vertical face with the bulge because I knew it was the most difficult and the one that Saša had certainly used. The first move from the ground was a lunge. So many people fell from that move that the desert dirt there had been churned into something like a child's sandbox. If you make the lunge, waiting for you is a pretty good hand hold, but it's the only thing. You hang by that hand as you work one of your feet up to find the one, single, solitary toe jam in a blown pocket that is about knee level from that position. With enough strength, meaning you can do a one-arm pull-up, you can bring yourself up to a place where there is a second hand placement, but I couldn't do a one-arm pull-up and had to find the toe jam before my arm gave out and I would have to let go. Saša stood on top like a temple statue and watched. The entire problem is composed of nebulous finger holds and spooky toe jams. The only really good, substantial hand hold is the first one, the one you make on the lunge. Even mantling over the top is scary, because there is then 18 feet of air behind you.

When I came over the top, Saša stepped back to make room, then we sat side by side in an area about the size of a car's backseat. I saw that she had shaved under her arms.

"Wery good," she said, as I got my breath and rubbed some feeling back into my fingers, "but I am sorry you leave school. Is my fault for offer you to climb."

"I'm a big girl. Besides, it's only English Comp, in which I'm pulling a solid A, and Intro to Psych, which is a zoo of two hundred and fifty students. I'll get the afternoon ones. It was worth coming out here just to do that," I added, looking over the edge.

Saša leaned back on her elbows. I noticed that she had apparently scrubbed her fingers and nails; they were almost clean. She raised her face to the morning sun.

"So, tell me about your job."

"You are embarrass to be my friend, I think."

I turned sharply toward her and put my hand on Saša's forearm, which was as hard as a log. "Don't say that! Don't even think it in secret! Nothing about you embarrasses me. I don't give a damn what kind of job you have. Did I give you that impression?"

"Then maybe I am embarrass for myself."

"You can choose to do it or choose not to, but you're free to choose either way."

"Now you are existentialist."

"Why not? I think it makes sense."

"It reflect only your experience, not other experience."

"Okay, we both know you know more than I do and you've had all sorts of amazing and adventurous experiences that I haven't had, but it doesn't mean I don't know *something*."

"Vhy are you mad vith me?"

"Shit, Saša! I'm not mad *at* you. And I'm not embarrassed about you being a topless waitress in a girlie club, if that's what you want to do. But Christ! You have a university education, you were almost a goddamn doctor. What I don't like is that the only way you can survive is to dig in other people's dirt or serve drinks without your clothes on in a sleazy strip joint."

Suddenly Saša was crying. It was as shocking to me as if I'd been struck. I put my arm around her shoulders but she tightened up and pulled away.

"I'm sorry," I apologized. "God, what did I say?"

"I think of my father," Saša said, making herself stop crying. "My father vas man of much dignity and much honor, a man for honest living, and man who believe ve have . . . duty for to do vhat is right thing. I am his only seed. I look at vhat seed grow to."

"Wouldn't he be proud of what a good climber you are?"

She ignored me.

"*Kúrva*," she spit the word.

"What?"

"Whore," she said.

"Working in a nightclub, topless or otherwise, doesn't make you into a whore, Saša. Besides, I am my father's only child, and, except that I am a climber, I can't say he would be too happy with my lifestyle."

Saša shook her head, indicating that I just didn't understand, and she was right. This was so out of the blue. Saša was hardly maudlin even when she was drunk. Saša, filled with ribald humor and laughter, smiling and friendly to everyone, sometimes combative, but meditative in her silences, not depressive. I didn't know what to make of this side of her.

"I miss my father," she said.

"Me, too," I answered.

She looked at me, and what can only be described as a knowing look passed between us.

"Don't come see me at my vurk," she said.

"Okay."

"Sometime can I talk to you about my father's life?" she asked.

"That would be great."

She smiled and impulsively kissed me. Then she stood and said, "Vhy not go vurk on Great Balls On Fire?" Great Balls Of Fire was a B-3 boulder problem about a hundred yards down the hill from where they sat. We had both tried it a dozen times, with no success. It was possible we might never succeed. It was the hardest problem in the area.

"Yes," I said and we slapped hands above our heads. "Today we do it!"

We didn't. We never did. And I never went to Les Girls during the three weeks Saša worked there before quitting and going back to her old gardening job. After all, she had taken the job only to repay the 500 dollars.

Tom

Pajštún is the ruins of a 1000-year-old castle perched on a limestone promontory high above the village of Borinka in the small Carpathian Mountains that rise from the Danube plain just east of Bratislava. There are vineyards in the foothills. Higher up in winter there are places for easy skiing and marked trails for hiking. It is possible to walk from village to village on trails through forested mountains. One can imagine gypsy camps, violins, dancing and vividly-painted wagons, although they no longer exist in Czechoslovakia, and now Romany inhabit blackened ghettos clustered around poisoned mining villages far to the east.

From the bus stop at Borinka we had to walk steeply uphill with the rope and our gear along a rutted tractor road for almost an hour. Water stood in areas of continual shade and often we had to walk in brush along the roadside to avoid thick, deep mud. It was so hot suddenly that it seemed the mud would turn instantly to dust. We passed a family having a picnic at the base of the hill leading to the crumbling castle: two men, two women, a grandmother, seven children, an old wooden table heaped with pots of steaming cabbage, which we could smell, and bottles of wine and beer. The men were shirtless with farmer's tans. The children stared at us and I waved at them. Emboldened by my greeting, they came closer and said in heavily accented English, "Hello, how are you? What is your name? Good-bye." I said we were fine, we were Americans, and wished them well. Two of them started to follow us up the hill, but the grandmother called them back.

The trees were full of light, which leaked onto the trail like smoke. It was calm, warm, and a good day for climbing on limestone.

I have always liked the purposefulness of climbing, which is an otherwise pointless activity. I came to it late, relatively, in my twenties as a college student. Molly has done it all her life. We agree that to work so hard to reach a spot on the earth easily accessible by trail or, except for the most impossibly high summits, by helicopter, doesn't make sense in a practical way. There is only one purpose to climbing, and it isn't simply to cover a vertical distance. Climbing is its only purpose and its only reward. It concentrates and focuses one's thoughts on a singular task, and for me that functions as an anesthetic to trouble or pain.

I was thinking about the climbing routes ahead until we came across that family. Now I was fantasizing that Molly and I were a part of their lives, and I began making up a story about us all, which led me to believe that Molly was all right and would always be all right. I had to believe this.

I was born in a deep green sea, a hamlet in a forest of pine trees, on delta flat land; the first hills I ever saw were in the Ozark Mountains of Arkansas, and I was already 12 years old. I never did have a real sense of family and now my parents are dead anyway. I have a sister, but we are so dissimilar that we are seldom in contact, and when we are, it is briefly and we are both bored. I don't know how to explain this, but I am a sort of story-maker. I mean, who I am is characterized by the story I have created, and I live for some time within its structures. I see in Molly's journal that she claimed this for herself, but it's not true about her. It is true about me. Molly is the most consistent and stable person I have known. But I imagine a world then inhabit it. I have had many lives. Molly said I am cursed by imagination, that I will never really be happy or satisfied because I cannot stop myself from imagining some other way, and wondering if it's better. But it is story-making that has saved me, truly. Now, if I am possibly going to survive Molly's death, it will be because I can wholly re-imagine myself without her, make a new story. If I am unable to do this, I will die. I have no doubt regarding this.

Of course, this isn't fair, because I'm writing some years after the events described here, and at that time, the day I am writing about now, I was not conscious of what I just wrote. Had I been conscious of it, I would have failed. And to have failed would have ended me, as well. I, at least, have the benefit of being able to look back and explain what I meant, or what I should have meant, or said, or done, or believed.

Molly walked a few steps ahead of me; her hair, pulled into a ponytail, lay over the top of the new green rucksack she bought in Paris. In blue jeans her ass was wonderful.

I was thinking that if she left . . . died, I would have nothing. Somehow, without intention, she had become the sustenance of my world. All my dreams of happiness, my hope for purpose, were placed with her. We had ten years, and it wasn't enough. That's the trick of happiness: it is something you only recognize in the losing of it.

Molly slowed and let me catch up with her. "Thinking about that family?" she asked.

"Jesus, it's weird how you get into my thoughts."

"Oh, I was thinking about them, too."

"What were you thinking?" I asked.

"I—wondering happy, maybe if they're . . . I was thinking—oh. Damn it! Just Goddamn it to hell!"

"It's okay. I understand. I was thinking the same thing." I slung the rope over my shoulder, took her arm and held it for a moment. "Do you remember when we saw the film of *The Unbearable Lightness of Being*?"

"You thought Saša was like Sabina. Not as pretty."

"Do you know what part I most identified with?"

"Tell me."

"Toward the end, after they come back from Switzerland, when Tomaš and Tereza come back to Prague and are stripped of everything, their freedom, their dignity, their hope . . . you remember? They go to the farm of the man with the pig. Tomaš operated on his brain in the beginning . . ."

"His name was Pavel and his pig was Mephisto."

"You see? There's nothing wrong with your memory."

"Some things are so clear, and some things are . . . gone."

"You remember this part? Tomaš is on a tractor plowing a brown field and Tereza is working in the garden. She wipes her brow and looks at him. I think she was never more beautiful than in that moment. We can see in her look that after everything, the turmoil, pain, sadness, they have become deeply happy. They have found this great satisfaction together. All this in spite of the terribleness of their times."

"Karenin is dying of cancer."

"Yes. It's a story about life, so naturally we must be surrounded by death and threats of it. But what sticks with me about the movie is how happy they were in the countryside, away from the ridiculous political, social life of Prague, away from the things that had kept them from giving themselves to each other. You and I have been lucky in that way. We haven't let our duties interfere with our life together, which in the end—that you have given yourself to another—is all that matters, I think. I was just remembering how happy they were those last days. The way they laughed, danced, made love."

"And then they died."

"Yes, they died. But was it a good death or a tragic one?"

"What would be good?"

"Remember? They are in Pavel's old truck, driving home in a rainstorm."

"Tereza asks Tomaš what he's thinking."

"And he answers: 'I'm thinking how happy I am.' Then they crash. They died together happy. There are two ways to think about this: that they died consumed by happiness in a perfect moment, or that all the future happiness they might have had was tragically taken from them the moment they achieved it. Tragedy or not?"

"We are happy, my own Tomaš."

"Yes."

"Do you know why we came back to Czechoslovakia?" Molly asked.

"I always knew."

"Will we be happy always?"

"We will be happy forever. I promise."

"So it is not a tragedy."

"No, it is not a tragedy."

We were finally there, near the bottom of the castle ruins. The smell of the earth was strong enough to be held in the hands, to caress the face. A group of young people sat in a ragged circle on the long new grass inside the disintegrated walls of the castle, and a boy held a guitar without playing it. They had bottles of wine, cigarettes, and a radio playing Czech rock music. A young couple lay aside and kissed nonchalantly. Two adolescent boys scampered dangerously atop the old decaying gate. A *babička* sat on a blanket with her legs in white stockings stretched out in a vee before her. She had removed her head scarf and her white hair was long and luxurious. An old man sunned himself using his shirt for a pillow. Two men seated opposite one another at a small wooden table played chess and drank beer. Their bellies showed below thin white undershirts. An old bicycle with a wicker basket on the handle bars lay on the grass—who could have ridden it up that hill? A man and a woman hiking with ski poles and their long socks pulled over their pant legs passed below the far wall on the trail to Stupava. There were climbers along the crag on top of which the castle was built. Pajštún was a short bus ride from Bratislava and the nearest good place to climb. It was summer finally.

"Nobody's on Zapletal's route," I said, and asked if she'd like to lead it. It's short and hard, a strength-sapper, but doable because it's not so high.

"I'll try it," she said. "Definitely," she added more confidently.

We walked through the old gate and around the rock face where other climbers were already working routes and recent arrivals, like us, were setting up. Ropes in loose coils and strands lay about like electrical cables on a carnival lot, along with colorful packs, discarded shoes and socks, a shirt hanging over a bush. Belayers and climbers called to one another in Slovak. On a boulder two young women wearing shorts and halter tops leaned back to watch, their skin red from the sun, their long legs unshaven.

Our gear was embarrassingly good. Most of these climbers were using protection made from tire lug nuts on clothesline and karabiners of a vintage 20 years old. They were fun to watch because they were so bold. They had to be. What they were using to protect a fall probably would not.

Molly's first move was no good and she came off.

"Well, shit! That was a plenty inglorious beginning," she said, brushing her hands off then re-chalking them.

"You'll get it this time."

"I've done this thing before."

"I know. You'll get it."

"I'm just glad Pavol didn't see me do that."

The route was named for Pavol Zapletal, the young Slovak mountaineer who made the first ascent, also one of Štefan Borák's students. Pavol was the other climber, the one who got down, with Štefan from the summit of Mt. Everest.

It wasn't a long route, less than 15 meters, and it ended at the base of the castle wall, requiring the climber to rappel down at the end, rather than walk off, the way one could from routes nearer the gate. There was a young tree at the end of the route for a rappel anchor.

Molly stepped off the ground and moved quickly, one hand in the crack, the other on a higher knob, then pushed up two more moves so quickly that they ran together, seeming like one long move rather than two short ones. I fed rope to her from a Munter hitch around a big pear karabiner.

A few meters to Molly's right, a muscular teenage boy hung by one hand from a crack halfway up a route called Half Moon. Until he moved again he looked like a piece of sculpted marble. I watched the young man swing his leg up for a hold and then, from a stem, lunge with his left hand for a widening section of the crack a meter above his head. Like a spider.

"Beautiful," I said.

"Thanks," Molly answered, thinking I had spoken to her.

"I was talking about him," I explained. Then I repeated the word in Slovak, *krásny*, and it occurred to me immediately that I might have just called him handsome rather than his move beautifully done.

Molly climbed well that day, and some other climbers came over to watch her. She reached the top in a few minutes and rigged a sling around the tree to make an anchor. After the anchor was secured, she rigged a rappel. I dropped my end of the rope and sat on a rock to watch her. A young man stepped up and squatted down in front of me. "*Dobrý deň*," he said. Good day.

"*Dobrý deň*," I answered.

"Anglicky?"

"American, actually."

"I speak English."

"Very well, too."

"Thank you, but I think not. I study in school, but not so good school in here. My mother live at Toronto. In Canada. I was there one time."

"We are from California."

"Ah, Hollywood."

"In our case, San Diego."

"Is close Mexico, yes?"

"Very close. Closer than you are to Vienna. You've studied your geography."

"Slovak people has many interest in world."

"I wish Americans did."

"Americans has no need."

"We could debate that."

He was about 18. He squatted and picked at the grass between his legs. He wore black lycra tights with gold lightning bolts on the sides and a red tank top with a fake Nike logo. His climbing shoes were made from cast-off soccer shoes with the cleats filed off. He had on a harness with a locking karabiner hanging from the belay loop. He was trying to grow a moustache. His blond hair fell over his shoulders as straight and thick as a mop. Whenever I looked up to keep an eye on Molly preparing to rappel, he glanced back at her.

"Is good rope," he commented.

"It's a Mammut."

"Swiss, yes?"

"Yes."

"We have Edelrid."

"That's a good one."

"Here is easier to find German."

"We can get Edelrid in America, too."

"I like go to USA one time."

"Maybe you will."

"Hah! Is not in our future, I think. Our government leaders want protect us from all your money and things."

Molly began rappelling and I looked up at her. He turned to look again.

"Your wife?"

"Yes."

"Is good climber."

"Yes, she is."

"She is oldest woman I see who climb so good."

I laughed. "Well, here she comes, and I don't think I would let her hear me call her old."

"I'm sorry, please. I say only as compliment."

"I understand. You're right. She's a good climber at any age."

I stood and so did the boy, offering me his hand to shake. "My name is Tom Valen," I said.

"I am Vlado Hargaš."

When Molly came over, I introduced her. "Vlado says you're a fine climber."

Vlado blushed.

"Thank you," Molly said.

"Is true," Vlado said. "But I must excuse. My friends wait me."

"Nice to meet you," I told Vlado and he shook hands very formally with each of us.

"Cute boy," Molly said when Vlado was out of earshot.

"Don't get too excited. He said you were old enough to be his mother."

"He did not!" She punched my arm. "Did he?"

"I was just teasing. He did say you were an excellent climber."

Molly started the figure-eight knot for me and then handed the end of the rope to me. "Are you going to try this, or stand around faking compliments?"

Later we left our packs under the protection of Vlado Hargaš and friends, with whom we ate lunch, and walked down the hill on the back side of the castle to explore a small valley. We found a stream running cold from the far mountains and were soon without our clothes, sitting on the bank with our feet in the water. I had one arm over Molly's shoulders, my hand possessively cupping her breast. It was not possible to do this without becoming aroused. Molly leaned her head into my shoulder for a moment, then let her head slide down into my lap. I lay back on the bed of grass with my arms flung to the side, an ersatz Jesus. Molly turned a little and made herself more comfortable. Her long ponytail swayed over my stomach when she began moving. Sunlight waffled through the thick trees and made a checkered pattern in her hair.

We stayed at Pajštún until sunset and walked back down the mountain in twilight, our boots coated in thick black mud from the road. We caught the last bus back to Bratislava from Borinka.

We spent a third night in the Carlton and cleaned our boots in the bathtub. There was no point in moving to another hotel since we were going to the mountains with Štefan in a couple of days.

Monday we had lunch in the old town with Pavol Zapletal and Štefan Borák, where we talked about mountains and climbers we knew in common. I mentioned that we had been to Pajštún on Saturday.

"We heard," Pavol said.

"I led Zapletal's route," Molly said.

Pavol nodded modestly, smiling.

"There are spies everywhere," I said.

"More truth than you think," Štefan said, inclining his head slightly toward the camera mounted obviously in a far upper corner.

Štefan pointed out that Molly and I were very likely the only two American climbers in Slovakia at the moment, so it was not hard to keep track of us among the locals.

"We know you've also discovered that Pajštún is a romantic place," Pavol said.

Molly offered a confused look.

"It's okay," Pavol said. "We all have done same there."

"How did you know *that*?" Molly asked.

"Spies," Pavol said.

Štefan was laughing.

"Somebody could *see* us," Molly said to me. I shrugged my shoulders and held out my hands in innocence. "Well, I don't give a damn," Molly said, crossing her arms defiantly over her chest, trying not to smile.

But I saw that Štefan's attention had suddenly strayed from their table to watch two men who took the table next to ours. It didn't occur to me not to look at them until I caught Štefan shaking his head.

"Is something wrong?" I asked, lowering my voice.

Štefan shook his head again, but he leaned toward Pavol and whispered in Slovak. I understood enough to know that Štefan was telling Pavol to leave. "Pavol must go," Štefan said. "Must go for work now."

Pavol stood, and so did we. He shook my hand and gave Molly a quick hug. He said he might see us in the mountains at week's end.

When Pavol left the café, the two men rose from the next table and followed him out.

"What the hell was that?" I asked.

Štefan waved his hand back and forth, saying, "Another time, my friend. Another time." I nodded.

"More pivo?" Štefan asked in a loud voice.

"But this wine cannot compete with the wine from your vineyard, Štefan," Molly said incongruously. We were drinking beer and he asked if we wanted more beer; Molly knew the difference between pivo and vino.

Štefan lay his hand over Molly's. "I must agree that you are true," he said. "This wine here is broken."

Štefan waved to the waiter and ordered two beers and a glass of broken wine for Molly.

"So," he said to Tom, "say me about Pajštún."

"What part?"

"Oh, the climb." He smiled expansively, then laughed.

Molly

I first saw Tom Valen on January 3, 1978. I was suspicious of him because of the way he stared at me so openly. Tom has large blue eyes and a penetrating gaze. His eyes are mesmerizing and a lot of people don't like it at all when he looks directly and at length into their eyes. At that time he wore a long, full beard and shaggy blond hair that made him look sort of like a skinny Viking. He has never been shy about staring intently at someone or something that interests him. Tom makes people nervous until they understand that he is only expressing his curiosity, interest, affection or love. Yes, and at times, his anger, his disappointment. I have never been afraid of his anger, which rises and falls like a steam-fed geyser, but his disappointment devastates me.

It was a cool, overcast day, and the Lizardettes were camping over the holiday weekend at Joshua Tree, in Indian Cove. Lizardettes is the name my father gave to Saša and me, and the third member of our climbing group, a woman named Laura Sommers. Laura, a year younger than I, was off and on Saša's lover. She was an energetic but new climber. By and large, we were the only three serious women climbers any of us knew about at the time. Sometimes there were women at the crags, but they were only groupies or beginners or both. In *Climbing* magazine there were occasional articles about young female climbers, but none of the Lizardettes had ever seen one alive and in-person.

Laura was from Taiwan and had that round, full Chinese face. Her hair looked like she cut it with a bowl over her head, but it wasn't unattractive and I could not imagine her looking any other way. She was adopted as a child and thus the American name. She was a little boyish, slim, short and strong. She liked being in groups and said she couldn't bear being alone. She was a member of everything from the Sierra Club to the auto club; she wanted to formalize the Lizardettes into a club and attract other members, to make T-shirts, caps, and go on big expeditions together. She could see us atop Everest, arms around one another, wearing Lizardette T-shirts with a logo of her design. She decided that her logo (an obviously female lizard, with definite breasts, climbing a slab with a pack on its back) would work just as well on a parka when I explained to her that the top of Everest would be quite a bit colder than the top of San Jacinto in July, which was then the highest mountain she had climbed. She talked constantly while she climbed, usually exhorting herself to make it over the hard places. She worked as a research assistant for a bio-medical company in La Jolla. She was attracted to exotic religions. She was in love with Saša. Saša was in love with me, and I had known it for a long time.

In October, 1974, Saša and I were camping near Idyllwild, the small town situated between two of my favorite climbing areas in Southern California—Tahquitz and Suicide Rock. My father had died in early July that year. Although Saša and I had been climbing partners for more than a year, it was only the second time we had gone out for more than day trips; the other time had been a month earlier at the same place, Idyllwild.

We arrived late because we couldn't leave until Saša got off work and my last class ended at 3:30; by then Friday traffic on I-15 was terrible. When we found a campsite, it was dark, and we had to set up the tent by flashlight. It was colder than the forecast had predicted, so we ate some sandwiches, drank a beer apiece, shared a joint, then crawled into our sleeping bags. But it was too early to sleep and we were too keyed up about playing on Suicide Rock the next day. We lay on our sides facing one another and shared another joint, talking about nothing much.

Later, apropos to nothing, Saša told me that I was beautiful. She said, "you have wery nice hair," and reached over to stroke the part of it that was hanging at the side of my face.

We often flirted and laughed at sexual innuendoes, and sometimes there was a rather highly charged sexual atmosphere around us, but at that moment, for the first time, I understood that Saša wanted to sleep with me, and I knew tacitly that I would like to at least try it. There were butterflies in my stomach the same way there had always been when I realized that I was about to have sex with a boy.

But nothing happened. Saša said she had to pee and got out of her bag and crawled out of the tent. We were both wearing polypropylene long underwear for pajamas and as I watched Saša crawling on hands and knees through the tent opening, I thought how distinctly un-sexy we both looked. I felt a little disappointed and thought about doing it to myself. Saša was gone a long time and I got drowsy. I had almost dozed off when Saša returned. She got into her bag, patted my shoulder and said goodnight. I heard the zipper. Probably because of the beer and grass, she fell asleep quickly.

I awoke because I could feel a body against mine; a hand cupped my left breast. I could feel air moving against the back of my neck and ear, and hear the quick, rhythmic breathing noises. I opened my eyes but it was pitch black inside the tent on a cloudy, moonless night. The hand on my breast did not so much squeeze as stroke. It moved my heart into my throat.

"Okay?" Saša asked quietly.

"Okay," I answered, lifting my left arm and moving it back to lay across Saša's hip. Saša was naked. Her skin felt cool and soft and a bit damp.

Saša's right hand was in my hair, playing with it, and her left hand moved slowly away from my breast and along my ribs to slip beneath the waistband of my pants and lay on the rise of my hip. Her lips lay against my neck, at the lobe of my ear, but without kissing. Her hand moved down and her fingers touched my pubic hair.

"May I do this?" she asked, and began at the same time to tug down my pants. To help her, I turned onto my back and raised my hips so she could pull my pants down and over my feet. I sat up, pulled off my shirt, then turned so we were both on our sides, facing one another. I avoided Saša's eyes. Our breasts blended. Saša ran her fingertips over my hip and along my thigh and I did the same to her, our arms crossing over one another. I first felt Saša's breath then her lips touching, softly, without opening; then a touching at the outside of my lips; I opened my mouth spontaneously.

Curiously, I cupped Saša's breast. She was very soft and the smells coming from her skin were pleasing, even the tobacco odor.

Saša moved her hand along my thigh until it was between my legs, her fingers stroking the hair there.

This went on infinitely. It was so unlike being with boys, who stroked your body only as a necessary precondition to being able to enter it, not because there was anything inherently satisfying in the feel, smell and taste of it. It seemed that Saša could spend all the night simply stroking and smelling me.

My immersion in Saša, while it seemed to last a long time, began to disappear, and I found myself unable to stop thinking about the fact that she was a girl and there was no penis waiting at the end of all this, and that while it felt wonderful, it did not feel . . . what? Momentous? Purposeful? As my curiosity began to wane, so did my ardor. I could tell that Saša had also sensed this.

At some point Saša spread my legs and replaced her finger with her tongue. I had a spontaneous and mild orgasm astonishingly quickly. After that she moved up to lay her head next to mine, her hand on my breast and mine on hers. I could smell myself blended with Saša.

"I want to do you now," I said.

"It's okay," she answered.

"Don't you want me to?"

"Let's leave it like it is. I'm wery content now."

I wasn't sure that I really wanted to do it, and it became obvious that Saša could sense it. In a minute or two, she kissed my cheek and got back into her own bag. I started to get a chill so I found my pants and shirt and put them back on. "Goodnight," I said, then added, "I liked that very much."

"Yes, it vas good."

"But it was . . ."

"Not so good for you."

"No, I mean, everything felt really, really good. That's not what I started to say. You need to let me finish my sentences. You don't always do that."

"I'm sorry."

"Don't apologize, Saša."

"Vhat did you vant to tell me?"

"I had an orgasm, you know?"

"That you don't have to tell me."

"You are my best friend, Saša. My very best friend in the world. I love you, in fact."

"But?"

"*But*," I said with some irritation, "I don't think I'm very gay."

"Wery gay? There are degrees?"

"You said . . ."

"Don't trust me. I say anything."

"Like you said you slept with my father?"

Saša stiffened. I had not meant to hurt her. I had never mentioned what Saša told me the night she was plastered and I bailed her out of jail. I didn't know why I brought it up then, at that time.

"I'm sorry I say anything about that to you."

"I'm not horrified. I don't even mind. I think that was between you and him and if it made him happy . . ."

"It did."

"Is that the only reason you slept with him? To make him happy?"

"It vas the best reason, but not only one."

"I would like to know, if I may."

"Because of you."

"Me? You slept with my father because of me?"

"Because I am in love with you."

"Shit."

"Everything not go in straight line, here to there, rational and clear always. Sometimes go back to go forward. Understand?"

I nodded my head, but I wasn't thinking about straight lines and rational or irrational processes.

"I vant to quit this talk now." Saša turned over and let me know that she was going to sleep. It was the only time Saša and I had any overt sexual contact until the day I met Tom on that climb at Joshua Tree.

Saša, Laura and I were on a route called Crown Jewels in the middle of this jumble of massive boulders called Feudal Wall. Tom and his friend Phillip had already topped-out on a shorter route to the left and were cleaning up; Phillip sorting and packing their protection and Tom coiling the rope.

I was leading and had just reached a bolt where I could set up a belay to bring up Laura and Saša. I could feel him watching me, and I could hear the two of them making small talk. It was a crowded weekend, there were climbers all over the place, and families hiking along trails through the boulders below the climbing walls. A dog barked insistently.

After I'd set up the anchor, Tom called out to me: "You're a damn fine climber."

"Thanks," I answered. I think I was a little surprised he was talking to me, given the view he must have had of Saša below. I could tell he was older than I was, but not how much. I assumed he was trying to pick me up, which is the principal reason men speak to women in climbing areas, but I didn't mind. He was really nice looking in his exotic beard and long hair and didn't seem to be a rock surfer. He had a Texas-ish sort of accent that made him sound like Dan Rather on the CBS News.

I started bringing Laura up. I didn't look over, but I could hear the two men talking and feel them watching. I tried to pay attention to Laura and not look stupid while I was at it.

At a point where Laura stopped to gather herself (and chastise herself) for a hard move, Tom called out, "Good luck," and offered a wave.

"Thanks," I said. "You guys, too."

And they disappeared to down climb the back side.

I am amazed at how things work. The utter randomness of it all. The blindness. I had just met and spoken to the man I would love and live with for the rest of my life, and except for this sudden and vague feeling of hunger, the moment passed with no more weight or importance than saying hello to a friendly passerby. Every moment of our lives is pure potentiality, Tom has said.

It was pretty much dark by six o'clock and we were in our campsite sorting out our gear by lantern light when Tom and Phillip walked up. Tom had a cooler in his hand.

"Would you guys share a beer with us?" Tom asked, holding out the cooler like an offering.

I glanced toward Laura and Saša for their opinions, and got a shrug from Laura and a vague nod from Saša. I pushed our stuff aside on the picnic table and we sat down, except Laura, who fiddled around the campsite in her usual evening routine, like some den mother.

We introduced ourselves. Tom said, "You don't see very many female climbers, certainly not any as good as you guys."

I thanked him, Saša cocked her head and eyed him suspiciously. Tom and Phillip were looking at our climbing gear piled at the other end of the table, appraising it by its beat-up usefulness.

I can't remember what we talked about. Just stuff. The way people do when everything is unfamiliar, yet portentous. I do remember that we ate together—sandwiches we'd brought from home, chips, dip, things like that—and drank all of Tom's beers, then all of Phillip's, then all of ours.

It got cold after the sun went down, and Saša made a fire. Every few minutes we would add more clothing. Phillip went off somewhere to pee, and came back with fleece jackets for Tom and himself, although they were still wearing shorts and running shoes without socks.

Saša went to pee and didn't come back. Laura crawled into our tent to read, but it quickly became obvious (she snored a little) that she had fallen asleep. We smiled and lowered our voices. A radio played somewhere not far away. After that, Phillip said goodnight and wandered off, I'm sure to look for something more interesting, or maybe to look for Saša, whom he clearly found attractive. Tom said it looked like we were the leftovers.

I think about that night fairly often, and I try to remember what we said to one another, and how by the end of the night I could have wanted him so much, but I can only remember the feelings, not the words. Of course it was just the usual conversation: we scrolled out the data of our lives in comments and little stories. Some things were special about him. For example, he occupied himself when tent-bound on expeditions by memorizing poems, and to prove it he quoted to me a few stanzas of a very long Rilke poem about the Orpheus myth. You have to imagine what it was like to have a little buzz on and be sitting in a beautiful place with a handsome and intelligent man quoting poetry in a Southern accent by lantern light. I remember being impressed that he was a philosophy professor (actually he was only a lecturer in his first year then), and I remember him saying that it should have been obvious that my father was Frank Cook from the way that I climbed. He said I was easily the best female climber he had ever seen. I was surprised that he was ten years older than me. He would not get around to telling me that he had been married before for nearly a month. By then I was hooked and would have stayed with him if he'd told me he was the son of Satan.

About ten o'clock, I think, he got up to leave. When I stood, he stepped forward and leaned toward me, so I let him kiss me. It was very brief, very soft.

"Wonderful," he said, stepping back.

And I said, "Then let's do it again."

The second time it was long, breathless, with our mouths open, and when he turned to walk away, I shivered from some chilly well of magical anticipation.

Saša woke me when she crawled into the tent and crinkled her body into the sleeping bag. I couldn't see my watch, but I had been sound asleep.

I asked her what time it was. She said, "I don't know." Then she giggled.

Laura moaned, turned over, and began softly snoring again.

Saša was drunk and smelled of sex and after less than a minute she turned on her side toward me and her arm came across my side. I could not imagine she had fallen asleep so fast. But she wasn't asleep. Her hand cupped my breast and held it. I could hear her breathing. I hoped that she was *really* drunk and had mistaken me for Laura. She took my nipple between her fingers and rubbed it gently. It was what I wanted the man I just spent the evening with to do. When she put her other hand between my legs, I said, "You turned the wrong way," then eased out of my sleeping bag. Saša didn't say anything. I grabbed a flashlight, slipped into my sandals, and trotted off to the latrine. It was a sparkling clear night and awfully cold. When I pulled open the door, the screech was absurd and obnoxious. The latrine smelled horrible.

After leaving the latrine, I walked along the road that winds through Indian Cove toward Feudal Wall. I was probably looking for Tom Valen's campsite, although I wouldn't admit it to myself. I wouldn't have recognized it anyway; not knowing what kind of car he had, what kind of tent, or anything. I wanted to see him again, and I was afraid I never would.

We spent another day at Joshua Tree, climbing on Feudal Wall again, but didn't see Tom and Phillip. They had to have left; Indian Cove isn't that big an area. I wondered what I had done wrong, and decided I was too aggressive when he kissed me. He hadn't asked for my phone number.

I climbed horribly, sick with dread and self-recrimination. We left Sunday night and drove back to San Diego. It was late when I got back to my apartment and my answering machine light was blinking like some Christmas star in the kitchen.

"Hi! It's Tom Valen. I got away without asking for your phone number, so I hope you don't mind that I looked it up and called you. And if M. Cook isn't the beautiful climber I had the nicest evening of my life with on Saturday, I apologize. I hope you'll give me a call."

He left both his office and home numbers. I jumped straight up and punched the air with my fist, screaming: "Yes!"

Tom

We spent two days alone in Bratislava. The weather turned bad again. Not cool, as it had been all week, but hotter and oppressively humid. We thought of going by train to Vienna, but we didn't have multiple entry visas and were afraid we might have some trouble getting back into Czechoslovakia.

We took a mud-streaked local bus to Devín and as we walked along a foggy, cobblestone country lane toward it, the old castle appeared like a Scottish ruin on the moors. There wasn't much remaining of the ancient Roman fortress built two thousand years ago on a high rocky promontory at the confluence of the Danube and Morava rivers. There the river formed the border. Red-and-white-striped poles symbolized the warning. Stretching along its banks on either side of the castle ruins ran a continuous double row of six meter high barbed wire fence with hidden cameras, guard dogs, and watch towers manned by soldiers with machine guns. Waiting for what? I wondered. The capitalists to attack from Austria? I knew it was serious, but it seemed so silly.

Below the castle adolescent boys played soccer on a muddy field near a cemetery. Their fathers drank beer they bought from a bar resembling a wood shed. In back a man stoked a barrel of sausages being cured with hickory smoke. A radio near him played violin music and sometimes he looked up at clouds floating by with the pleading look of a desperate hitchhiker.

A tour bus filled with East Germans, all wearing identical red conical felt hats, disgorged in the parking lot below the castle. A Slovak family getting out of their green Škoda stood watching the Germans for a moment, before returning to their car and driving away.

"I would love to climb this," I said, referring to the castle keep. A section of the castle on a rocky spire separated from the main section of the structure stood like a needle rising from the river below.

"Is it possible to climb here?"

"Probably not. It's really close to the border. I'll ask Štefan."

We followed the Germans up a winding lane filled with gravel to a kiosk where tickets to tour the castle could be purchased. We laughed about the Germans' hats. "It must be like the Japanese tourists wearing matching name tags," Molly speculated sarcastically.

We waited out a sudden thunderstorm inside a cave that had been converted into a small art gallery. A bronze Soviet soldier liberated a Slovak peasant woman and her adoring ragged child. There were replicas of Celtic coins and fertility statues: FOR SALE. The Germans smoked and drank from bottles held in their coat pockets. Soon it was impossible to breathe and we went outside. But the rain had stopped and it was a little cooler.

"I'd like to sit somewhere," Molly said. "Just for a little while."

"How are you feeling?"

"I have a headache but it's not . . . bad. Where are we?" she asked suddenly, a bit desperately. "Where is this place? Where are we?"

"We shouldn't have come all the way out here." I felt useless, helpless and stupid. This was the second time in two days she had completely lost herself. And just as suddenly she came back.

"Done what instead? Lie abed in the Carlton." She smiled and took my hand. "We could walk down the hill and watch the kids play soccer."

There were some benches in front of a small club house. One coach who was awesomely fat prowled the sidelines, yelling at his boys. Two women sat at the end of the bench with knitting in their hands. A man alone watched intently. The benches were still wet. Everyone else seemed to be having beer at the bar shed, grouped below sheltering trees.

I watched Molly go into the cocoon of her illness, becoming a prisoner inside her deteriorating body. I saw her try to watch the boys play, but clearly she couldn't concentrate. Their running, their gibberish cries, seemed to sadden her. I knew that Molly wanted one of them to be hers, one she could cheer for; now, *now* I would give anything to have a child with her. One day I would have nothing of her but memories. There was an evil inside her, robbing both of us of all hope and even the smallest happiness. No matter how hard she tried to pull away, the disease took her back, and me with it.

She told me that now her vision was only clear in one eye. From the other she could see, but everything appeared with indistinct borders. It seemed to be a little worse each day and problems of depth perception plagued her. The throbbing headache moved into her neck. She did not understand why what she thought wasn't always what she said, and she didn't know how much of it I was in fact keeping from her.

I did keep some things from her because I thought it couldn't change anything for her to know. It didn't happen frequently, but sometimes she would carry on an unintelligible monologue, often with her father, and she never seemed to realize this, during or after.

I took her hand and held it in her lap, she put her head on my shoulder. I feel it there still. The boys in the red-and-white shirts won, three–two.

We ate dinner at a nice restaurant below Bratislava castle, with white tablecloths and waiters in tuxedos with thin bow ties. There were Austrian tapestries on the walls. Scenes of hunts, of mountains, of the Vienna woods. The food was Austrian, as well, and I noticed that everyone spoke German. In defiance, I ordered a Slovak specialty: meat-filled pancakes, and the local Topvar beer, which I actually didn't much like. Molly ordered trout and white wine from the vineyards of Pezinok, near Štefan's field.

We walked back to the hotel as the fog crept across the road from the riverbank, through what had been the old Jewish Quarter of Bratislava. It was leveled, along with the oldest synagogue in Slovakia, to make way for the exit ramps of the SNP bridge. Sometimes at night people would come to the underpass below the bridge and with paint quickly recreate the Jewish Quarter buildings on the concrete, down to the details of flowers in window boxes. The authorities would have it washed off again and again. But outlines remained, clear shadows of hope's persistence.

She slept fitfully. I sat reversed on the straight-back chair and watched her. What were we going to do in the mountains? She couldn't even judge curbs along the sidewalk. I had kept her from tripping a dozen times. How was she going to climb? How could I keep her from it?

I knew she had come to these mountains to die, and for a time it had seemed all right, a glorious and appropriate way to take leave of one's life. But that was only the thinnest of intellectual constructs, and I had been thinking of it in my terms, not hers. I could feel it crumbling like the old city outside the window. She should be in a hospital. She should be making every attempt to let modern medicine bring her back from this horrible place, this business of dying. If there is a rope thrown to us, we should reach for it, no matter how thin or suspicious it might be. I could not remember how many doctors we had seen: five, six, seven? But what if the eighth could do something? Or the ninth, or tenth? What if she didn't have to die now? What if she could have another year, two? What if she died because we had not taken just one more step?

I could not bear to look at her struggling against the sheet, pushing her head hard into the pillow, twisting her feet, digging into the stiff sheet with her fingers. And I could not sleep next to her; her erratic movements continually awakened me.

I slipped on jeans, boots and a sweater and stood next to the bed for a moment, looking at Molly. Her hair was damp with sweat. On the bed table were four vials of pills and a bottle of the local fizzy mineral water. I started to touch her hair but withdrew my hand.

I hoped there was a God and I hoped I could be cognizant of this God when the time came, because for what God had done to Molly, I intended to torture and kill him. I was so angry that I felt like my body would explode from it.

I left the room quietly, ignored the whores in the lobby, and walked toward the music coming from the Hungarian café. I ordered a beer and the waitress who brought it smiled at my accent. A prostitute asked in Slovak if she could join me and I let her. She asked if I spoke German. I used the candle on the table to light a cigarette for her. In Slovak, she asked if I liked her and I said no. She crushed out the cigarette in the ashtray as if it were my hand and left the restaurant. I drank a second beer, left the waitress an obscenely high tip for her honest smile, and walked back to the hotel.

We woke early and I asked Molly if she was nervous. Only excited, she told me. There were no clouds. The sky was pale, a washed-out blue like old denims. The brown river was now silver and to look at it hurt our eyes. Even the gray endless concrete wall of high-rise apartments over the river in Petržalka looked good in the blinding glare of sunlight washing across hectares of glass, like a glistening ancient city on some vast desert plain, a bright sun shielding the ugliness with incandescence. A long barge pursued the river, beating against the strong current. A slipstream of turgid water raced past, straining channel markers. White birds hopped along the stone embankment, others cruised above the barge boat. A tram rattled along the riverfront street. Shoppers waited for the next one. A boy and girl kissed while they waited. A waiter in a shiny black suit set Pilsner Urquell umbrellas in sidewalk tables beside the Hotel Devín.

I held Molly's hand as we walked back across the road in the rising heat and went back to the hotel to get our things. We felt an incongruous nostalgia for the decrepit city, although we were excited to be finally heading for the Tatras. I wondered if Molly would ever see Bratislava again. I wondered how many things each day were done for the last time.

Molly had a mild toothache and I walked down to the *lekáreň* in old town where herbal medicines were kept in apothecary jars bearing hieroglyphic names on dusty unlighted shelves; I bought aspirin and buds of clove. We left the Carlton with all our gear: two backpacks and two large duffel bags. The duffel bags held our clothes, shoes, boots and books. In the backpacks were ropes, slings and runners, both alpine and rock harnesses, karabiners, rock shoes, crampons, helmets, nuts, hexes, cams, Friends, chalk bags, sleeping bags, and head lamps. Strapped to the backs were ice axes, adjustable trekking poles and sleeping bag pads.

Two trams went by with standing room only before we decided to take a taxi to the train station. The driver said he would take us to Poprad, the largest town near the Tatra mountain range, a five-hour drive, for one hundred dollars or equivalent in any hard currency. I explained that we had train tickets, and the driver offered to go for eighty dollars. He was sullen when that offer was refused and did not help with our bags when we reached Bratislava's *hlavná stanica*, main station.

Štefan waited for us near the entrance and took both duffel bags after giving us each great bear hugs. The duffel bags were preposterously heavy but Štefan hefted them casually by the straps and carried them high. Workmen stood at tall round tables and drank beer. A gypsy man kicked his wife hard, then threw her into the mud; she screamed at him in a gibberish language and two small children, apparently theirs, watched like statues with their thumbs in their mouths. Two policemen sauntered over, but only to watch. The man chased his wife into the station and the show ended.

Štefan, Molly and I moved quickly through the station, down the long stairs to the tracks and boarded the next to last car. A group of students carrying large rucksacks, some with climbing ropes tied across the top, milled around the platform talking, teasing one another, passing the time. A conductor in an ill-fitting uniform helped an old woman board. A fat man said good-bye to his wife or mistress. Sacks of mail moved along atop a pushcart. An old man slept soundly on the one bench, his head covered by a newspaper. Two soldiers drank beer at a kiosk and smoked listlessly; between them someone had vomited a while back.

A long train with forest green passenger cars pulled into the station, scattering cigarette wrappers and greasy papers across the platform. Two old men leaned against a wooden fence on the hill beyond and watched the trains. One smoked a pipe.

Štefan had commandeered a compartment for us and his friend Edo waited there, holding it. Štefan's backpack lay on the luggage rack next to Edo's. Our packs went on the opposite racks, our duffel bags in two empty seats. A woman and her two small children noisily passed in the aisle. Štefan introduced Edo, a climber who also lived in Bratislava, to us. Edo pulled fat brown bottles of beer from a knapsack on the floor and began opening them. Molly stood between where Edo and Štefan were seated so she could look out the window, and she watched passengers drag amazing suitcases along the platform. Bread and sausage appeared, and the close, crowded compartment confined those odors.

"*Na priateľstvo*," Štefan toasted after Edo handed him a beer.

"*Na priateľstvo*," Edo said and drank long.

"To friendship," I agreed and drank.

"Yes, to friendship," Molly said, impulsively leaning down to kiss my head.

We settled into our seats to drink, eat and talk about small matters. Štefan translated for Edo, who spoke very little English. After a while the train lurched once, twice, and began slowly heading out of the city. Molly stood by the window again to watch Bratislava's concrete suburbs fade away.

But after a few minutes she had to sit down. She had lost her balance. When she tried to explain, some of the words were ridiculous. She seemed to be most aware of Štefan watching her from the corner of his eye, and she pretended to sleep. She did not speak again, except to answer questions, until we reached Poprad.

Molly

It is certainly not that I had no life before Tom Valen, it's just that it has diminished so far into the background that it seems like the memories we have of books read a long time ago. Tom says that people resemble artichokes, that we are made up of prickly layer after sharp layer after spiny layer protecting our delicate and essential core. He does not say what that core is. There are, he supposes, countless ideas about it. I have never asked Tom directly what *he* thinks is at the core of our existence. But he is very much a pragmatist. He does not deal easily with things he considers to be unknowable. He is like those ancient cartographers who mapped to the outer limits of the known world, and when faced with the unknown wrote: beyond this place is the domain of monsters. Tom's known world ends at the limits of reason, although in his case those limits are quite vast. I also don't know if there's anything beyond, and I am very afraid that in fact there's nothing at all. But I like to think we are more than what Tommy refers to as temporarily animated mass. Otherwise life is pathetically pointless repetition. Of course, that may well be all there is. Sometimes I wonder if whatever the soul may be is what resides at the core of our being, but I don't know if some nebulous soul is enough for me. I wish we would talk about these things more often. We did in the beginning.

Tom and I didn't date for very long before we married. There didn't seem to be much reason: We were very much in love with each other, almost from the very start. He says he fell in love with me the first time we kissed. He is awfully romantic, my Orpheus.

I was afraid of him in the beginning. Not *of* him, of course, but the feeling of such utter dependence. I needed him and it frightened me. I did not want to live my life without him, which gave him the power of a god. As soon as I knew I could trust him with this power over me, we were married, and I understood that part of the vow: the two shall become as one.

We met in early January and were married on the first of August, 1978. Tom's friend Phillip lived on the bay in the peninsula town of Coronado, so we were married in his beautiful backyard, by a minister we hired from an ad in the newspaper classifieds, who charged twenty-five dollars and included a cassette tape of the ceremony. Mom came, and I think she was sort of happy about me getting married, although she had her suspicions about Tom: He had been married before, he was ten years older. But it bothered her most that he was a climber and a teacher. She thought I was marrying my father, and said as much.

Saša and Laura were there, a few of Tom's colleagues from the university, Phillip with the girl he would almost but not marry three months later, a few of my friends from the paper. That was it.

The Lizardettes wrote "Just Married" with soap on the rear window of Tom's old Toyota Land Cruiser.

We went to Switzerland for our honeymoon, but not to climb. I didn't have enough experience with technical high altitude alpine climbing and Tom said we would start on something smaller and less intimidating than the Berner Oberland. But just in case, we packed our boots, a pair of eight-millimeter ropes, crampons, picks, harnesses, and the usual odds and ends. We wouldn't want to find perfect conditions for a climb and not be prepared to do it, Tom said. I don't think it was possible for Tom to be in the mountains, anywhere, anytime, and not have his climbing gear. Just in case.

We flew to Zurich and took the train to Interlaken. The small town dividing a pair of large blue lakes is in the most beautiful setting I had and have still ever seen. In spite of horrible jet lag, I kept my face plastered to the train window, staring in disbelief and wonder.

We spent a blissful three days acclimatizing by jogging on steep trails below the Harder Kulm, taking the cog railway from Wilderswil to the Schynige Platte, then hiking along the high trails—along with a couple of million other people, speaking a dozen languages, wearing the most odd assortment of clothing, including a pack of college girls hiking in tennis shoes, cutoff jeans and bikini tops. In those days I had plenty of self-confidence, and Tom never gave me any reason to doubt it; I could hold my own with those college girls, and Tom made sure I knew it. Of course, I had myself only just graduated from college less than three months earlier.

Tom said that late summer was probably the worst time to be in Switzerland, but we, like all the rest, had no choice. Tom had to be back in the States for school by the first week of September, so we only had three weeks.

We had perfect weather for three days. Not a cloud until late in the afternoon when big, cotton-ball cumulus built up over the mountains. The Berner Oberland rose unrealistically above us, like a 1940s movie painted backdrop, and it was impossible not to go high into it. On the fourth day, Tom decided we could climb the summer route to the Jungfrau, 4158 meters.

There would probably be gaping crevasses in the glaciers, Tom said, and a lot of bare ice this time of year. He had climbed all three of the famous peaks in the northern wall of the range—Eiger, Monch and Jungfrau—but in late fall, early winter, when rock fall was diminished

131

and the glacier approaches not so severely crevassed. He had never been here in summer, but said he could guess what it would be like up there.

In spite of all his warnings, I was excited and intent on climbing the Jungfrau, which I had admired from our hike above Kleine Scheidegg. Because of the danger of crevasses in the Jungfraufirn, which feeds into the distant Aletsch Glacier, Tom decided that we would start from the Jungfraujoch railway station and take the alternate normal route up the northeast spur of the Rottalhorn to connect with the ascent ridge rising from the Rottalsattel Couloir.

Then for two days it rained without letup. In the afternoon, giant bolts of lightning crashed over the mountains and reverberated through the town like a cannon assault. I wondered what it must be like on that long, exposed ridge I had seen in the photographs of the Jungfrau. I was more afraid of being hit by lightning than anything else in the mountains, and had once had my hair stand on end while hiding from a storm in a cave-like depression high on Mt. Wilson in southern Nevada.

We stayed in the hotel sorting, re-sorting, packing, re-packing our climbing gear, although we wouldn't need very much. We would take the ropes, harnesses, axes, a few karabiners, helmets, and crampons for the glacier and higher up. The hotel kitchen would pack a lunch for us. We would be up and back within the day. I thought of it as the mountain equivalent of Joshua Tree, where climbers drive up in their cars, park, slip on their climbing shoes, walk a few feet and start climbing. Here we would take the train to the Jungfraujoch station, climb the mountain, then return and take the train back to the hotel.

We sat on the big, sagging bed playing with our gear and looking out the window at the rain. We could see young tourists in every manner of parka and poncho dashing along the streets, skipping over puddles and dodging splashing cars, and insistent shoppers carrying large plastic bags with cord handles. Sometimes in the middle of it all we would stop and make love, the bed squealing like a poor lost pig. Tom phoned down to the desk three or four times a day to check the forecast.

On the third day the rain lightened to a misty drizzle and we went for a long walk through the town. Tom bought an expensive Swiss watch for me. I bought for him a Swiss Army knife climber model and had his initials engraved on it. (He still carries it; I still wear the watch.) We had dinner at a sidewalk cafe across from our hotel and watched the mountains appear like a developing photographic image through the thinning clouds. There seemed to be new snow, and I remarked how odd it was to see so much snow in August. By sunset, which came late that time of year, the sky was clear and the air cool enough for a light sweater.

The next morning we took the train to Kleine Scheidegg, and from there to the Jungfraujoch, the highest railway station in Europe. We disembarked to join a thousand other climbers and hikers, and another two or three thousand day-trippers. It was like trying to work your way through the crowd outside a rock concert. We started out from the station in a single-file line, but began to split off after a while as a few more serious mountaineers headed for the East Face route or the Northeast Ridge. The rest of us, actually down to a number somewhere less than a hundred, slogged along on the glacier.

I could see that this sort of thing embarrassed Tom, but he never said anything, and his spirits were high.

After less than an hour, hikers began turning back in rather large numbers. Some had no crampons and we were often crossing icy patches. Others were not acclimatized and couldn't maintain a strong enough pace to have any chance of reaching the summit. Others seemed to have been watching the ridge line rising ever more steeply above them as we approached and had second thoughts. We slogged on in a group now down to about thirty.

There were crevasses, but easily avoided. I had never seen a crevasse before, and such a yawning chasm of blue ice, dark and deadly, both fascinated and repelled me. Clipping into the rope and belayed by Tom, I approached the edge of one and looked down. I could not see the bottom, there were ledges and sharp ridges at various intervals, and the ice reflected the blue sky. I wouldn't have survived a fall into it.

We reached the Rottalsattel at one o'clock, and all but 12 of us turned around. From here I really began to notice the altitude and level of exertion. We were ascending at an angle of 35 to 40 degrees on mixed ground, with snow and ice. I believe the temperature was near 40° Fahrenheit, but we had taken off our jackets, sweaters and gloves, and were climbing in helmets, T-shirts and wind pants over jeans. Tom and I were in front. There was a mixed group of men and women behind us, stretched out along the ridge for a hundred meters. It was getting a bit exposed. A misstep here would take you back to the glacier in one long, tumbling, deadly fall. Tom and I roped up, with Tom leading. I looked back and saw that the ten had become six, and they were also roping up in pairs. I was surprised to see anyone turn back now, because the summit was not very far away. Less than an hour, I thought.

It was a strikingly beautiful day. There wasn't a cloud. The glare was so ferocious that even wearing mountaineer's goggles, I was squinting. A breeze had come up and because our shirts were damp from sweat, we stopped to put our jackets back on. Some places were more steep, and although I planted the ice axe now and then, I seldom needed to use my hands; it was all fourth-class climbing. I was having a great deal of fun and Tom said later that every time he looked back at me, I was smiling.

I did not realize that we had made the summit until Tom stopped walking and turned around. "Well?" he said, opening his arms expansively, as if he had just created all this for me.

I had sort of expected a peak, a rounded point like the top of a cone. But the top was more a long, narrow platform, littered with stones and patches of snow and ice. The final ten meters had been a gentle rise rather than the steep slope we had been on. Now everything dropped away. Far away.

Tom and I hugged each other, then he began naming the peaks we could see, and the glaciers twisting away from the mountain ridges like the neck, tail and legs of a fossilized albino dinosaur. I took a picture of Tom and he took one of me, then we asked one of the other climbers to take a picture of us together. Tom put his arm over my shoulder and I held up my ice axe triumphantly. It was a perfect moment in time. That picture is framed and sits on the mantel above our fireplace at home.

We sat down to eat and rest. By now four of the other six climbers reached the top, five men and one woman. They greeted us in German.

Holding a sandwich in one hand and a bottle of water in the other, I lay my head on Tom's shoulder. "This is where I want to live, Tom."

"It's pretty cold in the winter," he teased, kissing my hair, which I imagine was still sticky with sweat.

"Tomorrow let's do the Eiger."

He laughed. "Why not? Then we'll just stroll up K-2 to cap off the week."

I jabbed him in the ribs, then he took my chin in his hand and kissed me.

"Bravo," an Austrian behind us said, and we gave him smiles in return.

"It is wonderful," Tom said after a while. We stood and prepared to descend. Now all eight of us were on the summit and it was rather crowded. Suddenly Tom put his arms around me again and held me tightly. He said, "I will always take care of you, Molly."

"I believe you."

Then we started to descend.

There was a message at the desk for us to call Laura Sommers in San Diego and I told Tom in the elevator that something had happened to Saša. I trembled with fear and Tom kept his arm around me as we went to the room and I placed the call.

I thought that if I began in a bright and cheerful manner that some-how I could change what I knew was coming. When Laura answered, I said, "What a surprise! How did you find us here?"

"I called the university and someone told me—Molly, Jesus Christ, Molly, Saša fell."

I was shaking my head and could not speak. Tom took the phone and I heard him talking with Laura:

"But how?—"

"But I don't understand—"

"How high was she?—"

"But why would she do something like that?—"

Suddenly I had a fever. My face was so hot that I thought I would melt. I was going to be sick.

"Okay—Uh-huh—Yes—This is terrible."

I ran to the bathroom and sat on the edge of the bathtub, crying. When I came back he had hung up and was pouring scotch into two glasses. I lay on my stomach on the bed.

"Is she dead?"

"Yes, Molly. I'm very sorry. I liked her very, very much."

"What happened?"

"It's not clear." I felt his weight on the bed and his hand in my hair, stroking it. "They were at Tahquitz, day before yesterday, I think. They had topped out and were coming down. There were two full-length rappels."

"What route?"

"I didn't ask, she didn't say."

"I wish you had asked."

"I'm sorry. We can find out."

"What happened?"

"Again, it's not clear. Laura was on the ground, waiting, cleaning up. She saw Saša rope down from the top and reach the belay ledge. A minute later she hit the ground. She was not on the rope." He took my shoulder and gently turned me over, then he lifted me and put a glass of whisky in my hand. "Drink this." I did in one big gulp and it burned my throat. I pulled away and swung my legs off the bed, then stood.

"We have to go," I said.

"I know. I'll call the airline."

"We have to go now, Tommy."

"I'm just going to call . . ."

"Now! I mean right now! We have to go home right now!" I was screaming and crying and suddenly I was punching Tommy in the chest and trying to slap him. I don't know why. I just don't know why.

Tom

Edo was asleep when we got to Poprad and Štefan shook him awake so we could leave the train, which would continue on to Košice. We had a short wait before we could board a smaller train, hardly more than a tram, for the short ride into the cloud-shrouded mountains rising abruptly east of the wide valley like a saw-toothed granite wall.

Inside the Poprad train station a stream of campers, hikers and climbers ascended a wide stairway leading to the upper level station for the mountain train. Large windows were streaked by a steady drizzle inching through dirt and railroad grease. The smaller train was crowded but not full. Storm clouds formed behind the mountains, typical for July. By August the villages, the hiking trails and even the more arduous routes to higher summits would be choked with Hungarians, who have no mountains of their own, East German workers getting their holiday reward for showing up at work sober three days in a row, poor Austrians who couldn't afford resorts in the Alps, and Czechs and Slovaks on summer vacation. Only in the most winter of winter days did this place belong to the mountaineers and skiers; it was in that season I first took Molly into these gorgeous mountains.

We disembarked in Tatranská Lomnica, one of a string of small villages lined up along the short baseline of the mountains. There were a few hotels, one beautiful old baroque hotel high on the mountain side, and some restaurants, a bookstore and a tiny climbers shop. There were also many state hotels intended for the use of state-sponsored workers and unions. Štefan called them "houses for rewards."

Štefan had arranged for us to stay in a small chalet hotel managed by a friend, while he and Edo hiked up to one of the climbers huts in the high valley between the two main ranges: Belianské and Vysoké.

The hotel had no sign and we could not determine its name. It was made of cedar planking, small, with maybe a dozen large rooms on three narrowing floors. It was a short walk from the train station, very near the post office, which seemed to be the only official government building in the village.

We ate dinner with the manager and his family and found out that we were the only guests in the hotel, which was owned by a large communist workers union and reserved for their exclusive use. Molly only spoke when it was necessary to be polite. The pain medication left her feeling empty and useless.

After dinner we went for a walk. It was drizzling steadily and the ground was soft and muddy below the slick grass. We could see a few lights well up the side of Lomnický Štít, the high, jagged peak nearest the village. There was a lake up there, and next to the lake a building where the cable cars for skiers went 'round about. There was still plenty of snow higher up, but not for skiers. It was only in those places where it could make progress more difficult or more hazardous for climbers.

We both stared at the distant lights.

"I guess it's from that café up there," I said, making conversation, but also thinking how nice it would be to climb high.

Molly nodded. She took my hand and held it.

The restaurant where we thought to have some espresso was full of soldiers, so we returned to the hotel.

For a few minutes we sat in the soft chairs just inside the large glass door that led out to the balcony. With the lights off, we could see outside, the thin rain making the branches of the tall fir and pine trees glisten with weight.

The rooms—there were two, one with a steeply slanting roof for sleeping and one with a small stone fireplace, a long sofa, furniture made of heavy, dark wood—were enormous. There were bookshelves without books built into one wall. On an antique table postured an East German black-and-white television set, which we never tried. There was a bar without liquor but with enough specialty glasses to serve thirty people. The curtains were intricately woven lace with blackout curtains behind them. There was a green lava lamp on the coffee table, but it didn't seem to work. There was a good painting of the Tatras in summer.

In a little while, Molly went to have a bath. There was no shower. I stepped onto the damp balcony and looked through the trees toward the dark mountain, not visible. On the street beyond the nearest trees, a police car slowly passed. I watched a man step quickly off the street and disappear into the tree line.

I was making a fire when Molly came out. With all her clothes off she looked almost like a teenager; so slim still, with hardly evidence of a stomach, the hair between her legs so light as to be nearly indiscernible, her breasts maybe too large for a girl's, but still high on her chest, and the muscles in her legs so long and tight from all the years of climbing. Where was the disease that was so rapidly murdering her?

Her hair was not quite dry and wound itself in tight curls around her face, curls that would relax later, when the moisture was gone.

She came closer to the fire, leaving the towel over the back of a chair.

"It's nice," she said.

"*This* is nice," I answered, looking at her.

She came and sat on my lap. The firelight reddened her skin. Her hair smelled of soap. I kissed the valley between her breasts, smelling her. Then I raised my head, brushed my cheek against hers and said, "Do you remember the last time we were here? Sleeping up there in a tent, in a blizzard, listening to rocks tumble down the slopes?"

"No talk, please."

"Good idea."

I hurried out of my clothes and we made love on the couch in front of the fire. It was the last time.

Before we went to bed, Molly sat at the desk and wrote what she said were letters on paper she found in the drawer. The hotel's logo, a stylized A-frame building flanked by twin spruce trees, was on each sheet. I left her there and went to bed. When I bent over to kiss her, she covered the paper with her arm.

The next morning I found the papers wadded up in the wastebasket and took them out, carefully unfolding each. There were six sheets. One was filled with gibberish. I couldn't tell the order in which they were written. The next one read, in a cautious penmanship: *My name is Molly Louise Cook Valen. I was born in La Mesa, California, on November 5, 1955. I am 33 years old. I may never be 34.* There were a dozen incoherent words after that. The next sheet had only these words, begun as a letter: *My dearest Tommy, You are the only man I have loved. Because of you I have horn beautiful incredible fortune to hill hap. . . .* On two other sheets she had obviously tried to write the same thing, with less success. The last sheet I straightened held only my name, the word "confess," some scribbles, and the word "NO" marked deep into the paper.

Molly had not gone to bed. I found her asleep on the couch, curled tightly against herself, a couch pillow pulled over her head. It was just dawn. Although I very much wanted to keep those notes, I knew Molly would not have wanted me to know. So I wadded each sheet up again and put them all back into the wastebasket.

We walked by the white church, its spire mimicking the shape of Lomnický Štít rising directly behind it, to the café where we were to meet Štefan. As the morning fog lifted, the mountain seemed to be thrusting forward from inside a cloud, although the meteorological station on the summit remained invisible.

We walked in the damp street. There were almost no cars there in summer. It had been decided that automobile pollution was bad for the mountains. Only government officials and persons of anachronistic privilege were allowed to bring their cars, so that a few dumpy black Tatras and the necessary service trucks were all one saw.

I thought this was a good idea and told Molly that it might be an even better idea to extend this theory to include protecting people who had to live near the coal-fired power plants and chemical factories.

We were aware of the changing light as more of the sun made its way through thinning fog. The dew brightened. Vertical surfaces became distinct. We moved aside to let pass a black Tatra carrying a fat man reading a newspaper alone in the back seat; it turned onto the steep gravel road leading to the Grand Hotel Praha.

Five men, boys really, carrying ropes and heavy packs, walked toward the cabin lift station. There were crusted patches of black snow in the ditches and in the places of continual shade. On a late July morning it was cool enough for a jacket or sweatshirt.

The fog lifted suddenly and the light seemed inexhaustible. Through the new green leaves we could see the mountain with its snowcap nearly as far down as the small round glacier lake lying above the tree line. Now in the sun, we removed our jackets at the same time.

Štefan waited outside the café, watching for us.

"*Ahoj, dobrý deň.*" I waved.

"*Dobrý deň*," Štefan answered, holding out his arms, waiting to hug us. "*Ako sa máš?*"

"We are fine," I said.

After hugging one another in that great and affectionate Slovak manner, Štefan opened the door and we entered the smoke. Two men standing in the lobby had drunk their breakfast and were very pleased about it. Štefan found a table by a window. It was hard to breathe through the acrid smoke, so I leaned over and opened the window, asking if anyone minded. "All right?"

"Of course," Štefan said. "We smoke much. Maybe for some, health have no reason." He shrugged. "How you like *chata?*"

"It is fine, although we seem to be the only guests," I said.

Štefan looked at Molly, waiting. His question was to her, but I had answered for her. Molly smiled then picked up a menu and hid behind it.

"This *chata* can be full or empty. Not between."

"But we seem to be between."

Štefan laughed heartily. "Because you are my friends, all is possible. Understand?"

Štefan glanced at Molly then back toward me. I realized he wasn't going to keep quiet with his concerns about Molly anymore.

A sluggish, offended waiter appeared and flipped open a small notebook with an angry flourish.

"What for eat?" Štefan asked.

"Molly?" I asked.

"Egg." She said the practiced word without looking up from the menu.

"Eggs," I said to Štefan, "and maybe some toast for both of us, and I'd like a piece of cooked ham, if they have it; also any kind of fruit."

Štefan repeated the order in Slovak and a quick, sharp argument followed. I followed enough of it to understand that nothing we ordered was available.

"I am sorry," Štefan said quickly, then turned his attention back to the waiter.

Molly looked out the window. The cool air made her cheeks red. Her gaze distant.

"Coffee, he will bring," Štefan said after a moment. The waiter flipped closed his order book and about-faced. "And I help him to find some bread, some cheese and two apple."

"That's enough," I said.

"I hope apple will be good."

"It's the season, so we can hope."

"Here is only one season: season of stupid."

I shrugged in sympathy.

"Is big wish for me before death I might have some chance for live in my country as normal country. Ah, but enough!" Štefan leaned across the table on his forearms and lowered his voice. "I have some bad news." Molly turned back from the window. "Edo is taken by police. Not VB," he whispered: "StB."

The State Secret Police agency.

"What?" I said.

Štefan nodded to enhance his confirmation. "During night three men come to Brnčalová *chata* from helicopter and he must go with them."

"Do you know why?"

"Is no need for why in our *normal* country. They come in helicopter! Too lazy for walking in beautiful mountains."

"Edo," Molly said, as if testing her ability to speak.

"Yes," Štefan nodded. "But there is more. We plan also for meeting Pavol at Brnčalová, where he come day before today to wait. But no Pavol. Not day before. Not in night. And no one of us see him or hear something about him."

"Pavol is missing?" I asked.

"Yes, missing. Pavol is missing."

"This is crazy."

"Is crazy country."

"Why?"

"You are *filosof*, Tomaš, so you tell answer."

"I mean, why would the police take Edo, and I presume you think they have taken Pavol, as well?"

The waiter appeared phantasmagorically, a macabre pop-up from the magic lantern. On a round Formica tray he carried three bruised and misshapen apples, three small plates holding dark rolls, a plate of butter, a small jar of red jam, a pile of utensils and napkins, and three small cups of coffee.

"We can eat," Štefan said, "then have some small hike. Near here is nice park. Moja Molka, would you like have walk in such nice park?"

"Yes," Molly nodded.

Štefan saw me about to pay the waiter and reached over to stay my hand.

"*Zaplat'im*," Štefan told the waiter and quickly handed him some crown notes.

I put my wallet away and thanked Štefan. I learned long ago that this argument could not be won.

We ate quietly for the most part, or talked a little about mountains. Štefan watched Molly, waiting. Sometimes she smiled, but she seldom spoke. Only yes, or no, maybe.

"You know where Pavol is, don't you?" I asked.

Štefan nodded. "In our country we know where disappeared people go. Is only one place for disappeared. Police keep them. We will speak on this later."

It was hard to eat in all the smoke. In deference, Štefan waited until we were outside to light his own cigarette.

Molly put her hand on my arm and leaned toward my ear to whisper, "I have to go back."

"Back?"

"To the room."

"Are you all right, Molly?"

"Just a headache. But I'd like to lie down."

"I'll go with you."

"No." Then softer, "No, Tom. Go with Štefan. I can find my way okay. I'm just going to sleep for a little while."

"I don't mind going with you. I mean I would rather go with you."

"You can't do anything to help me. Go with Štefan. I want to be alone to get rid of this headache. Your hovering around will just make me nervous."

"You're sure?"

"Please."

Abruptly Molly kissed both of us.

Before Štefan could mount his protest, Molly told him that she had slept badly and had a headache, that she wanted to rest. Štefan took her hand for a moment, then let go and said good-bye to her. Štefan and I stood quietly, like men waiting for a bus, and watched her walk away.

When she had disappeared beyond the church, Štefan turned on me and closed the space between us, almost in anger.

"Now you say me what is wrong with Molly."

"Let's walk up there, my friend."

Molly

I daydreamed absurdities. My mind latched hold of nothing long enough for me to create sense from it. There were maybe 20 people in the chapel and I only knew four of them. Saša was not there. Saša was not anywhere. What she left behind was radically altered by fire and the residue put into an urn, the urn into a box and the box shipped to Vienna, then to Prague, then, I suppose, to an unknown village near the East German border. I tried to picture the house her ashes went to, and where they rested there, but all my images were formed by movies and none satisfied. The 20 of us, no, 21, because there was the woman playing an electric organ, were in the memorial chapel of some mortuary in San Diego that I couldn't find again at gunpoint. Tommy had his arm around my shoulders for a long time and it must have been uncomfortable for him. Laura sobbed in a soft, infectiously sad way. The mortuary's minister uttered the traditional homilies. Saša had other friends and I had never seen them before. Some of them did have sort of a gardener look. On a table sat a framed photograph of Saša amid bouquets of flowers; they were natural and appropriate and I thought they had come from gardens Saša tended. I wondered who took the picture. It was quite good, artistic, or did it seem so because it was black and white? Saša was sitting on a grassy slope with an endless forest of aspens in the background, her legs were bent and held with her arms, and she had been smiling with her lips closed. Maybe Laura took it; Laura arranged everything. An oval karabiner with a narrow band of black tape around the gate hung from one corner of the frame. When it was over we went out into a diffused but bright sun and like in a cartoon all put on sunglasses at nearly the same time.

I have remembered this throughout the years as vividly when it comes to mind as if it were the present moment, but it is not of course the only memory I have of Saša, just the most immediate.

This is what happened, as far as anyone knows.

Laura and Saša were in Tahquitz for the weekend. They had climbed two long routes the day before. That day they were on So's Your Mother, which is two full pitches with a 5.11 roof crux move on each pitch, but rated 5.10 overall. Laura said it was a normal and perfect Southern California day. Laura led the first and easier pitch, Saša the second. Laura said it was one of the hardest pitches she had ever led and she took a 15-foot fall halfway up and had to hang on the rope to rest before doing the roof crux. Saša cleaned the pitch without a problem and led the next one slowly, but also without problems. They saw a vulture's nest. So's Your Mother doesn't have a walk-off. It comes to an end at a wide belay ledge where there are three bolts and a chain for the rappel; it is impossible to continue free climbing from there; the route does continue, but as an aid route, A-3.

Laura rappelled to the mid-point anchor, clipped herself in, and waited for Saša, who came down in a minute. Laura asked Saša if she wanted to go next, but Saša told Laura to go first and she'd follow. "She blew me a kiss when I went over the bulge," Laura told us, weeping again.

Laura got off the rope when she reached the bottom and yelled up to tell Saša she could come down. Then Laura begin picking up their loose gear and packing it away. "I couldn't see her because of the overhanging bulge," Laura said.

Laura was not watching when Saša fell to earth. She only heard a cry and when she looked Saša was already crashing through a pine tree about twenty feet to the side of where Laura stood. A limb broke her back as well as her fall, so she did not bounce. Laura saw it.

She had not been on the rope. Her figure-eight was still attached to her harness, but she had not been on the rope. Laura remembered seeing Saša clip into a safety line while they re-rigged the rope for the next rappel, so she must have taken herself off the safety line before rigging the rope in the figure-eight. Laura said it was not a very wide ledge and it sloped downward and it was filthy with dirt, grass and pebbles.

Saša was semi-conscious. She would open and close her eyes and she looked, Laura said, surprised. They were afraid to move her, but it was obvious she was bleeding internally, as well as from the compound fracture just above the knee of her right leg. It had taken them forty-five minutes to hike up a scree-filled slope to reach the start of the climb. They could not imagine a way to get her down without killing her, and a helicopter couldn't get in to their location because of thick scrub brush and stunted trees.

By the time other climbers reached them, there was no point in going for help. Saša had died. She spoke once, but it was in Czech and Laura could not understand any of it. It took almost two hours to bring her body down on a rescue stretcher. Laura cried all the way.

I told Tom that I didn't think I ever wanted to climb again, and I went to bed as soon as we got home. I could hear him later in the closet hiding my climbing gear. He said that he was afraid I'd just give it all away and we'd have to replace it when, inevitably, I started climbing again.

Losing Saša made me absolutely terrified of losing Tom. He was right, I started climbing again, but three months passed before we went back to the rocks.

There was a short article in the mainstream San Diego press about Saša's accident, and a three-paragraph obituary edited down from the ten paragraphs I submitted. Saša's memorial appeared as I wrote it only in my paper, the *San Diego Reader*.

Freelance work I'd done for more than a year had turned into a real job, my first full-time, non-student job, with the *Reader*, an alternative newspaper that featured an in-depth, investigative feature story in each weekly issue, as well as reviews and art news. I did some features—bogus drugs being sold under U.S. labels in Tijuana pharmacies, the plight of an immigrant family living under a freeway overpass in El Cajon, the destruction of wilderness areas by the park service, and things like that— and after a few months, I got a column. It was called, *Beside the News*. There I often wrote about climbing and climbers.

Because now I wanted to write about Saša, I began reading about the history of Czechoslovakia, and particularly about the events of 1968.

On the last day of September, 1978, the day my article about Saša came out, Tom asked if I'd like to visit Czechoslovakia. He said he had a friend there, a climber he had met on Nanga Parbat. It would be my Christmas present. Anyway, I had fancied myself a writer until I tried to write about Saša, and found out that language is horribly limited; but this is the inadequate memorial printed in my column:

Beside the News . . .

By Molly Valen

Let's take a look at some of the important news events of the past month.

Of course the biggest story in San Diego, probably of the year, and one of the most dramatically tragic, is the collision of the PSA airliner with a private plane that killed 150 people, including casualties on the ground in the neighborhood where the flaming wreckage fell like deadly rain.

In Nicaragua, Somoza is struggling to put down a rebellion led by the leftist Sandinista group, and now there is speculation that Carter is urging Somoza to resign in hopes further bloodshed can be avoided.

A state of emergency was declared in Chile due to violence and labor agitation.

There were riots in Iran following the imposition of martial law, and on the 16th, some 25,000 people were killed in an earthquake there.

Mandatory busing of school children has begun in California.

Ali beat Spinks to win the Heavyweight Championship for an unprecedented third time.

Just today we learned of the tragic death of Pope John Paul I only one month after being elevated to the papacy.

Begin and Sadat came down from the mountain to announce they had reached an historic agreement at Camp David.

Over the Labor Day weekend, Alexandra Jandova was killed in a fall at Tahquitz, in Riverside County.

Who?

She was called Sasa by her friends and, besides my husband, she was my best friend.

Sasa was born in Prague, Czechoslovakia, on August 22, 1935, to Juraj and Alexandra Janda. Her mother had been a photographer's model and stage actress. Her father was a photographer and mountain climber. He was also a well-known Czech dissident.

Sasa was a beautiful young woman, much like her mother, but bright and inquisitive, like her father. She excelled in sports and science. After graduating with a diploma in chemistry from Charles University, she enrolled in medical school.

But three years into her medical studies, her father was arrested for the first time for his anti-communist writings. Sasa was not allowed to continue the final year and receive her medical diploma. She lost her job as a research assistant for a major Czechoslovak chemical factory and eventually found a job as a field worker on a potato farm.

Her father would be arrested and spend a total of thirty months in prison during the next ten years, from 1958 to 1968. Sasa picked potatoes, treated the farm animals when they were sick or injured, and perfected her climbing skills, which were prodigious.

Then in January, 1968, Alexander Dubcek was elected leader of the Communist Party in Czechoslovakia, defeating the hardliner Antonin Novotny, and Dubcek began a program of reform and liberalization—"socialism with a human face."

Juraj Janda was released from prison that spring, the "Prague Spring." Sasa and her father were able to climb together in the Tatra mountains after a separation of almost two years. Juraj took his last mountain pictures during that trip.

Winter came and went. Then spring. Sasa told me that there was hope and the real smell of political freedom mingling with the flowers of spring. Czechs and Slovaks were like teenagers, hugging each other in the squares, yelling happy greetings to each other, embracing like reunited lovers. It was a true picture of joy, she described.

On Sasa's 33rd birthday, August 22, 1968, Soviet tanks invaded Prague.

"We fought them," Sasa told me one day when we were sitting on top of a mountain in eastern San Diego County. "A few of us had guns, but we fought with sticks, with rocks, with our own bloody fists."

And they hoped for saviors from the west. They waited for the cavalry to ride over Charles Bridge with their sabers flashing in the late summer sun. All they had to do was hold out long enough for salvation and freedom to be returned.

Her cousin died in her arms as she tried vainly to stem the gushing blood from the bullet hole in his neck. His body lay in an alley covered with a blood-soaked Czechoslovak flag until a platoon of Soviet soldiers took the flag and dragged his body off to an armored car, followed by rocks and taunts from the Czech resistance. A Soviet soldier bloodied Sasa's jaw with the butt of his automatic rifle when she tried to pull him away from her cousin's body.

The U.S. cavalry, afraid of the nuclear-toting Indians, hid in their fort; the Czechs died; Dubcek and President Svoboda were escorted to the Soviet Union for a special history lesson.

Juraj Janda was killed by police thugs in the street only two blocks from his apartment. They took his tongue to insure the silence of the dead.

Pursued by the secret police, Sasa managed to make her way across Moravia and swim the turgid, fast-moving Danube to freedom in Austria. She arrived in America as a refugee in 1971, where I was lucky enough to find her and become her friend.

I met Sasa on a rock. She was the best female rock climber I have ever known. She was virtually fearless without being reckless. I thought I knew a lot about climbing until I met her.

But it is not the new skills as a climber for which I remember Sasa. It is for the gift of vision. From Sasa Jandova, I learned that the world extends beyond my backyard and that being human comes with a given set of responsibilities; you may reject these responsibilities, but you do it in shame.

I am ashamed of myself, and of us, those of us who have the indulgences of freedom as a gift which we did not earn and for which we have not yet given thanks. Not really.

We owe Sasa and her nation an apology. But she would only laugh if we tried to make it—tell us we were being silly. She had always believed it was her fault.

But if not us, who?

Tom took me to Czechoslovakia, as he promised, during the university's Christmas break, 1979. We flew Pan Am from Los Angeles to New York, then on to Vienna; the air tickets and new climbing equipment devastated our savings account, but Tom wanted me to meet the Slovak mountaineer who had been so important to him on Tom's first (and only) trip to the Himalayas. Now I know that he thought meeting and climbing with Štefan would revitalize my interest in mountaineering. I had another motive: I wanted to see where Saša had formed her life, the earth from which she sprang.

It was snowing slightly in Vienna and just starting to stick, but the ground was bare, like the trees and the gray sky, and everything looked cold and dead after the green and abundant life of Southern California. We rented a car at the Vienna airport, which is on the far eastern side of the city, and continued east through farm fields with patches of old snow in the furrows, past a family of deer standing in the stick trees, and the ruins of a castle on a hill above a small, modern hospital, just before we left Austria and the western world. After thirty minutes we reached the Czechoslovak border.

On the Austrian side there was a small kiosk with a candy cane-striped pole hanging across the two-lane road, and a short backup as the guard looked at passports. We were behind a bus belching horrible fumes; through the mud-splattered rear window, a man sat sideways watching us blatantly. There was a Škoda behind us, and a dirty white Mercedes behind it. After ten minutes, the bus took a separate lane and we inched forward behind a black car of a type I had never seen before.

"It's a Tatra," Tom said. "The favorite car of the Communist nomenclature."

"Is there really such a thing as a Communist nomenclature?" I asked with a smile. "Or did somebody make that up?"

"I don't know. I've never seen one. But if there is such a thing, it, or they, would have such a car."

We stopped laughing when we reached the customs official and tried to look serious. Tom held our passports through the partially opened window.

The officer didn't even take them—if we were crazy enough to want to go over there, he had no interest in stopping us. He just waved us through, and we got into a much longer, much slower line creeping toward the Iron Curtain; which actually was made of wire topped with coiled strands of razor concertina and woven with electrical lines. We could see the fence stretching in both directions until it disappeared in the frozen haze. On either side, the earth was a bulldozed gash a hundred yards wide. There were guard towers and young, heavily bundled soldiers with machine guns. Two guards, both smoking cigarettes, automatic weapons hanging from their shoulders, walked the fence with a German Shepherd straining against his leash.

Suddenly the black Tatra pulled out of line and sped forward, passing through the narrow gap between our line and cars going in the opposite direction.

"R-H-I-P," Tom said.

"What?"

"Rank Has Its Privileges. Well, shit."

"What's the matter?"

"There's only one lane open."

"Oh."

"That means we'll be stuck here for at least an hour."

"An hour? But back there he didn't even look inside our passports."

"We're not in the free world anymore, Toto."

"You make it sound so ominous. Too bad we aren't doing this late at night, in a fog, with searchlights washing across our faces, with cigarettes dangling from our lips, the microchip planted . . . where did we put that damn microchip anyway?"

"It's funny from this side of the fence, but from over there—" Tom nodded toward the country we were creeping toward at one car length every ten minutes. He just shook his head. I understood we were to stop joking now.

Going in the opposite direction, picking up speed, cars of types unknown to me, largely unrecognizable in the road grime and frost covering them, looked like an exodus of refugees. Most of the windows were fogged over, but sometimes you could see part of a face or a hand, heads in wool caps, earmuffs, head scarves. The cars were mostly full of people, families, sometimes just groups of men. Cigarette smoke streamed from slits in windows, like steam from a train engine. Sometimes a bus passed, its rumbling engine rocking our car, its exhaust choking us for a moment. There were massive trucks parked along the side of the road, so filthy with road grime that the signs on them were not legible, although on one we noticed Russian letters; their drivers stood in groups, smoking, slapping their arms, kicking their feet in the gravel, and passing around what was probably a bottle inside a paper sack. No one we saw seemed to have anything to do, anyplace to go.

We had a Milan Kundera novel and an Ivan Klíma novel in Tom's pack. We had exchanged their dust jackets with those from a pair of bodice-ripper romances. The books were gifts for the wife of Tom's climbing friend, Štefan Borák. Her name was Anna. Now I began worrying about the books being discovered. Would we be arrested? Deported? Imprisoned after a show trial? Of course it was silly; you had to be there.

It took more than half an hour before we reached the Czechoslovak border guards, and we had covered a distance across the no-man's-land between the two countries of maybe 500 yards. By then we could see the line of cars, buses and trucks waiting to leave Czechoslovakia stretching back toward the dim outlines of Bratislava, the end of it lost in the frozen mist. We were pulled to the side, into an empty parking stall just vacated by a Škoda, its back doors secured with wire, that had what seemed to be a refrigerator in a box tied to its top.

They made us get out of the car and go into a small building that looked like a cheap roadside café somewhere in Texas. When I looked over my shoulder, I saw two officers taking our packs and bags out of the trunk.

The customs office was smoky and smelled faintly of urine. There were a couple of round tables with bottles of something like ketchup on them, empty beer bottles and full ashtrays. In one corner a woman in a gray smock and scarf on her head stood behind a counter lined with bottles of clear liquors, small pieces of pottery painted blue and white, greasy boxes of sausages, and a rack holding key rings, car deodorizers shaped like breasts, and cigarette lighters.

I leaned close to Tom and whispered, "God, this is Saša's home."

"Not quite, she was Czech, but close enough."

Along the back wall, two open doors led obviously into the toilets, which at the time I badly needed. But the smell changed my mind. Between the two doors, a woman wearing an identical gray smock and scarf, sat on a wooden folding chair with a box containing a few coins and a roll of brown paper in her lap.

Two men dressed in quilted jackets and baggy denims like the truck drivers we had seen standing around outside were leaning against a counter along the wall, smoking and drinking beer. They stared at us openly, but without any recognizable feeling or opinion, other than maybe bored curiosity.

We were beckoned toward a uniformed officer seated behind a table that held a stamp pad, a fat notebook, a box of stamps, and a full ashtray. Tom said hello in Slovak, which he did not speak then as well as he does now. The officer asked for our papers, flipped through our passports to find the visas, then found the right stamp and plastered ink all over the visa page.

"Change money," he said, handing back our passports. He inclined his head toward the woman behind the souvenir counter, while scribbling a number on a small piece of paper. He handed the paper to Tom and we walked over to change dollars for Czechoslovak koruna at the ridiculous artificial rate of eight to one. (A few hundred yards away, in Austria, koruna sold at ninety koruna for one dollar, if you could find a place willing to trade for them. It was highly illegal to bring koruna into Czechoslovakia, or leave taking any with you.) Based on the number on the paper, we had to buy more than 300 dollars of the stuff.

When we got back outside, all our things were lying on a long table near the car. Both our suitcases were open, but the backpacks were closed.

When we approached, one of the officers asked Tom: "You have Bible, short-wave radio, magazine, tape recorder?"

"None of that," Tom answered.

"Change money?"

Tom held out a handful of paper notes and said, "Lots of it."

"You come here tourist or business?"

"Tourist."

The officer nodded and looked us over. He was sort of fat, or maybe broad is a better word. Bullish. He had no neck. His uniform shirt was unbuttoned at the top, his tie pulled down an inch. His shiny green uniform coat with a fur collar was open. He wore a big round cap with a small patent leather brim. A cigarette smoldered between his fingers. His younger and slimmer companion, whose uniform did not fit, was still picking somewhat daintily through my duffel bag.

"Go," he said, gesturing with his hand as if he were banishing us from the kingdom—go ye forth and sin no more.

Both officers abruptly walked to the next stall, leaving us to close our bags and re-pack the car.

When we drove up the ramp and back onto the road into Bratislava, I felt like a big gate had just closed solidly behind us. "What did you think of that?" Tom asked.

"Astonishing, but I have to pee in a really bad way."

"I'm looking for Štefan. He's supposed to be waiting at the first big intersection we come to. I think that's it ahead."

"How did he know when to come?" I asked.

"He knew what time our flight arrived. I suppose he just calculated how long it would take."

"You mean he might have waited along the side of the road for hours?"

"Probably."

The winter mist was heavy and we could only see about a mile ahead. To our right was a gray wall of high-rise buildings with no vegetation around them, like concrete spontaneously replicating itself. At the first road leading off that way, we saw an old primer gray Škoda parked on the road's shoulder. "That's Štefan," Tom said. There was a woman waiting with him.

I thought Štefan was attractive, nearly handsome. His eyes were compelling and pastoral at the same time, and he looked at me over Tom's shoulders while they hugged in greeting. In another man such a gaze would have been annoying, but from Štefan it was pleasantly unsettling. "You are Molly," he said, stepping around Tom and walking toward me. He reached out for my hand, then put it to his lips for a kiss. "Welcome my country. You see already most bad part. Now only see good."

"*Ďakujem*," I thanked him with one of the four or five Slovak words I knew at the time.

Suddenly he threw out his arms and pulled me into a tight hug. "Molly, Molly," he cried, "You have good Slovak."

"Oh no. Thank you, but I've been practicing for days."

"Tomaš," Štefan said, stepping back from me, but holding my shoulders and still looking into my eyes, "I have fall in love on this woman."

"*Je bláznivý muž.*" He is a crazy man, his wife said, and I saw her come around the car to join us.

Tom shook Anna's hand politely and I could tell that they did not know one another very well, not considering the depth of the friendship between Tom and her husband. I had not asked before, but assumed then that Anna did not climb, which turned out to be the case.

Anna Boráková was slightly taller than her husband, and the amount of gray in her hair made her seem much older. She wore a plain dress under a massive simulated fur coat, and black boots. She was a doctor and knew some medical English, could read it pretty well, but her conversational ability was only a little better than mine.

"Come, come," Štefan said suddenly, taking my arm and leading me back to the rental car. "We go now. You follow okay?" he asked Tom.

Tom was watching the police car that had slowed as it neared us.

"*Samozrejme*," Tom answered. It means, of course.

"Oh such memory," Štefan said. "But now we go."

We got into our cars and pulled out following the Škoda toward the city. Tom looked in the rearview mirror and told me that the police car had made a U-turn and was also following.

"This is really spooky," I said.

"Don't worry about it. Nothing ever comes of this stuff. They just do it because they can. It's a power thing."

The road was beginning to ice over and I thought Štefan was driving at a precarious speed. Just ahead, through the sleet, appeared a monstrously ugly bridge with a giant flying saucer perched atop a pair of thrusting pylons. It crossed the Danube. Already a car had slid sideways against the low bridge railing on the opposite side, but Štefan in his Škoda whizzed across like a speed skater, we following like a sled. I looked out and tried to see the Danube.

Štefan's apartment was in an old building above a clothing store near the city center. We parked next to him in a small lot behind a modern hotel.

"We must walk," Štefan told us, "but only short way."

I thought Štefan was going to try to carry everything at once. Before Tom or I could pick up any of our gear, Štefan had my backpack slung over one shoulder, and had lifted out both our large duffel bags. There was nothing left but Tom's backpack and my airplane carry-on.

"Come, come," Štefan insisted, and took off before Tom or I could take something from him.

Tom picked up his pack as Anna grabbed my carry-on. She smiled at me and would not argue.

Off we went along a pedestrian path connecting two busy streets, me feeling ridiculous following empty-handed the luggage bearers.

The sleet was changing to snow and I saw Saša everywhere.

Tom

Štefan turned and walked a few steps. He stopped in front of a tree, as if it had suddenly appeared there just to interfere with his life. He reached out one arm and put his hand against the trunk, leaning into it the way a drunk might lean against a wall to piss. He lowered his head, spoke softly only to himself for a long time.

We were in a park between two workers hotels. The hotels were both rectangular, four stories high, made of bolted-together concrete slabs sealed with graying black tar. The windows were surrounded by aqua green plastic frames. I could not stop myself from wondering why, in this gorgeous natural place, everything man-built had to be so cheap and so god-awful ugly?

In winter a cable ran between two large pulleys and children could hold the cable to be pulled back to the head of a small ski slope. During summer the cable was taken away, but a worn path in the grass marked its location. Now children played on the morning damp grass. Two grandmothers sat on a bench, their faces turned toward thin sunlight. In the chill of altitude many children wore jackets or light sweaters. Some children ran and some laughed and some only stood wistfully watching. Mothers mingled, talked, smoked, some bored. There were no men. A crude, smoke-belching lawn machine came up from a lower driveway at the back of the nearest hotel. The fog was nearly gone and the high mountain seemed to slide closer and closer by the minute. Bacon cooked nearby. There were white birds high, brown birds hopping on the ground. A ball rolled into a narrow creek and a boy cried out for it.

I took the few steps that separated us and put my hand on Štefan's shoulder. He turned his head to look at me; his face seemed besieged.

"I want you say me everything. Is hope?"

"There's always hope. Isn't that what they say?"

"Is not in your voice."

"This is one of those times choice is taken away from us. She is dying. I see life flying away from her every day. Every day she is worse. If the choice were there, I would die in place of her. You know that."

"Maybe another doctor . . . ?"

"I can't even count the doctors we've seen. Two of them were the best cancer doctors we could find in the United States."

"How much time?"

"I don't know. Not much. At first I could see her changing from month to month, then week to week. Now it's every day she's worse."

"I see these things in her, these changes and . . . problems. She . . . how you say it?" Štefan demonstrated with a lurching motion.

"Stumbles."

"And words she say in wrong way, with no sense."

I explained how the aphasia affected her, what I had been told was happening in her brain, about the headaches and now the blindness in her right eye. I told him that she would die either from uncontrolled swelling in her brain, or much quicker if the tumor ruptured or she had a major stroke.

"But she say to me she want to climb now."

"Yes, she wants it very much."

"How can it be possible?"

"I don't know, Štefan."

"What to do? I want say you how broken my heart is . . . "

Suddenly Štefan punched the tree hard and I had to grab his arm to stop him from doing it again. I told him to stop.

"I cannot say you what is here," Štefan pounded hard against his chest with his fist. "I have no English."

"I know what's there, my friend."

Like a dog throwing off water, Štefan shook himself. It surprised me, but it calmed him.

"Now? She is okay now?"

"I imagine she is asleep. The pain pills make her very sleepy."

Štefan grabbed my arm and said, "Come, we will drink now and . . . and I don't this word." Štefan hugged himself.

"Hug?"

He shook his head and hugged himself more tightly, almost passionately.

"Embrace?"

"Ah, maybe. Okay, yes. We must go embrace our sadness."

"Or drown it."

"Of course. Drown, like under the water. Yes, we go drown now."

We sat in a wooden booth near a window spotted with raindrops dried in dust. We sat across from one another, leaning forward on our elbows like men about to arm wrestle or exchange a deep confidence. An empty beer pitcher waited to be refilled; our fat half-liter mugs were still filled with amber beer. A bottle of Polish vodka sat to one side with our shot glasses turned upside down—we'd had more than enough vodka. There was bread debris, one lonely bit of sausage and a piece of hardening white cheese on a plate. The tin ashtray contained three extinguished Sparta cigarettes. The roadside bar was filled with men who had no jobs, along with workmen who had nothing to occupy them on their jobs. Two men wearing bus driver uniforms sat in the booth behind us drinking shots of brandy with their beers. There were no women. Smoke wandered the room pushed along by a fan in the kitchen doorway. There was no laughter and very little talking. The men had come to drink. A man at the bar had drunk enough and was now passed out at the bar with his head resting on folded arms.

Štefan and I had already been there for three hours, and long ago had found it too difficult to keep talking about Molly's condition; it was like continually stabbing oneself in the stomach. We just had to stop talking about it. It was rough when I said, "I don't know how to live without her, and I don't know if I'm capable of learning," and I thought Štefan would cry. I was surprised how strongly he felt this. But we had to change the subject.

From time to time men had stopped by our booth to say something to Štefan, but he usually sent them away with a gesture or a look. The bar man filled the pitcher whenever we emptied it. A large black-and-white television hanging from a platform near the ceiling at one end of the bar showed a German language variety program involving singers; it was the loudest noise in the room.

Štefan's conversation now made me feel conspiratorial, and I noticed that a man seated at one of the tables seemed only to be pretending to read the newspaper he held, and another man at the bar always turned his eyes away when I looked at him reflected in the mirror. I pointed these things out to Štefan, and in a lower voice he said, "We bring not permit things across border."

"You mean smuggling? Who?"

"We. Climbers."

"What sort of things?"

"Things we need here." He touched an index finger to his head. "Things to make Jakes and Husak spend too much time in toilet from worry. *Samizdat*. You know this word, yes?"

I nodded, also smiled at the image of the Czechoslovak president and Communist Party first secretary hunched over matching side-by-side toilets, straining to pass rabbit pellets from worrying about what people might be reading.

"Is not so funny," Štefan said. "Maybe for you is only some newspaper, book, some *noviny*. For us is normal. For us, desire for to have knowledge of truth is treason and crime against Party."

"That's not why I'm smiling. I was just picturing Husak and Jakes on the toilet."

"Ah, on toilet. I say in toilet. Maybe same."

We had a good laugh over that and Štefan reached over and slapped my shoulder. Then he gestured for the bartender to refill our pitcher. After the bartender left, I asked Štefan how they smuggled *samizdat* over the border.

"Rucksack," Štefan began, as he topped off our beer mugs and spent some time fishing out and lighting another Sparta. The smoke smelled of diesel. Then he leaned even closer to me across the table and whispered, "Most come from Polsko. *They* are not so worry from this." He pointed to his head again. "Climbers go from their side, Slovak climbers go from this side. At summit . . . " he brought his hands together and clasped his fingers to indicate the joining of these climbers at the top. "One climber of each country carry same kind rucksack. On way down, rucksack go on different back. Understand me?"

I nodded. "How long have you been doing this?"

"I?"

"You, anybody. How long has this been going on?"

"Long history have this. In war, before war. I go first time in 1968. Same year I quit Party."

"You were in the Communist Party?" I was surprised to hear this now, after knowing him so long and never suspecting it.

"Not for to advance for me, you know. I believe then. Is not to join for some job or some special treatments. I am Socialist then, believer.

Not after 1968. Friends die. Friends disappear. Friends go away. Friends go to prison. Understand me, what I say? In 1968, my brothers and sister immigrate to Canada. Only parents and me stay."

"Why didn't you all leave?"

"I am Slovak. I don't know how to be Canadian."

"I think there's more to it."

Štefan shrugged. "One day I come home and my father he not come from office. My mother make me look everywhere. I go to favorite pub. Go to clinic. Go to police. To Father's office at university. Colleagues there say only my father go for lunch and not return. My mother say me: Father find some new woman. She is crazy from this worry. We cannot sleep. In morning we have visitors from StB, you know, secret police. Now we know Father is arrest and there will have trial for him. Others, too, of course. Is time of purges. You know?"

Štefan poured another shot of vodka and offered one to me, which I refused, and then he filled our mugs again.

"Father is idealist. In war he is fighter for Slovak National Uprising against Fascists. He is teacher in Comenius University more than twenty years. But because he is Dubček supporter and have powerful position in university he must be for trial. My mother and I hear trial on radio and hear my father say what crimes against Communist people he has done. He say this confession in voice like man reading from telephone book only names.

"After trial they allow me to see him in prison. First time since day of arrest. Even after this time I see they have torture him. I see they have break his life.

"He stay in prison six years, four months, four days. In that time he is not allow to have paper for writing, or pen, or even book to read.

"One day they let him go from prison. Is no announcement. He only come home one day like from office. But of course he no more have some office to come home from. No more biology, only trees for counting. They give him job of counting trees in Malé Karpaty east from Bratislava. With Dubček."

"I'm sorry," I said. What else could I have said?

"After 1968 there is only two ways for living in my country—with anger or giving up."

"You stayed while your brothers and sister left. Why?"

"I am youngest of my brothers. Anyway, is duty for parents."

"Is that what they wanted you to do?"

Štefan shook his head. "They do not say. I know. Father try to send us all away from our country. But I believe one must stay.

"Tomaš, you must see I have no regret. I love my country."

"Is this the reason Edo and Pavol have been arrested? For smuggling?"

"Edo yes. Pavol I don't know. Pavol say many things, write things, sign his name to papers. But is hard for government to arrest one of only two Slovaks who stand on highest mountain in world."

"Here's a toast to you, and my hope that they don't also arrest the other one." I raised my beer mug to Štefan.

We were pretty drunk by then and decided not to get any drunker. When we got up to leave, I saw the man with the newspaper and the man watching us in the bar mirror get up and follow. I started to point this out to Štefan, but he indicated that he knew and made quite a show of us going our separate ways. I don't know where he went. I headed back to the chalet to see how Molly was feeling.

Molly

That first night I spent in Czechoslovakia has stayed fresh and real in my mind over many years, more so, I think, than any other place I've been. Tom's love for the place and its people was partly responsible I'm sure, and then there is the connection with Saša, but otherwise I am not able to explain this, because there are no rational reasons, no specific details or events to support the persistence and value of those memories to me.

At first I was dismayed: everything so bleak, so disheartening. New snow on the ragged cobblestones lay treacherously disguised over old ice; all of us sliding our feet along as if on cross-country skis. A narrow, faded red-and-cream-colored tram passed just before we reached the street, and we had to stand waiting for it to unload and reload its two cars before we could cross. It disgorged old women in long black skirts and black or gray sweaters and polyester overcoats and black felt boots that looked like the inner liners of plastic climbing boots, a few hard and scraggly-faced men in grimy workmen's clothes and probable secretaries in colorful cheap overcoats. Almost everyone carried some kind of plastic bag, and more than a quarter of them had one of those fat furry Russian hats on. I couldn't see very much of what was in the shop windows, which were all fogged over with ice crystals and streaked with condensation. Next to us was a bookstore and it felt strange to see a bookstore in which there was nothing I could read. Tom noticed a title in English and pointed it out to me: *Cuba's Miracle*. On the other side, a shop selling lace or folk clothing. Of course, all the signs were unreadable. People did not speak, nor did they look at one another. Only at us. Everyone gave us at least a glance. I realized it had to be our clothes. Tom and I looked like Christmas decorations; he in his red parka, me in a green one, and our multicolored ski caps, Gore-tex gloves, expensive hiking boots.

Then I realized what I was not seeing. It was only a week before Christmas, and there were very few decorative lights, no wreaths on the lampposts, almost no evidence of the season. Except the new white snow. It was a colorless world of gray, black and white. Some of this was due to the winter weather, the late-afternoon early dusk and the funeral pall of coal smoke laying like a shroud over the rooftops, but this was also the theme of the architecture, the odd, trembling machines and the clothing.

Tom and Štefan talked continually in a mix of Slovak and, mostly, English. Often they laughed, and I'm sure they simply forgot to include us. Anna and I stood next to one another, and when we happened to look at each other at the same time, we smiled politely. Once Anna shrugged, and I shrugged back. "Sorry I don't speak your language," I said. Anna looked at me expectantly, her eyes dark and deep and really very beautiful, then she said, "I try."

In the middle of a sentence, Štefan stopped and translated something for Anna. She answered, and Štefan turned to me and explained, "She is more sorry not speaking English. Is important language. She spend many years learn German and Russian."

"I would think German would be more valuable where you live," I said.

The tram pulled away and we crossed the street with our packs and bags like camp-bound trekkers, with me the pampered client.

Štefan led us into a narrow, deeply shadowed passageway next to a large clothing store. At the back was a door and a large trash Dumpster. There was a horrible odor of urine and I think that's why Štefan hurried with the lock. There were twelve buttons with small white name tags beside each one; number ten had *Borák* typed on it. Štefan unlocked the door and held it back for us, and we entered a bare, industrial gray and military khaki two-tone foyer. Štefan, still carrying the two duffel bags and my backpack, hurried by us to pull open the door to a minuscule elevator. There wasn't room for more than three people, and certainly not with any baggage. It had gray Formica walls and floor. A long crack ran from top to bottom on one side wall. There was a little graffiti, including *fuck you* in English.

Štefan explained that he would ride up with Tom and me, while Anna stayed with the bags until he returned for them. Tom argued uselessly for a moment.

In the elevator we were all touching. Štefan was polite and stared at the tiny door. Sandwiched between these two men, I embarrassed myself with an erotic thought.

Tom had been to Bratislava once before, two years before we met, and he had stayed at the hotel near where we parked. From the States we made reservations at the same hotel for this trip, but Štefan canceled them. He was not going to allow us to stay anywhere but with his family. Tom told me that it was a matter of both hospitality and pride.

There were a pair of large locks on the door. I had thought the Communists didn't allow crime. Štefan unlocked each of them hurriedly, then pushed the door open and led us inside through a small hallway. We hung our coats and took off our boots while Štefan went back to get Anna and the rest of our bags.

"I wish I could have slept more on the plane," I told Tom.

"I'm sure they won't mind if you take a nap."

"But I don't want to miss anything."

Štefan returned with Anna and our bags. Anna pulled off her boots, hung her coat, then disappeared.

"Please," Štefan gestured for us to follow him, and we padded in our socks behind him through the apartment, passing the open door to a small kitchen where I saw Anna loading a serving tray with cookies and small cakes. Behind her, a door with a glass panel looked out over exhaust vents and coal chimneys atop two- or three-hundred-year-old slate roof tops.

Štefan showed us through a dining area, which was actually an open space in the center of the apartment, where to find the bathroom, the toilet (in a separate room), and then we looked into a small bedroom with bunk beds, a larger bedroom with a double bed, and went into the living room, where double glass doors opened onto a narrow balcony that overlooked the street five stories below. In one corner, atop a bureau, sat a small Christmas tree strung with small blinking lights, a half-dozen small, plainly wrapped packages beneath it.

The apartment was filled with a mountaineer's expedition memorabilia: a Kurdish sword, an Afghan woven mat, a Chinese opium pipe, a squat, barrel-shaped storage container with the words—1975 CZECHO-SLOVAK NANGA PARBAT EXPEDITION—written on a banner round it. Framed behind glass the small blue Slovak Climbers Club flag that had been to Everest hung on a wall. Everywhere there were photographs of rugged mountains and equally rugged mountain climbers, base camps and expedition convoys, and in frames on the bookcase pictures of people who I learned were family members. In an open cupboard that covered one side of the wall in the hallway we saw hanging an extreme cold weather suit, ropes, crampons, boots, skis and ski poles, helmets, lamps, tents, a red-and-green expedition pack, a small rucksack, rolled topo maps, a canvas bag filled with karabiners—all the accouterment of the climber's world.

There were many books, including sets of medical texts in German and English, as well as Czech and Slovak, a small Tesla color television set, a Fifties-style box radio and a record player. Behind the couch, which was covered with a blanket-like brown material, there was an enormous blow-up of a black-and-white photograph of Everest mounted on a board. I walked to the photograph and put the tip of my index finger against the peak.

"You have stood right here," I said.

Štefan shrugged in a charming, shy manner. Then, before I could pull my finger away, he took my hand in his, moved my finger down an inch along the ridge line to the right, stopped and said, "I lose my best friend here."

I did not want Štefan to let go of my hand, but he did, and immediately I turned toward Tom and mouthed the words, *I love you*. He raised his eyebrows, the way he does when he doesn't understand something I've done, then took the hand that Štefan had just let go of, and we followed Štefan's orders to sit and rest. Anna came in carrying a tray filled with cookies, thickly frosted cakes, breadsticks, pieces of white cheese, some thick grayish slabs of a mysterious translucent substance that smelled quite like bacon (which turned out to be smoked bacon fat), pearl onions, a tub of horseradish sauce, dark bread and butter. Štefan produced a bottle of borovička, and white wine in a corked bottle without a label. Later I would find out that Štefan had a small vineyard in the hills outside Bratislava, and the wine was his.

He poured an inch of borovička (a juniper brandy that smells like gin) into tiny crystal glasses for each of us.

"Health," Štefan toasted.

"*Na zdravie*," Tom said in Slovak.

I watched as Anna, Štefan and Tom knocked back the drink in one swallow, and did the same. They laughed when I nearly coughed it up. Anna patted my back, laughing. I liked her and wished we could have long, long talks together.

Štefan filled larger Bohemian crystal glasses with wine. Anna handed plates to us and ordered us to eat. Both of us were hungry, we hadn't eaten in six or seven hours, and we filled our plates.

Then I found out we were eating, basically, raw bacon fat.

That small meal was the precursor to an evening out with some of Štefan's friends at a massive beer hall called Stará Sladovča, the Old Malt House, which Štefan thought might be the largest beer hall in the world. I could see no reason to disagree. It was four stories high and covered half the block.

Štefan, whom everyone in the beer hall seemed to know, gave dozens of hearty greetings, then commandeered a long table and over the course of an hour or so, some twenty people gathered; we plowed head-first into the smoke, music, beer and wine of a long winter's night, conversing in a mix of four languages—principally English, then Slovak, Czech and German. At the faraway end of our floor, an oom-pah brass band played a kind of Christmas folk music. Pitchers of frothy, amber beer made a tubular glass wall the length of the table; smoke rose from ashtrays like steam from city sewers; laughter roamed the room like a jolly host.

I could only manage the names of the people nearest me, with whom I talked most of the time, including Štefan, who sat at my side. Tom was across the table, smilingly sandwiched between a woman with large breasts (whom Štefan described as having a "grand balcony") whose body reminded me of Saša's, and one of the most beautiful women I've ever seen, a member of Czechoslovakia's Olympic volleyball team—in Paris she would have been contracted to *Vogue*, I'm sure.

There were well more than twice the number of men as women, so lavish attention was paid to the few of us. The men around me were climbers, all members of the Czechoslovak Climbers Club, although not all the people in our large group were climbers. The woman with the grand balcony, who in the thickly overheated room had stripped

off her coat to reveal a black-sequined sleeveless T-shirt, was introduced as a musician, but I've forgotten the instrument, something
classical, I'm sure. The volleyball player, Tom told me later, was not a
climber, and I got the impression that it was an important distinction
for him. She had once been married to a climber, he told me later, one
who died in the Atlas Mountains.

One man told me he was an English teacher, but he spoke very
nearly the worst English of any of the ones attempting it. He asked
me what I thought of the Czechoslovak government and I told him
that we get the government we allow. He took this as some sort of
somber truth and spread my little axiom around the table. All the men
flirted with me, but he was the most flagrant. Of course, all the climbers, except Štefan, had other work. There were teachers, coaches, an
engineer, a translator of Russian scientific documents, a doctor. I don't
remember all of them. Some of us were only smiles and polite nods to
one another during lulls in other conversations. I wanted to know everything about everyone.

Štefan orchestrated. He had that year just been elected president
of the Czechoslovak Climbers Club, and I could see why. He made
sure that no glass remained empty, that no one missed the punch line
of a story, and that each one had a story to tell. When necessary, he
translated into English, although two of the women there spoke English much better than Štefan.

Štefan did not last very long as club president. He was not a member of the Party, and although he had been voted into the position by
the climber members, the government, who funded all the sports
clubs, appointed a new president and made Štefan the vice-president.
But this happened after we were back in the States.

Some people danced. There were maybe three hundred people
on our floor, the second, and all of them were quite certainly drunk.
As were we.

There was no sense of time passing, and I was surprised when I
saw that our pitchers had not been refilled with beer, and that three

waiters hovered near us with cleaning towels dangling from their hands. I looked around to see that more than half the floor had emptied, and the band had cleared away from the stage. When I looked at my wrist-watch, it was only five minutes after ten o'clock.

"Is not weekend," Štefan explained when he saw me glance at my watch. "Nights of week bars must to close now, this time, because of morning workers. Because early hours for workers."

There was a rush for the toilets, which were in the process of being locked as we started out. By the time we got there, the women's toilet was locked. The woman with the grand balcony, whose name I later found out sounded something like Galena, in a huff marched us into the men's toilet. Tom was pissing when Galena led us in and she said to him, "You alone?" Tom, befuddled to find four women standing behind him—I was laughing like crazy by then—looked around in a serious way and said he supposed he was, or had been. "Good," Galena said. She headed into one of the open stalls and lifted her skirt. Tom, surprisingly quite the gentleman, zipped up and left us alone. Galena told me while we were peeing that I had a handsome husband. I was drunk and said, "You have a magnificent chest." She laughed like an explosion, then thanked me politely. She asked if we would come to dinner at her flat in a suburb across the Danube and meet her husband. I would like to have gone to her apartment and gotten to know her better, but we never saw her again. Like the others, her accented English reminded me of Saša. While we were peeing, a cleaning woman equipped with pail and mop found us there and a hilarious and heated exchange took place in Slovak. The cleaning woman tried to lock the door while we were in the toilet, but Galena snatched the keys from her and threw them some distance across the floor. Properly relieved, we four adventurous women went out to join our companions.

Many farewells were said in the main lobby and our group shrank every few minutes by twos, threes, or fours. The rest of us—Tom and I, who spoke to one another for the first time in nearly three hours without shouting, Štefan and Anna, a very handsome young climber named Pavol who had also stood on Everest's summit, his wife Línda, two other climbers named Medved and Peter—maneuvered ourselves out to Cintorínska Street like bumper cars at a carnival, careening off each other, then trying to hug each other in ever-expanding groups, laughing in the silliest ways. The street was virtually empty. A solitary drunk pissed against the cemetery wall. I watched him turn, stick his penis back into his pants, zip up, then without ever noticing us, bounce off the frosted stones and turn the corner. A police car seemed to suddenly appear in front of us, but I realized it had all the time been parked a dozen yards down the street. There were no markings on the car, but I could see the two men inside had on uniforms. The Slovaks in our group became quite nervous. The tone of the whispers changed, and even in Slovak I could tell that what they were saying was sarcastic and bitter. Good-byes were said, but in whispered voices. The police sat in their patently ugly little car and watched until our group split up and went in three directions. Tom and I, Štefan and Anna made our way along the wall of the dark cemetery to the street where they lived. It was bitterly cold and after the hot, smoky beer hall, I began to shiver. Tom put his arm around me and pulled me into his side. Ahead of us a couple of steps, Štefan took Anna's hand and they talked quietly in Slovak.

At the Borák flat there was an extended argument about the sleeping arrangements. Štefan and Anna had given us their bed, and they were going to sleep in the bunk beds in what had been the room of their two daughters before each left to be married.

We ended up in their bed, snuggled in each other's arms beneath a thick down comforter.

"I have never felt so welcome anywhere, by any people, in my life," I said to Tom.

"Told you," he answered.

We made love as quietly as possible, because we could easily hear through the walls. We were trying to get pregnant then and I found Czechoslovakia to be an aphrodisiac. I wanted to make love three times a day! My period was already a couple of days late and Tom and I were offering secret wishes with every toast we made.

We held each other afterwards and I whispered to Tom, "Wouldn't it be great if we conceived here in Czechoslovakia? If we had a girl . . ."

"We would name her Saša," he finished my sentence.

I don't know how Štefan avoided a hangover because Tom and I sure had a pair of great ones. At breakfast he was full of energy, making plans, running to the market down the street for more coffee and something resembling muesli for me. I thought of going back to bed, but there was such excitement in the apartment that I was afraid I'd miss something. Although our stomachs were hardly up to it, we attacked breakfast. It was astonishing, both in amount and quality. After Štefan had gone to the market for cereal, I felt obliged to eat it; but that didn't stop me from eating a potato pancake filled with jam, fresh tomato slices with melted cheese on top, and a couple of pickles. When I reached for the second pickle, Tom gave me a curious glance. I shrugged and smiled and said, "Who knows?" Was it too soon for food cravings? Desperate hopes.

Anna let me help her clean up the debris. She turned the radio on, I think so we wouldn't feel obliged to try making conversation, and I was surprised to hear old American rock and roll. We nodded and used sign language, and through point-and-mimic I learned some new Slovak words. She practiced her limited English with me. Tom and Štefan sat in the living room with coffee; I couldn't hear them except for occasional laughter. Finally Anna got tired of me messing up her kitchen system and shooed me out.

I sat on a stool across the coffee table from Tom and Štefan, who were on the sofa.

"We're going out to Štefan's vineyard in a little while," Tom said. "There's a small chalet there that Štefan built himself."

"Sounds great. Is it big?"

Štefan laughed heartily. "About so," he said, holding his hands about three feet apart. "Not big, but big enough for one man."

"I like the wine we had with dinner last night."

Štefan nodded his modest appreciation.

I turned to Tom and said, "Did you ask about going to Prague?"

"Not yet." He told Štefan that we would like to go to Prague and see Bohemia before we went back to the States. Štefan nodded, put his hand up to stroke his beard.

"It's a favor for me," I explained.

"Then it is done," Štefan said expansively.

I smiled and said thank you, adding that, "My best friend was Slovak. She immigrated from Prague in 1968 . . ."

Štefan nodded with a serious expression.

"I guess many people did. But she was born in a small village somewhere west of Prague. I don't suppose there's much chance of finding that, but I would at least like to see the countryside around where she lived."

"Your friend is Czech if born nearby Prague. Is not same like Slovak."

"I'm sorry. I forgot."

"Oh no, do not be sorry. Only to explain this difference. For some is important. For some not. Go to Prague is easy. Only say when. But there are many villages near Prague. You have maybe name from this village?"

"No. I'm afraid not. I have her name and she wasn't married, so I think it would be the same as her family name. Saša, or Alexandra, Jandová."

"Say again, please."

"Maybe I'm not pronouncing it right? Alexandra Jandová. Is it a hard 'J' or like in Spanish, *ja*? Saša pronounced it with the *ja* sound . . ."

"No, no," Štefan waved his hand back and forth to stop me. "Saša Jandová? She is close my age, or a few years older?"

"Jesus, Štefan! Did you know Saša? That's unbelievable! Yes, Saša would have been around your age." I looked at Tom incredulously and he shook his head in amazement.

"Her father was climber Juraj Janda?"

"Yes, yes. Of course, he was a famous climber here. This is just too amazing!"

"But please, wait. I no understand. Maybe is my bad English. You use past verb, is true?"

I finally figured out what was causing the dismayed look on Štefan's face, the tremor now in his voice. He must have known Saša or her father—of course, it is a small country with an even smaller population of climbers, and Štefan is the leader of the climbers club—and Štefan did not know Saša was dead.

"Štefan, you knew Saša?"

"Yes. Something happen to her?"

"I'm very sorry. Saša was killed in a climbing accident about a year ago, in August."

Štefan sat on the edge of the couch with his arms resting on his knees. He lowered his head for only a moment then looked up at me again. "Please you can tell me what happen," he said quietly but urgently. It was still not easy—it would never be—to talk about Saša's death. I glanced at Tom and he took over for me. I got up and walked to the kitchen so I wouldn't cry in front of Štefan. Instead, I cried in front of Anna and she held me politely.

It changed everything, this news about Saša. Štefan and Anna had a long discussion in Slovak, phone calls were made, Štefan apologized and went to his office, and finally, Tom and I went out and walked around the old town of Bratislava, which was stark and cold in the new snow.

Later that afternoon, Štefan told us that Saša's mother was very ill and in a Prague hospital, and she could not have visitors. She did not know Saša was dead; no news had come to her. No one had known. I asked Štefan if he knew what had become of the urn with Saša's remains. He said that it had never passed through customs and now it was lost. "Friends try to find some informations," he added.

"Do you want to cancel the Tatra climb?" Tom asked me.

"No," I answered, maybe too sharply. "I want to climb." I did not say that I wanted to climb because Saša would have been deeply offended had I not.

Now every time I looked at Štefan, I saw a man who had known Saša, and that made him seem closer to me than I could have imagined anyone I had just met being.

I suppose it may also have been then when I began falling in love with him.

Tom

It was difficult to wake Molly. For those few moments I was terrified. I could see that she was breathing, but I thought she was in a coma. It took more than a minute of trying to rouse her before her eyes opened and she tried to sit up. When I asked if she were all right, she seemed not to understand the question. Something had happened while she slept, maybe a stroke. I brought her a glass of water, then sat next to her on the bed and stroked her hair. Physically she seemed the same as that morning, but mentally she seemed very drunk. She swallowed a bit of the water and then suddenly lurched toward the toilet to throw up. I wanted to call a doctor, but for what?

Ten or fifteen minutes later she become more coherent. We sat on the sofa in front of the French doors where we could look out over the balcony into the thick grove of evergreen trees beyond. We held hands. The first words she spoke to me since waking were:

"What did you and Štefan talk about?"

"I told him about the cancer."

"I really wish you hadn't."

"Molly, he was tormenting himself with unanswered questions about the changes he could see in you. Don't you think it was fair to tell him?"

"Now he will start treating me differently. I can't stand that."

"Štefan will treat you the only way he knows how, the way he always has."

Molly looked at me for a moment and seemed about to say something, but she paused, looked outside again, then said, "It's okay he knows."

"Štefan told me an interesting story today." I related to Molly what Štefan had told me about his family, his Communist past, but mostly about how the climbers were involved in smuggling *samizdat* and forbidden materials over the mountains along the border with Poland. I told her who had been arrested and who was missing. At this point she put her hand on my shoulder and interrupted.

"Tommy, I want to go."

"Go where?"

"With Štefan when he . . ."

I could see she had forgotten already either the word or what they were doing. "They meet on the summit of Vysoká," I said. "It is a very demanding route, Molly. Okay, even easy for you . . . before."

"Will not be babied!" She screamed into my face.

I got up and walked onto the balcony. The smell of pine was thick. I could see mountain peaks above the trees. At some point Molly joined me, stood next to me with her hands on the railing.

"Some days are really not bad, Tommy. I could probably do it."

I turned and put my arm around her shoulder. "Some days you can't get out of bed."

"That's only because of the headaches. I can take something stronger."

"But then you'll just be more sleepy."

"Please let's don't argue about it."

"I don't want to argue, Molly."

"Then let's do it. Let's go with him."

"Look, in the first place, I don't even know when or if he will go again. He is being watched all the time. It's pretty obvious. In the second place, my darling, what they're doing is considered treason in this country. Not only might they go to prison, they could be executed! What do you think they would do with us, Americans caught smuggling political materials over the border into a Communist country?"

"I want to do it."

I started to simply say that even if we were going to do something so stupid, hadn't she considered what a handicap she would be? But telling Molly she can't do something is the best way to insure that she will.

"Why?"

"Because I've never done anything meaningful or important."

"Oh, come on."

"It's true."

"Just because you aren't a political person doesn't mean that what you do isn't meaningful or important. What about the impact some of your writing has?"

"Writing, not doing. I want to do one important thing."

"Your life is filled with important things. I know. I've shared a lot of it."

"I want to do one important thing."

"Molly, please be reasonable and listen to what I'm saying."

"I want to do one important thing."

I could see that now it was taking concentration and a strong physical effort for Molly to stand and speak. There was sweating on her forehead and along her upper lip. Her eyes were glazed, staring into the trees. Then I saw that she had started to cry.

I could only put my arms around her, but she only barely accepted the comfort. I wanted desperately for Molly to have everything she wanted, to fulfill every wish she expressed. I don't know where this sudden desire to become a smuggler came from, or even if she understood what was involved. She certainly had not recognized her own limitations now as a climber. I knew it would be impossible for her to climb Vysoká. Impossible. In fact, I now doubted her ability to walk up a hill.

Tears streamed down her face but she made no sound. Her hands gripped the balcony railing as if she were on a tossing ship.

"I'll go talk with Štefan about it," I said.

Molly nodded and kept staring into the pine forest.

I found Štefan in the Hotel Uran's coffee shop. When I left, Molly was asleep on the sofa, curled up into a tight ball. I told Štefan what Molly wanted to do. Štefan said he would try to take her, or at least let her think she was going, but that now, the way everyone was being watched, there were no such climbs. I told Štefan that Molly couldn't climb anything anyway, but he waved me off and said we would find a way to carry her if necessary. "But we cannot go now," he added.

"What happened? Something else happened?"

"Everyone is arrest. Edo, Pavol, Andreka, Milan, Eva, Miro . . . all but me, and maybe soon also me."

"I can't believe this, Štefan. This is crazy!"

"This is my country. Here it is normal life. Know you are lucky you don't understand and think is crazy."

"I can't believe they would arrest you . . . Pavol." I began looking around, expecting to see some sort of Communist Gestapo charging us.

"Is better you not look for them," Štefan said.

"I suppose not."

"There are three, at least. Two by the door over there and another is the girl who bring your coffee."

"Christ."

"I think now I have put you and Molly into this trouble. We are together so many times, you have visited me many times in past."

"Don't worry about us."

"I do."

"What are they being charged with? Edo and the others."

"Not charged. Only arrest. Only taken to police for asking some small questions. Sometimes it can take many years to ask small questions."

"I feel like I've stumbled into a cliché."

"Cliché? What cliché? This is not cliché, my old friend. This is real life."

"Yes, I know. I'm sorry."

The fake waitress, who was unusually pretty and young, brought the ham and cheese toast we'd ordered and I paid. Štefan lit a cigarette and I watched how his eyes scanned the room behind the exhaled smoke. When the waitress left, I said in a low voice, "This is only about the special climbing trips?"

Štefan shrugged. "Can be about something, about nothing, about who knows? I think they are special crazy now because of Gorbachev reforms and those eastern part Germans running across on country on way to Hungary, where they can escape to West. Hungarians cut their wall to Austria. One cut and now the whole wall start to crumble like one old dry cake. Husak and his friends are special busy now try to hold together all falling pieces. They are afraid. Like animal. It is most dangerous time."

"What can I do?'

"Take Molly and go back to normal world."

"That is the one thing I can't do. Even if I wanted to, and I don't, this is where Molly wants to be and she won't leave. We won't leave."

Štefan put his hand over mine on the table; I wondered what the spies thought of that. He said, "Molly is most important from this other business. Molly first. We worry about other business later."

I didn't know what he meant.

"If is important for Molly have this feeling in her soul, then we must give to her this feeling."

"Yes, I agree. But it's impossible, Štefan. She can't climb. Even if she could, with everyone already taken in by the police, and who knows when they will take you . . ."

"I get Juraj and Malý Tomaš to go with us. They are not part of this group. There is easy trail to summit Východná Vysoká. It is only walking. Sometimes steep, but we can carry her. We three go on trail, Juraj and Malý Tomaš go up other side on technical route and we meet at summit for changing rucksacks."

"Molly knows Juraj. She will recognize them and know they aren't Poles."

"Ah. Okay. I can get other climbers."

"If this is at all possible, Štefan, I would give anything . . ."

"We will do it."

"Východná Vysoká is not close to the Polish border."

"Molly do not know this."

"God, I hope this can work!"

"We make it work, my friend."

"Thank you, Štefan."

He shrugged. "Is for Molly."

"Let's go back to the *chata* and tell Molly together."

Two men followed us obviously when we left the hotel.

I opened the door and called Molly's name in an excited voice, but there was no answer. She wasn't on the sofa where I'd left her sleeping. I went to the bathroom and Štefan walked to the balcony.

I found Molly on the bathroom floor, in a fetal curl wedged between the toilet and tub. I cried out for Štefan and we got her up and out to the sitting room. She was drooling down her chin and her pupils were pinpoints. I thought she was dead. I suppose I must have been hysterical at this point. Štefan said she was breathing and he helped me get her onto the sofa. He said he would get a doctor.

That's where we still were when Štefan returned with the doctor. I had Molly in my arms and I was sobbing.

Molly

We drove from Bratislava to the Tatra Mountains, 350 kilometers away, in our rental car because it had front wheel drive for the snow and it would hold all our gear. Anna could not go, so it was just the three of us. It was two days after Christmas, 1979.

The plan was to traverse the length of the main High Tatra range (Vysoké Tatry), more or less from east to west, following the highest ridge line (Štefan called it "the comb"), crossing the summits of most of the major peaks. It had never been done before in winter—not that particular high line. Tom and Štefan cooked up this idea a few years earlier while anchored to base camp during a blizzard in the Karakorum of Pakistan, waiting for the weather to clear on Nanga Parbat's Diamir face.

Actually, Tom, who likes to be precise, would immediately correct me. Nanga Parbat, ninth highest mountain in the world—8,125 meters, is in northern Pakistan, near the central Karakorum range, but it is actually part of the Himalayas, marking the far western end. Nanga

Parbat means naked mountain. Before it was climbed by a German expedition in 1953, thirty-two mountaineers died trying. Thanks to Štefan, the man who would become my husband made it to the summit of the highest mountain he had ever attempted without adding to the continually increasing number of deaths.

There are hiking paths and climbing routes all through the Tatras. What made this scheme different was to follow the highest ridge, the very spine of the mountain range, in one go, carrying everything we would need and not coming down until we had done the deed. We would start from near the village of Lomnica and traverse the highest ridge line to the summit of Kriváň at the western end. Our first peak would be Svišt'ovka.

The snow was very deep. On the ski slopes there was a 15-foot base. There had been a continual cycle of freezing and thawing throughout November and December, so there was a significant avalanche danger. One of the principal ski areas was closed because of this. A lot of people thought we were crazy to be doing this in January. But isn't that precisely the point of any adventure?

We started out at dawn on the last day of 1979, on the trail from the village to Svišt'ovka peak. We planned to celebrate the new year's arrival camped on the ridge between Svišt'ovska and Kežmarský.

We had to post-hole through the valley. First Štefan led, or is plowed a better word?, and Tom and I slogged through the holes he left behind. We rotated our positions every half hour. It was a drudge. Uphill, uphill, uphill. We were carrying heavy packs; mine weighed 40 pounds. We had two 8mm ropes and a 10½mm rope, plus an assortment of artificial protection.

It was only an uphill walk for the first few hours, with switchbacks and long slope traverses. We added an hour going around a windblown wall of tottering snow that didn't look any too stable. From the summit we could look back toward Brnčalová chalet, at the large, featureless, snow- and ice-covered Zelená Lake. I thought the smoke rising from Brnčalová's chimney looked too inviting.

"We go now," Štefan announced.

We began heel-kicking our way down a steep slope toward the rising ridge line that would lead us to Kežmarský. At one point the slope became more gradual and we could safely glissade, which would let us cover an enormous distance in a couple of minutes. We sat down in the snow, lifted our cramponed boots to keep them from digging in and flipping us over, and using the ice axe as brake and rudder, we slid screaming down the hill on our Gore-tex-clad butts; doing in three or four minutes what would have taken half an hour of heel-stepping.

The days are short at that latitude in January. That was one of the central problems of the timing of our traverse: less than eight hours of useful daylight. We ended up erecting the tent by the darting yellow glow of our headlamps.

I don't know how Štefan and my Tomaš felt—I had taken to calling Tom "Tomaš," as Štefan did—but I was exhausted. And now cold. Štefan melted snow over the stove for soup, and I put my feet in the general direction of the minuscule blue flame.

"That's the hardest work I've ever done," I said.

Štefan and Tom looked at each other for a second, then burst out laughing.

"Okay, it's no goddamn Nanga Parbat." I couldn't keep from smiling.

Tom reached over and rubbed my thighs. The pressure of his fingers, even through the layers, hurt in the most wonderful way. It made me want to make love. Not a good idea, under the circumstances, but I let myself enjoy a few seconds of fantasy about sex with Tommy in the sleeping bag, knowing Štefan was nearby. I embarrass myself sometimes.

The wind came up and the side of our tent snapped back and forth in that obnoxious, sleep-depriving way they do. We ate soup, bread and sausages. Štefan pulled a bottle of wine from his sack and we couldn't believe he had packed it. On the other hand, it would have been strange had he not. If Štefan had not been a mountaineer, he would have been a vintner.

But the wine made me have to pee. The boys just stepped outside and quickly did their business. But I had to go through all these clothing contortions and stick my butt out in the snow. Toiletry chores are abysmal while mountain climbing, and I found myself wishing nature had given us a way to cork everything up for a little while.

We squeezed into our bags early. I was in the middle—democratic geometry. Tom read by the light of his headlamp for a little while. In the shadows I could see Štefan lying on his back, his hands laced behind his neck, staring up at the top of the tent. He seemed completely at home with himself. Content. I admired his sense of personal peace, which was particularly evident in the mountains. I said good night to them and turned on my side, facing Tom. Eventually the light in my eyes made me turn the other way. Štefan smelled like those old Sparta cigarettes he indulged in now and then. I wondered how he could smoke at all and still be able to climb the way he did. He had enormous stamina. I supposed it was some genetic gift.

I awoke some time later; I don't have any idea what time it might have been. There was a hand on my breast, cupping it through the silk undershirt I wore, just holding it without moving. It took me a few seconds to figure out whose hand it was: Tom's. He was asleep. He often did that in his sleep.

Štefan's back was to me and he snored lightly. It wasn't snoring as much as ragged breathing. The chest cold he had been fighting all day was now clearly worse. He had pulled a ski cap over his head, and his long hair exploded from below it.

I moved Tom's hand without waking him, then extricated myself from the bag to go out and pee. That required pulling on my sweater and parka, wind pants, two pairs of socks, my boots, cap and gloves.

No wonder it was so cold. There wasn't a cloud in the sky. A crescent moon had risen from the southeast and was now overhead; there was a dim ring around the moon. I could see the Milky Way. We were surrounded by peaks larger than the slope where we camped, so it was like being in a bowl. There were no signs of life. I squatted not far from our little dome tent and looked at it; like some outpost of human life adrift in a white, empty universe, or a red-and-gold life raft on a white sea.

Štefan coughed. It startled me like a pistol shot.

Maybe I was a little frightened by all that darkness, the ragged peaks surrounded our small tent, enclosing it like a spectral barrier. For a moment I had to fight against an urge to pack up and hike down to the wide open valley, with its villages, cars, lights and sounds. I had learned first to like my rocks dry and warm.

Štefan coughed again. It did not sound like a cigarette hack. He sounded congested. It sounded, I feared, bronchial.

In the tent's vestibule, I quietly undressed down to silk underwear and wool socks, leaving on my ski cap, then crawled as quietly as I could into the tent. The zipper on my sleeping bag sounded like cloth ripping when I pulled it. Tom stirred, turned over, but never woke up. Štefan's back was to me and I don't know if he was asleep. I listened to him breathing.

It felt like I had only been asleep a few minutes when I was awakened by Štefan unzipping his bag and crawling out to the vestibule. Tom sat up, unzipped his bag, stretched, kissed my forehead just below the ski cap, and began fishing around in his pack. We heard Štefan go outside. It was still quite dark, but when I found my watch and shined my headlamp on it, I saw that it was a little after six.

"Did you hear him coughing last night?" I whispered to Tom.

"Uh-huh. Sounds like he's getting a bitching cold."

Tom came up from the bag with some granola bars and offered one to me. Štefan came in with a pot of snow to make coffee.

"*Šťastný nový rok*," he said, lighting the stove.

"Shit!" Tom said. "I completely forgot last night." He turned and gave me a kiss. "Happy New Year, Molly."

"I don't believe it! How could I forget?" I kissed Tom back.

"We all forget," Štefan said.

"Happy New Year, Štefan." I leaned over and gave him a kiss.

Our headlamps and the flickering blue stove flame looked surreal. Tom was getting dressed to go out. I had to pee again, too. "Wait for me," I told him.

"I have to take a dump," he said.

"All right. You go your way, I'll go mine."

After Tom left, I asked Štefan how he felt. I said I'd heard him coughing.

"I am sorry," he said, "if I wake you."

"It's all right. I just wondered if you're okay."

"Am okay," he answered, but not very convincingly.

After some breakfast and a series of toilet runs, we packed up and prepared to leave. The sun was just coming up and snow crystals glistened in the bright patches. But there were ominous-looking clouds to the north and east.

Three large peaks completely blocked our view to the south. We would be heading toward the one on the left: Kežmarský. To the right were Lomnický and Pyžný peaks, and the lower but much nearer Spižský Peak. Now I could see that the range dropped away from us to the northeast, into a wide valley of low, rounded hills. Poland lay beyond. It was probably already snowing there.

"Today," Štefan said as we hoisted our packs, "we go down in small valley there," he indicated the direction with a look, "and find way to Kežmarský."

"It's a beautiful valley," I said. "Does it have a name?"

"Malá Zmrzlá Dolina. Mean small frozen valley."

"Isn't *zmrzlina* the word for ice cream?" I asked.

"*Ano, dobre*," he said, patting my shoulder. "You have good memory."

"Just for special words."

"Pronounce Slovak good, too."

"Careful, you'll turn my head."

I could see that Štefan did not understand the idiom, so I just smiled, then said, "I like little ice cream valley better."

"Then it is so," he said.

"It looks like ice cream."

"Shouldn't we start our trek through the ice cream now?" Tom said, looking over his shoulder at the clouds.

We made the summit of Kežmarský by midday, and by then we were in a thickening fog. For two pitches we ascended fixed ropes that Štefan took up on lead. We climbed on a mixture of snow, ice and inconsistent rock, following the outside lip of a natural avalanche chute. The peak was in the clouds and we descended to the spinal ridge before we could see the attention-getting amount of open air there was on either side of us.

We rested for ten minutes before starting up again. It was three hours later, during the climb to Lomnický that it became obvious Štefan had to go down. We were on a 60- or 70-degree wall with a deep couloir marking its right side. I couldn't see the top of the mountain, although it was supposed to be only a couple hundred meters away. We were blocked from the wind, which blew out of the north, but the spray of ice crystals and snow mist blew off the top and settled over us in a wet, cold cloud. The route ahead followed a narrow snow gully with bulging rocks on one side and an avalanche chute on the other.

Štefan's cough had become much worse. During one fit, Tom reached out to hold Štefan's harness, in case he coughed himself right off the wall. Tom told Štefan that he had a fever and Štefan said, "Not so bad."

"I can feel the heat from here," Tom told him.

It was true. I looked at them, and while Tom's beard was white with ice and snow, Štefan's beard dripped like tree limbs in a spring drizzle.

From that point to the summit, we needed a fixed rope. Tom took it up and I belayed, staying back with Štefan.

Tom began kicking steps and planting the ice axe to pull himself up. It was not insecure, only desperately exposed. I could see how he tried to move steadily, but sometimes the snow and ice just crumbled away, showering Štefan and me as we ducked against the wall and covered our heads.

To the left I could see where a massive cornice had broken off. Beyond it was a free-standing rock tower. The snow was unusually deep, given the angle of the wall, and crusty, not holding steps well.

I could see impact marks from falling rocks or ice. Although not as defined as the avalanche funnel to our right, which I could no longer distinguish through the mist, I realized that the narrow face, wedged between a mountainous cornice structure and a rock tower, would carry a lot of the debris being swept off the mountain by wind, avalanches, diurnal freezing and thawing, and simple fate. The sensation of being in a shooting gallery was intensified by the narrowing field of vision as Tom disappeared into the cloud, the rope dangling and twisting in the wind behind him.

"Tomaš *je veľmi dobré,*" Štefan said as he looked up.

Those words I knew. Tom is very good. He is. "*Ano,*" I said. "Yes, he is."

Štefan would not allow me to remain on the ledge alone, so I had to go up next. I couldn't see twenty feet ahead, so it was a surprise when I reached Tom and found that the end of the rope was secured to an ice-crusted iron railing and Tom was sitting with his back against the wall of a building; it was the meteorological station and we were on the summit of Lomnický.

The cable cars that descended to a plateau lake, then continued into the village, were not running because of the storm, so we spent the night in the station.

I think Štefan expected to be miraculously cured by morning so we could continue, but he wasn't, of course. During the night he began throwing up. It was still too windy to run the cabin lift that morning, but they turned it on long enough to get us down. Štefan had the flu, and two days later Tom got it.

I never told Tom what happened between Štefan and me that time in the Tatras, when both of them got the flu, and I don't think Tom knows any other way. He wouldn't be able to hide it, the way I have hidden it from him all these years.

It is a strange thing, something like that in your past. It is an exhilarating memory, even while it saddens me. I don't know if I would do it again, knowing what I do now, but we never know what we ought to know when knowing it counts, which means I'd probably do the same thing. I am only sad because Tom wouldn't understand and it would hurt him. No, not only Tom. I hope Anna doesn't know and I don't think she does. Still, I am not sad for doing it.

What we did could not be called an affair, it didn't last long enough, and we only had sex once, which does not mean we didn't talk about it all the time and almost do it again. I was in love with him; I am still in love with him, and I don't know any more appropriate word I can use. I love him without having to love Tom any less. They, Tom and Štefan, are not so different: I love Tom more deeply and more profoundly because we have a shared history, we have a commitment to living our lives together, we are bonded together, but had I known Štefan first it could have as easily been him. If we have souls, or maybe I want the word spirit, but if we do, Štefan's and Tom's are like twin pearls from the same oyster. I am not making excuses. They are so much alike that it would have been odd if I didn't love them both.

That day we came down from Lomnický, the cable car swinging wildly in the freezing wind, Štefan had a hundred and four fever. He was deeply embarrassed that we had to come down from the mountains. I think he would have stayed up there and died if we had not insisted on calling it off.

195

I sat next to Štefan with my arm around him; he shivered against me like some unsynchronized motor. Tom sat opposite, facing us, and sometimes he would put his hand on Štefan's knee and say something meant to be soothing, like, "Molly and I are just happy to be here in the Tatras—it's enough for us—don't worry about it." Štefan knew it wasn't enough, but what could he do? He was terribly sick. "We'll do it again," I told him. "We've got all the time in the world." Štefan had nothing to say to our stupid palliatives. He smiled politely and shivered, his eyes bloodshot and watery.

Someone from the meteorological station had radioed down that we were coming. Juraj and Tomaš, two of Štefan's friends from the Mountain Rescue Service, met us at the cable car station. Juraj had the largest forearms I've ever seen; he was built like a bear. Tomaš was nearly the opposite, a skinny, short, elf-like man whom Štefan called malý (little) Tomaš to distinguish him from my Tomaš.

We had left our clothes at Sliezský Dom, the mountaineer's hotel on the plateau above Tatranská Polianka. To get there we would have had to take the mountain train between the villages, then hike through deep snow for two or three hours to reach the hotel. So Štefan's friends met us with snowmobiles. They took Štefan on one and much of our gear strapped to a sled pulled behind the other. We all waved as they departed in a roar of blue smoke.

Tom and I walked on into Tatranská Lomnica where we sat in a café and drank espresso; we were quite disheveled and probably a little smelly. We could see Lomnický peak where we slept last night and where we were standing only an hour or so ago. It is a beautiful mountain, rugged, vertical and draped in heavy snow. It is a compelling, magical mountain.

After coffee we took the electric train to Tatranská Polianka and made the hike along a forest trail to the climbers' dormitory. Without our packs it was really very pleasant, in spite of the wind and still-falling snow. We passed a family of four (two sons) on cross-country skis going in the opposite direction. On a distant slope we saw a small herd of chamois, smudges seen through the gauze-like curtain of snow.

That night Tom began to feel bad, and by the next morning it was obvious that he was also coming down with the flu. I expected to be next. It hit Tom so hard that he only got out of bed when he had to drag himself to the toilet. I brought soup and water to him. There weren't many climbers in the dormitory-style hotel. The beginning of January wasn't exactly the climbing season. Sometimes in the bar there would only be four or five of us. The only other woman seemed to be the waitress, although once through the kitchen door I might have spotted a woman dressed in cook's clothes, but it could have been a fat man with a ponytail. No one spoke enough English to converse with me. I had learned some food words and I knew how to offer polite greetings, so I did all right alone. Everyone respected my privacy, although I was the obvious object of much respectful attention.

Everything happens in Czechoslovakia on a small scale; it is a small country. This is particularly true of the Slovak part. The mountains are beautiful and rugged, but very small. The language is understood by fewer people than live in Los Angeles County. There are only two real cities in Slovakia: Bratislava in the west and Košice in the east. Most of Czechoslovakia is made up of villages and small towns—Prague and Brno are the only major cities in the Czech part. The community of climbers is more closely knit than many families. I doubt there was a climber anywhere in Slovakia that January who did not know about the two Americans who were going to do a mid-winter traverse of the Tatras with Štefan Borák.

So in the bar, in the café and when I took walks around the frozen lake in the afternoon, I was aware of being watched, even if it was in a friendly and curious way. This did nothing to mitigate my boredom or moderate my loneliness. After three days, I wanted to talk to somebody who didn't just moan and turn over.

I suppose that's partly why I went to Štefan's room that night. Although it's probably not why I took a bottle of *slivovice*.

Štefan opened the door wearing house slippers, long underwear bottoms and a T-shirt. "Feeling good enough now for a drink?" I asked, holding out the green bottle.

I had surprised him. For that one, long moment, he looked be-fuddled. Then he smiled, took the bottle from my hand, and gestured grandly for me to enter the room.

Štefan's room was much smaller than ours, and not as well fur-nished. It was almost a closet. His climbing gear almost filled it. The contrast was so distinct that it struck me that Tom and I were in the larger and more lavish room where normally the head of the mountaineer's club would stay. What I had taken for granted was very likely a singular honor.

Štefan's window was open a crack and a bit of snow melted from the sill onto the floor. Away from the window the room was hot. Ours was, too. We had not been able to figure out how to regulate the tem-perature of the steam radiator, apparently a common problem.

Štefan pushed a pack onto the floor so I could have the only chair. He produced two glasses and poured shots of *slivovice*. We clinked glasses and toasted our health. Štefan sat on the narrow bed, among books, web slings and a rope. He leaned over and refilled my glass, then leaned on the rope like an armrest. He asked how Tom was and I said he was terrible, but sleeping well enough. Štefan blamed himself for Tom getting the flu.

I don't remember everything we talked about, because most of it had to have been trivial, only conversational. With Tom he could use a lot of Slovak, but we had to very nearly pantomime anything beyond common civilities and sentences using my thirty or forty words of Slo-vak and his few hundred words of English. In spite of this, I had the sense of talking incessantly, using my hands a lot. We kept refilling our glasses, clinking them each time and toasting our health, until the bottle was two-thirds empty.

Štefan told me that his parents were still alive and they were very old; his father was almost eighty-five, and his mother was seventy-nine. I knew that Štefan was forty, so his father had been forty-five when Štefan was born, the last of a family with five sons and one daughter. He told me about his first climbs in the Tatras when he was still too young for school; then his father was a professor of mathematics at Comenius University, but they spent the summer holidays in the Tatras. All the brothers became climbers. Štefan's oldest brother was killed on Peak Lenin in the Soviet Union. Another brother died in a crevice fall in the Himalayas; Štefan was with him. Of the two remaining brothers, both had immigrated to Canada in 1968 and Štefan had not seen them in the eleven years since. But he got letters. One was a guide near Banff and the other taught Slavic languages at a college in Toronto. Štefan's sister followed her two brothers to Canada and married there. Štefan had only seen his nieces and nephews in photos.

"What can you tell me about Saša?" I asked. "What was she like when you knew her?"

"Ah," he said with a smile. "We were young. I were young. Saša is four years more old from me."

I think he stopped because he had used the present tense. His smile faded for a moment, then he gathered himself and continued.

"Her father was one my teacher. Was camp for mountain sports in Tatras for summer. Is continue here now. I was student this camp from years twelve to seventeen. Some women climbers are . . . you know how I say? They are not much pretty. Saša was beautiful girl. Like you are beautiful."

"Thanks, but you don't have to say that."

"You know this truth. All men in camp have their eye for her. All men here have eye for you."

"You, too?"

"Of course." He laughed. "Maybe I most."

The contrasting heat and cold and the *slivovice* combined to make me feel dizzy, but in wanting to stand by the window I got up too fast and had to lean against the wall to keep from fainting. Štefan rushed over and took my arm.

I told him I was all right, only a little dizzy from getting up too fast. I turned and we were face to face. He was holding my arms above the elbow. We were so close that his breath felt like a small, tobacco-laden breeze on a warm day, and I could see the spot of light from the ceiling lamp reflected in his pupils.

If a woman really wants to be kissed, I think a man knows it, if he is paying attention. So we did not have to be quick, the way you might if you were afraid of being rejected, and we were drunk enough to have lost our futures. It seemed to have taken minutes for our mouths to come together, and then they only touched, only the softest skin of our lips, while Štefan's right hand left my arm and came to my breast.

After a moment, Štefan pulled back and said in a soft voice, "Is wrong do this, but not possible now, I think, not do it."

"I know."

We kissed again with more passion.

I knew what we were about to do and was both embarrassed and excited. I wondered what he would think of me naked. Would my breasts be large enough and well-shaped? Would he think I was fat? I had not shaved my legs in two days; what would he think of that?

I felt his sudden erection against my lower abdomen. His under-wear was so thin that for a moment I thought he had somehow removed them. My hand appeared beneath the back of his T-shirt.

I almost thought of Tom, but that would come later; now I shut him out of mind.

We sat on the bed and Štefan shoved off the rucksack with his left hand. His right hand had not left my breast. The rucksack thud-ded onto the floor and I wondered if someone in the dorm below heard it, and what he might think. The bed squeaked when we lay back and I knew it was going to be loud when Štefan made love to me.

I don't know why those things came into my mind and not some thoughts of Tom. We made love, sweating like workhorses, among ropes, slings, and books. We did it for a very long and wonderful time. We never spoke once.

I went back to our room at two A.M. Štefan and I were wise enough not to talk about what had just happened, and in that way it could remain a part of the almost mystical event it had seemed to be—that it was. We seemed to know that we would probably never do it again. I knew, anyway. It had been enough, that once. We had shared something important, we had become special to one another; that was all we wanted, I think.

Tom was sleeping on his side, facing away from me. I went to the toilet and undressed, washed myself. The room was like a sauna. I opened the window a few inches and stood there for a moment, naked, feeling the freezing air against my chest.

I got into bed and slid close to Tom. He was very hot, his back was dry. I put my arm on his shoulder but he didn't stir. I put my ear to his back to listen to his heart; he was so still it was like death.

"I love you very, very much," I whispered.

His fever broke a few hours later, in chills and sweats, and I held him against the shivering, telling him he was all right, that I was there, that I would always be there—forever.

Tom was too weak to climb during the rest of our stay in the Tatras, and in fact we left two days earlier than planned and went back to Bratislava, where Anna babied Tom with cookies, cakes and hot soup, and Štefan tried to cure him with three-times-daily doses of *borovička*. Štefan and I were seldom alone and we did not try to be. I could barely face Anna. I don't know how Štefan felt around Tom, but I could sense no difference in their friendship. Maybe it's something men can do.

The first night Tom felt like sitting up with us, Štefan brought out a large box filled with photographs from various expeditions. All the pictures were black and white, printed on cheap paper and the edges were curling. Some were fading and I could imagine that one day there would nothing on the paper at all. Štefan did not only take pictures of mountains; many, maybe most, were of villages and villagers, often full face portraits. There seemed to be thousands of photos, and it was obvious Štefan was looking for something in particular. He would fish around in the box, pull something out and look at it, maybe make some comment as he passed it around, then fish in the box again. Anna sat next to me on the sofa, so close that we almost touched; I could smell her soft feminine odor mixed with the vinegar she had used to clean her hands after peeling onions. Tom sat cross-legged on the floor and Štefan sat on a stool made from an ox hide. We were drinking white wine from the small Borák vineyard.

"Ah," Štefan said, at last pulling from the box the picture he had so obviously been searching for. With the flair of a waiter in a posh cafe, he presented the picture to me. Anna leaned against my arm and looked over my shoulder.

Amid the typical debris of base camp—storage barrels, lines strung with frozen laundry, ski poles with gloves atop them stuck in the snow, scattered tents, packs and ropes—eight men stood with their arms on one another's shoulders.

"Is Nanga Parbat," Štefan said.

"I see you," I said to Štefan. He was second from the left.

Tom scooted over and leaned against my knee so he could also see the picture.

"God!" I cried when I recognized Tom. "That's you."

"So it is," Tom said.

"My Viking."

"Viking," Štefan wondered.

"Doesn't he look just like a Viking with that beard and hair?"

"Ah, Whyking. Yes." Then he turned to Anna and said something in Slovak, which I assumed to be a definition of Viking.

"*Horal muž*," Anna said, which I knew to mean "Mountain Man."

"Who are the others?" I asked.

Tom pointed to the man on the end, on Štefan's opposite side, and said, "That's Peter Kubyni. Next to me is Miro Šušor . . ."

"Slavo Šušor," Štefan corrected.

"Of course. Slavomir, not Miroslav."

"Is Miro here," Štefan said, pointing to the man on the other end of the row. "Miro Šivčík."

Tom named two climbers: "This is Tom Blackford—he was with the British team, and Rick Roybal. This is . . ."

"Ivan Rajniak," Štefan filled in the name.

"Juraj took the picture."

"What happen with Tom and Rick?"

"I don't know about Tom. He was from England. He wrote a book about K-2 two years ago. Rick works for the U.S. Park Service in Colorado. Or he used to. I haven't seen him in three or four years."

"Ivan die . . . dies?"

"Died," Tom said. "Ivan is dead?"

"He is died on Everest attempt."

"On your expedition?"

"No. Not with my. One year before."

"To Ivan," Tom said, raising his glass of wine.

"Ivan," Štefan said and they clinked glasses.

"What happened to him?" I asked.

"High altitude edema," Štefan explained.

"I thought Ivan was good at altitude?" Tom said.

Štefan shrugged. "We all think this."

"True," Tom said. "Anyone else?"

"No. Peter immigrate to Canada. Slavo is work now in Tatras with rescue service. Juraj is in Bratislava, at same office like me."

"And Miro?"

"He also live Bratislava. But this time he is with Czech climbers on Fitzroy, Patagonia."

I handed the picture back to Štefan, but he refused it. "Is for you," he insisted. I had wanted it very badly but would never have asked. I thanked Štefan and sat looking at the picture while he took others from the box and passed them around.

The talk turned to dead climbers. There were very many. I didn't want to think about death. I went to bed earlier than the others and through the wall I could hear them talking still about death in the mountains. I listened to Anna's accent and thought about Saša.

When we returned from Czechoslovakia on the tenth day of 1980, I found in our mail a note asking me to call my mother's doctor. He said Mom had breast cancer and it had metastasized throughout her lymphatic system. She had known for five months and I don't think she would ever have told me.

She died in a San Diego hospice in March. I tried to reconcile with her, but she wouldn't allow it. She died in the night, alone, believing that her secrets went with her, I suppose. Just as well, of course. Some secrets should go with us, advice I am obviously not taking for myself.

I had Tommy and that was everything. But after Mom died, I felt very much alone in the world. Our family was small and I was all that was left. Mom was an only child and I was an only child. Daddy's brothers, my uncles Bob and Willy, were killed in Korea. My paternal grandfather died before I was born and grandmother went when I was two. I was not quite twenty-five years old and alone, the last one of us. My family's tiny spark in the human current was about to extinguish.

I have thought of human life that way, as a continually flowing current, sort of an electrical surge through the universe, the power surges from births regulated by the constant drain of death. Our family made a spark that flared and faded before it could be caught by the eye. Poof!

Tom

I thought she would die that day. But for the next three months she maintained her tenacious grip on life. She spent those months in the Poprad hospital and I took a room at a hotel a few blocks away so I could be there every day. Half the time—more than that really—I don't think she knew I was there. The important thing was when she did. Those were the days I lived for. There were times I thought seriously of finding a way to die before she did. It was a stupid thought, because Molly needed me. Afterward I would have all the time I needed for dying.

Fall began spectacularly. Often that's what we talked about, when Molly was at all coherent: the weather, the trees and sky, the mountain hues, remembering special routes we had climbed, with whom. For eight weeks she never responded to me, but I knew she heard, I knew she understood, I knew it gave her peace.

The stroke she had in the mountain chalet had left her paralyzed on her right side, her mouth twisted into a grimace. She was blind on that side, and had no peripheral vision in the other eye. I bought a Walkman and put the speakers into her ears so she could have music sometimes.

Molly was in a room with up to seven other women, although the number changed as some got better and others died. There was only one toilet and one shower area. Often I cleaned it. It didn't seem to be specifically anyone's job. Some days I hated the hospital staff. Some days I pitied them. Some days I loved them. Anyway, for more than a month Molly didn't use the toilet or shower. She eliminated waste through tubes into bags and we cleaned her body with cloths dampened in a white tin basin.

They called me Dr. Valen, I suppose from something Štefan said, or maybe from the forms we filled out, and I continually had to explain that I was a teaching doctor, not a medical doctor. But I was around so often that it didn't seem to matter, or there seemed no difference. I think some of the patients who shared Molly's room and their families decided I was really some sort of special foreign doctor and they literally begged me to give them some sort of answer, some sort of solace. After a while I just didn't see what it could hurt and found myself offering advice. Most of it was simply common sense, but in fact mostly I just offered advice of a spiritual nature. How stupidly ironic! My own spirit was destroyed. But I have to say that all of them broke my heart again and again.

Amazing things happened that fall in Europe. I knew it from Štefan. He came often, always on Sunday, and sometimes other days. Although he lived in Bratislava, much of his work was in the Tatras, so he wasn't far away. But I know of times he took the train from Bratislava, a journey of more than six hours one way, only to visit Molly. Had I known then what happened between them, it wouldn't have mattered, because his love for and attention to Molly was too important. But I didn't know until I read it, and by then it could and did matter.

Štefan described a climate of intense paranoia in the world outside. He expected more purges of the 1968 variety. He said it was like a ship splitting her seams in stormy seas and the panicked crew rushing about helter-skelter trying to patch leaks. A flood of refugees roamed across Czechoslovakia trying to get into Hungary, where borders to the west were virtually wide open. East German refugees had gone to Prague and were climbing over the walls of the West German embassy, which, Štefan described, looked like a refugee camp, not an embassy.

Štefan was wrong about purges. It's amazing that the most astonishing changes in Europe since World War II were only weeks away, and we didn't have a clue. Not one. Štefan expected to be arrested and taken to prison any day, yet in a few months he would be an elected member of a free parliament.

Toward the end of October, Molly seemed to get better. She was able to sit up, to speak, even if in a halting, senseless way. I suppose she did this from pure strength, since in all ways her condition worsened by the day. Sometimes she could get out of bed and go to the toilet if someone held her up. It was amazing to see her do this and hopefully I imagined maybe she would really just get better and better.

I apologized to her for not giving her the only thing she had ever really asked me for: to let her die in the mountains she loved. It was obvious that she was going to die in an ugly, smelly hospital room at the edge of an ugly, smelly industrial town. She didn't even have a view of the mountains from her window.

On the last day of October, a few days before Molly's 34th birthday, Molly stopped getting better and got dramatically worse. The pain must have been horrendous and her morphine was increased. Her doctor, one of Štefan's mountaineering friends, told me that he thought her pain would be intense, no matter how much morphine they gave her. If they gave her more, the morphine itself would kill her. He told me that he did not think Molly would live to see her birthday.

That night as I sat beside her bed, Molly said my name. I leaned close to her face. She repeated my name. Her breath was husky, sulfurous. I told her I was beside her and held her hand. A skeleton's hand.

I remember this as distinctly as any memory I possess; I hear it every day. She said, "Tommy, it's time."

From a pay phone in the lobby I called Štefan in Bratislava and told him what I wanted to do. I stayed all night with Molly in the hospital. Štefan took the night train and came to the hospital at dawn. We put Molly into a robe and wrapped her in a blanket. The weather outside had turned cold and snow spit from dark, low clouds. We carried Molly between us out of the hospital and put her on a cot in the back of the mountain rescue service's truck.

"She wants to die in the mountains," I told Štefan.

He understood. "We will take her."

"There is a place she described to me. She saw it when we climbed Gerlach in 1980. A wide ledge up high, beyond Polska Hreben."

"Very high, near summit?"

"Yes, less than a hundred meters back. You know it?"

"I know. Is place enough for one tent or bivouac. Only approach is technical. Is impossible for Molly."

"I intend to carry her."

Štefan considered this. We drove into Starý Smokovec and it was snowing.

"Is only way," Štefan said.

"Whatever it takes. I will go to hell if that's what it takes."

"And I go next to you."

"Then you think it can be done? We can get her up to this ledge?"

"We will do it."

"I owe you a big debt."

"You owe me nothing. Never say this again."

Molly

I only saw Štefan once more after January of 1980, and that was when he came to America in the spring of 1982 as a UIAA representative and met with the American Alpine Club in New York. Tom was in school so I flew to New York alone to see Štefan. We had four days together before he had to return to Czechoslovakia. On the last day I tried very hard to convince him to request political asylum and stay in the U.S., but he wouldn't even consider it. I tried various temptations, but the only real one we had forbidden ourselves. The day I arrived we sat in a café near Grand Central Station and tried to talk through the unasked question of what would happen next. The very fact that Tom had let me go to spend that time in New York with Štefan created an enormous guilt. It is not easy to be trusted. Štefan and I hugged and kissed when we met, but it was by obviously tacit agreement a kiss of friendship. Maybe we had already answered the question in the kiss. We were romantically charged, but there seemed no outlet for it. We dedicated ourselves to tourism and common talk.

"How is our Tomaš?" Štefan asked.

"Busy as all hell," I answered.

"He work too much."

"You don't?"

"We should ask Anna."

"Yes, we should ask Anna."

"What have you climb this year?"

"Mostly rocks. Tom and I went to Denali, but I wrote to you and sent pictures."

"Yes, good letter, good pictures. Best is picture from summit."

"It was really, really hard. Weather. But I wrote everything . . ."

"Yes, good letter. Like I am being there."

So went our conversation in the café.

It was my first trip to New York City, so Štefan and I were both like children at Christmas. Everything was bright, filled with wonder and exciting. Štefan was traveling on money from the Czechoslovak mountaineer's club, a fortune on their standards and a pittance in New York, so he was staying in a room at the YMCA—a very nice room, he told me, although I never got around to seeing it; I had a room at the Algonquin (I'd always wanted to stay there). I know it bothered him that I arranged to pay for so much of what we did: restaurants, two movies, the Natural History Museum and a Gray Line tour. I didn't mind at all, but it was so noticeably hard for him that finally I arranged for us to eat our last dinner together in my hotel room so I could just add it to the bill. I was embarrassed, but only for him.

I brought with me pictures from our home and our lives in Southern California and we spent our last evening together sitting next to one another at the room service dining cart with photographs and the debris from a supper of club sandwiches, french fries, dill pickles and beer spread over it. Štefan did not understand or approve of the principle of a sandwich. He took off the bread, which he pronounced to be a foul substitute for the real thing, and just ate the stuff inside. The only beer I could find that he liked was an amber Mexican beer called Dos Equis. He got up and washed his hands carefully before he would touch the pictures.

He could not believe the size of our house and the palm trees in front. He kept shaking his head and saying, "Is paradise, is paradise." He studied each picture of Joshua Tree, a place with a well-deserved international reputation among climbers, like an art historian trying to date a painting. He would run his fingertip along a crack line or arête and ask me if that was the route, and listen carefully as I described and rated it.

But the picture he studied most attentively was one I'd brought of Saša. It came at the end. Actually there were two. The first was of Saša and me at Joshua Tree, taken by Laura, clowning around by our campfire. Saša had stuck out her tongue at the camera and I was holding my hand behind her head with my fingers spread to imitate horns. Saša held a can of beer and I a box of chocolate chip cookies. Our eyes glowed red from the flash. The other I took of Saša alone on the trail from the parking pullout along the road to Tahquitz. A Tahquitz wall is visible behind her, and the route from which she fell can be seen. I had not known this until one evening when Laura had come over for dinner and we were looking at old pictures. She showed me the route. Saša looked especially beautiful in that picture: wearing cut-off jeans and a bandana halter top, her hair piled up on her head and held with a red ribbon, a climbing pack slung across one shoulder, a rope on the other, and her old EB shoes tied to a belt loop on her shorts; almost identical to the way she looked the first time I saw her at the Santee boulders. I thought Štefan would like to see how she looked in her American incarnation.

"That's Saša," I said when he got to the first picture, and he smiled as he studied it. "We were camping at Joshua Tree. Apparently we were a little drunk." Štefan nodded but didn't say anything. Slowly he put that picture on the cart and looked at the last one. "Saša at Tahquitz," I explained. "Is that a mountaineer, or what?"

"Is Tahquitz?" Štefan asked for confirmation.

"Yes. And that . . ." I put my finger to a spot on the rock wall, "is the route." He knew which route I meant. "But this picture was taken almost a year before. We climbed farther to the right that day, a route on this dihedral called, Falling Off A Log. It's five pitches."

Štefan looked at that picture for what seemed an awfully long time. I actually think it was some minutes. Maybe not. It just seemed so. Then he said abruptly, "Good pictures," and began helping me gather them up. It was a moment before I noticed that his eyes were glazed, damp. I asked what was wrong, concerned that I had said or done something without realizing it. He looked like he might leave.

"What did I do?"

"Nothing," he answered. "I am sorry."

Štefan got up and walked to the armchair by the window and sat with his chin resting in his hands and his elbows on his knees, looking at the bed.

"If you have negative from that picture of Saša, the last one, maybe I can have this one?"

"Of course, let me get it out." I retrieved the picture from the bag and handed it to him.

"Thank you wery much." He did not look at it.

There was a very strange and uncomfortable feeling in my stomach.

"Molly," Štefan began, and I could tell from the tone of his voice that he was going to say something difficult for him, "I was lover of Saša from before she immigrate in nineteen and sixty-eight."

It was probably the last thing I expected him to say. I was sure I had done or said something to offend or upset him. Now my mind was trying to process *this* information. I think a smile came to my face. Instantaneously I realized that Saša had in her own mysterious way connected people who needed to be together, if only through her: Saša had slept with Štefan, then my father, then me, and I had lost my father because I dreamed of sleeping with him; and I slept with Saša and I had slept with Štefan. Saša was our common bond within the little community of people who climb. But I did not relate this to Štefan. I did not want him to know about that part of the relationship I had with Saša. He was still looking at the bed, not at me. I got up and walked over to sit on the corner of the bed. He had continued talking:

"Saša is four years more old from me. Her father is one time teacher of me; I have then seventeen years. Many times in summer we go to Tatra Mountains. Is big group, not only Juraj Janda, Saša and me. In summer, Juraj has many students for mountain sports. I am one. That summer, nineteen and fifty-seven, Saša is my first lover. You know is saying that first time for love make most strong memory. Is true for Saša, for my memory.

"I only see Saša at summer climbing program in Tatras. She is live at Prague and I Bratislava. I do not ask her about any other man. I have other women. But there is only Saša, you know? I think we will have marriage together, but she never agrees on this. Is only my wish. She tell she love me, but not for marriage.

"In nineteen and sixty-two, I meet Anna and next year I have marriage with her.

"But sometimes in summer—now I am teacher of mountain sports—I am continue to have romance with Saša. Anna knows this."

"Does she know about us?" I interrupted.

"No," he answered, shaking his head. Then he continued: "In nineteen and sixty-eight, after Juraj is kill by secret police, Saša disappear. I never see, I never hear again from her until you sit at my flat and tell me she is dead."

"I'm sorry, Štefan."

He looked up at me for the first time since he began talking about Saša and our eyes connected.

"I understand about Saša. She was impossible not to love."

He nodded.

"She was my best friend, at a time when I really needed a best friend."

He turned the picture over in his hand and looked at it. I thought for a moment that he might cry. I stood and took the picture from his hand and put it on the night table.

We had a nightcap and he left before midnight.

I thought of Štefan and we wrote letters back and forth, four or five times a year. Actually, Tom wrote more often than I did, and I would add comments to the bottom of Tom's letters. We sent pictures and books as gifts at Christmas. There was nothing particular or methodical about the decisions we made regarding where to climb on our holidays, but we didn't get back to the Tatras. We went to Alaska and failed because of weather to climb Foraker. We spent two summers in Colorado doing routes on Long's Peak and climbing in Eldorado Canyon. We went twice to the French Alps, and once to England and Scotland. We tried Ben Nevis, but were weathered out; we even tried and failed to walk up the road.

I don't think Tom had an affair during our marriage. I think he burned himself out on all that before he met me—he had an active romantic life. I think he had opportunities—some of his students were atrocious flirts—but I don't think he pursued them. I don't know. It's just a feeling I have. I don't think it would make me feel one bit less guilty if he had. Marriage is not tit for tat. If he had an affair I would have been deeply hurt. I cannot imagine the possibility that anyone could have loved me as much and with as much single-minded devotion as Tom. In fact, it is a little scary to have someone love you that much. It's a gigantic responsibility, and one I came awfully close to screwing up: the cry of Antithesis on my shoulder, which over the years I have become more and more successful at ignoring.

At the end, it wasn't Antithesis at all who fucked it up. It was only fate with a barely pronounceable name.

It was not a perfect day, more noticeable in a place so littered with perfect days, it was hazy and heating up, especially for November. I had lived in Southern California all my life, so I was used to fog and smog and all the stuff that clutters up the air, but I still wished for vistas, for a view.

Tommy and I were climbing The Screaming Meanies, and I was belaying him from a ledge we had named The Window Sill. I was trying not to be distracted because Tom fell so infrequently that I just had to keep up with feeding him rope. I was unusually tired and surprised that the previous (the first) pitch had taken so much out of me. I was embarrassed to have taken a fall. When I craned my neck back and looked up, I still couldn't see Tommy because he had gone over a bump and gotten onto the ramp. I expected him to top out in a minute or two.

The instant I heard the sound I knew it was a rock, even before I heard Tom's voice yelling, "Rock!", which I heard very nearly simultaneously with the lights going out.

I have thought of this a thousand times. I am unable to separate what I remember from what I imagine from what I hope and from what I know. If I remember it, is it real? Is a dream recalled real? Was it ever? What I remember is that Saša spoke to me as I dangled unconscious from a perlon safety line and the rope connected uselessly to my husband's harness.

Saša said, "Wake up, Molly! Don't be such a vuss." She said it twice. Then I felt her hands on my shoulders as she pulled me from thin air and plopped me steadfast on the tiny ledge. I saw her plain as day, as clear as a crystalline sky. She held my arm as if to stay me and said, "It won't be all that bad; I'll stay with you until it's over." After that came the hellish odor of struck flint and my husband's voice and the enormous, infernal headache.

I knew even then, as I was being strapped onto Tommy's back, days before the tests and the doctors and the terrible reports, that I had begun the final and inevitable process of disappearing, and that Saša would guide me through the darkness.

I don't know what Tom will do. It is like him to become completely focused, absorbed in something (or someone) he is interested in and be virtually incapacitated if he loses it. That Tom loves me and that we found each other is a miracle. Tom often said that my existence was proof of the existence of God. He was telling me how much he loved me and being sarcastic at the same time. He does not believe in God. He quotes a favorite Spanish existentialist: *The will not ever to die, the refusal to resign oneself to death, ceaselessly builds the house of life, while the keen blasts and icy winds of reason batter at the structure and beat it down.* Tom is cursed by reason; condemned by imagination. He has the soul of a poet but the mind of a logician. He will not accept the unreasonable but he craves the romantic; his house of life is always under threat from the rational part of his mind. The inexplicable angers and frustrates him. He will be angry when I die, and hurt, and I don't know what will console him. So I am worried about him. There is nothing I can do, and in the end, isn't that what death is?

It seems that I have lived with all these whispered thoughts for an awfully long time, but actually they have existed for only moments.

I have not told you what I wanted to tell you. Except that I don't know what I wanted to tell you. Something more. Something with weight and real lasting value. But I have given you just particulars and altogether they seem, well, light. I know that's not what Kundera meant by his unbearable lightness of being, but it could have been, or should have been. I just wanted to leave you with something more than simply a poof.

I came into being. I was named. I inhabited spaces. I did things. Things were done in spite of me, to me. I will cease being. It is the most common of human stories. I don't know another way to tell it.

I only sought a way to say, I am . . .

And if the earthly no longer knows your name,
whisper to the silent earth: I'm flowing.
To the flashing water say: I am.

Tom

The truck took us up to the mountain hotel at Sliecký Dom in light snow. We strapped Molly into a rescue chair and put her on my back. Štefan took everything else, our climbing gear, tent, sleeping bags, some food and water. Juraj and Malý Tomaš would have gone, would have helped us, but Štefan wanted them to stay back fresh, if we needed them later. We started up the mountain. I looked back and saw Juraj and Malý Tomaš standing by the lake watching us ascend. I think Molly knew. She did not speak, but Štefan told me that from time to time her eyes were open and she seemed to be trying to focus.

It was excruciatingly slow, but before noon the weather cooperated by clearing off and warming. The dusting of snow disappeared under the sun in minutes. By the time we were on the narrow ridge of Polský Hreben we could see eternity, a view of epic dimensions. I tried to keep talking to Molly, telling her as often as possible where we were and what we could see and how the weather was. We stopped to rest before the technical ascent to the ledge and I leaned sideways against the cliff face.

"The valley is still green, Molly. I can see Poprad in the distance and the long highway. The summit of Gerlach is not far above now. We are at the technical section. Don't worry about us getting up there. You know I can climb with you on my back. I'll be on a rope with Štefan. Back there, Polský Hreben looks like a dragon's spine. I can see Východná Vysoká. It's snowing again over there. I suppose we'll be getting snow again pretty soon. Are you cold? Štefan says we're ready. He's fixed a rope."

I don't know if Molly heard any of this, but I choose to believe she did, that she knew everything we were doing.

It was snowing when we reached the ledge. It was sticking to the rocks and cliffs. It had held off long enough for me to get up the wall with Molly on my back. I don't think I could have done it in the snow. Štefan put up the tent while I got Molly out of the rescue chair and into a mummy bag. We were exhausted. Sometimes Molly opened her eyes. Sometimes, I am sure, she tried to smile.

We put Molly between us in the tent and Štefan gave me a candy bar. We were too exhausted to do anything else and were asleep in minutes.

In the morning it was obvious Molly was worse, not even conscious. Štefan waited outside in blowing snow while I took off enough of Molly's clothes to clean where she had fouled herself. God! She was such a skeleton. I put clean clothes on her and bagged the dirty ones. I zipped her tight into the mummy bag and went outside with Štefan. It was snowing heavily; Štefan's beard was white with it.

"She is . . . ?"

"Alive. But I think she's gone into a coma. She's unconscious."

"Storm." Štefan looked to the northeast.

"I see it. What do you think?"

Štefan shrugged. "We are here now. No matter." He finished a cigarette and looked at the wall that needed to be climbed to reach the top. He said, "I think I go to summit."

"Now?"

"Is not so far from here. Fifty or sixty meters."

"I have to stay. You'll climb alone?"

"Of course."

"Then I'll see you later."

"I come back in two, three hours."

I nodded. I knew that Štefan was going to the summit mainly to leave me alone with Molly. I also believe he could not watch her die. I think he hoped it would be over when he returned. I stood by and watched as he attached his crampons and stuffed a day pack with some extra clothes. He pulled his old red wool knit cap over his thick hair and picked up his ice axe. He gave me a wave with the axe and then disappeared around a buttress that blocked my view to the summit route. After he left I got out the stove and melted snow for water.

I lay next to Molly and listened to her ragged breathing. I never thought to hear her voice again, but I hoped she might still hear mine. I put my mouth near her left ear and told her how much I loved her, described how long I had loved her, and promised that I would always love her, for the rest of my life.

I lay my head on her shoulder. Her mouth was horribly twisted at both corners and bubbles of saliva popped from her lips.

In the middle of the afternoon I heard the crunch of Štefan's crampons, then the click of his cigarette lighter. Molly had not stirred once the entire time he was gone. I think he smoked another cigarette. Finally he crawled into the tent and sat in the vestibule removing his boots. He asked how she was and I said nothing had changed. He told me that from the summit he could see how bad the storm was going to be and said it was good we were already in place.

He said her breathing had the same rattling sound as high altitude edema and I said, "Edema is edema, I guess." Sometimes her eyelids fluttered but never actually opened and her breaths came in shallow, quick cycles, punctuated by really horrifying gasps.

I lay on my right side facing Molly, who was on her back and zipped to her chin inside the mummy bag. Štefan squirmed out of his parka and heavy red sweater and stared for a moment at Molly's face, which had once been the most beautiful sight in the world to me, and now looked like a skull painted to resemble skin. I put the back of my hand near her lips from time to time. She made no sound but for the ragged breathing. I have no idea what she felt, if anything. I can only hope the pain was over by then.

Then suddenly Štefan said simply that he was going down. I don't know if he wanted us to have the chance to be alone at the end or if he just couldn't stand to be there when she died. It was obvious she was dying as we spoke.

"What time is it?" I asked.

Štefan put his head through the sweater and looked at his old Russian wristwatch, which hung around his neck from a leather cord. "Fifteen and twenty," he said.

"You can't see fifty meters now. It'll be dark in less than two hours."

"Is enough, fifty meters."

"I wish you'd wait until the storm lifts. I mean, you aren't required to stay up here no matter how long it takes, but at least wait until the weather improves."

"Now is time for only two people. I stay on this mountain forever if is some help for you, for Molly. No, is time now for two people here. These are my mountains, Tomaš, so not to worry. I know way down like I know this . . ." He held out his hand, then pulled a glove over it. "Alone I move fast."

He promised to come back in 24 hours with the unstated intention of bringing help to carry her body down. I didn't try to stop him, in spite of the storm. Štefan was like that when he made up his mind. He was going down. So we said farewell and shook hands. He pushed his pack before him into the vestibule, then turned and leaned over Molly, touching his cheek against her face. In a low voice, barely audible above the wind snapping at the tent, he told her in Slovak that he loved her and asked that she go with God: "*L'úbim t'a mojá Molka. S bohom.*"

Štefan raised up, offered me his hand once more, which I grasped in both of mine. Then he pulled away and backed into the vestibule to put on his boots. I heard the tent fly unzip and then zip back as he left. Wind shook the tent and made it seem like a thing alive.

Molly died before Štefan reached the mountain hotel, I'm sure. I was laying next to her, asleep, when the change in her breathing woke me. She was gasping for a breath. I saw blood trickling from her ear. She struggled for air less than 10 seconds and then stopped. Everything stopped and there was only the wind buffeting the tent walls. I felt for a pulse. I put my hand on her forehead and pushed off the knit cap to uncover her hair. She wouldn't be cold now. I ran my fingers through her fine long hair.

She was dead.

On a cold and drizzly day in November, only a day after Molly Valen would have become 34 years old, 18 climbers hiked slowly and in single file from the chalet at Popradské Pleso to the Mountaineers Symbolic Cemetery, which is covered with memorial plaques attached to the rocks along the mountainside like shiny plates held in warm hands. Folk Totems there seem to have fallen randomly from the sky and embedded themselves between and among gigantic boulders and against cliff faces. There is a chapel. It has a red tiled roof and white-washed walls. The roof is round with an onion dome peak and Slavic cross on top. It is not large enough for five people to stand inside at the same time. Štefan stood just in front of the chapel door. He wore a red parka with black patches on the elbows and the logo of the Czechoslovak mountaineers club on one arm. He had on the same red knit cap he put on when he left Molly and me alone on the Gerlach Ridge. There wasn't much white in his beard for a man who had just turned 50 years old. He had removed his glasses which were useless in the steady drizzle and held them in clasped hands in front of his waist.

The weather was bad and so not many people had come up from the village for Molly's memorial service. There is a supply road up from the village of Štrbské Pleso. From this road, high up the mountain, a trail splits off and winds up a slope to the symbolic cemetery. I have never seen a place more appropriately and dramatically situated.

Among the climbers present, some had known Molly, but most had not. There were old men whose lives were the history of the Slovak Tatras, men who came from respect and from anticipation of their own memorial in that place, and there were young climbers who came because they thought Molly was a good climber; there were three women who came because a woman climber had died in their mountains. Anna Boráková stood with those women. Behind them were the two men, malý Tomaš and Juraj, who helped Štefan and me bring her body down.

I looked at the plaques on rocks nearest me. They contained the names of climbers who had died in these mountains and were decorated simply. One showed only a pair of rugged hands reaching high, another had crossed mountain axes, another a coiled rope and axe, and all had names, dates of death, and the route and mountain on which it occurred.

Štefan did not look at us as he spoke in soft Slovak the words of Molly's memorial. His eyes were turned up toward the gray and relentless sky. Near his feet, not yet affixed to its place on the rock walls, was Molly's plaque. This was on it:

Molly Cook Valen
1955–1989
United States of America
Climber

Possessed by Shadows

I am still possessed by the shadow of Molly in my life, casting by turns both light and dark over everything I do.

I went back to California a few days after Molly's memorial service, taking with me her ashes to bury next to her father. I was not able to get over this. Maybe I relished the pain, as if I might gain some moral strength from suffering. Maybe I made a religion of suffering. Maybe Molly was right to worry about me the way she did. No "maybe" about it.

I can't remember when I was able to read her journal. It was sometime after Christmas, alone in the house I was about to be forced to sell. I was broke, but I had a good job, even though I was also about to lose it. I just couldn't afford to keep the house. It wasn't my house anyway, it was our house. I needed to leave it behind.

Then I began to self-destruct.

I only lasted one semester, and even it was wasted. I was often drunk, and more often skipped classes. I am not proud of this, of course.

Alcohol was not an anesthetic, it was in fact a knife stabbed directly into my heart, again and again and again, the weapon of an unrepentant sufferer.

I remember they were knocking on the door for some time, becoming more insistent about getting in. But I don't remember how long I'd been locked in my office. I'd made a real mess of it—the books with their colorful spines on the floor, the desk and all around it littered with student papers like jetsam after a storm, papers I should have dealt with weeks before. I was drunk. I was blind, deadly drunk. They stopped knocking and started banging.

This is what I remember most clearly: On the corner of the desk lay a shard from the bottom of a broken drinking glass, the paper beneath it stained with condensation circles. Sunlight passing through the glass made of itself a prism that flickered against the opposite wall in a Technicolor sort of Platonic cave show. I looked at the sharp edge of the glass, touched a fingertip to it, drawing fascinating blood. I lay my wrist over the glass and thought to myself, there's nothing like taking phenomenology by the balls and giving them a little squeeze.

Do you remember Molly writing about hearing Saša's voice after the rock hit her? I sat watching the blood ooze from my wrist and suddenly there it was, as plain as that fascinating blood: Molly spoke to me. "I would never have fallen in love with you if you were this weak." That's what she said.

Someone had found the key by then and when Helen, the department secretary, and Dr. Thomas, my chairman, came into the room, my blood dripped over the edge of the desk and spotted a pile of final exams.

More or less, that's why I am no longer living in California.

For the last 10 years I have been living in the mountains where Molly died. I work for the Mountain Rescue Service based in Starý Smokovec. Štefan arranged it. Until the split between the Czechs and

Slovaks, which Štefan opposed, he was a member of parliament. He resigned in 1993 and went back to the (now) Slovak Mountaineers Club as president. In a way that makes him my boss, since the club is the parent organization of the rescue service.

I avoided Štefan after returning to Slovakia. I had a room in a cheap hotel, appropriate for someone with my financial status, and spent most of the time walking. Some days I walked for seven or eight hours with only brief stops. I needed to move. When still, I could only sleep, drink, or cry. But I was sort of all right when moving.

I had on one of those walks come across a large cemetery in the Palisady district of central Bratislava. It was thickly wooded and generally unkempt. There were some very old graves, going back 300 years in some cases. Lots of Hungarian and German names. Most of the benches were broken down, few of the flowers were fresh. It was quiet and beautiful, and I was more at ease among the dead.

Štefan, who until then had no idea I was in the country, came up behind me as I sat on one of the benches, elbows on my knees, staring blankly at a gravestone. He circled the bench at some distance to be sure before shouting my name and throwing out his arms as if he thought I would rush into them.

I said hello but didn't get up. Štefan dropped his arms; I noticed he carried some flowers. He stayed back, nodded. It was not a difficult assumption to figure out that I knew about Molly and him. It would under no other circumstances have been possible for me to be in Bratislava and not have contacted him. He knew.

It was probably only seconds, but it seemed like we stayed in those positions for a very long time. Finally Štefan said, "My father is here. Not far." He glanced over his shoulder. "I come sometimes."

"I found this place yesterday. I never knew it was here."

"I am sorry, Tomaš."

I stood. I think Štefan thought I was going to hit him. "I still can't really believe it happened."

"I also not."

"Why?"

"I have no answer."

"Did you love her?"

"Of course. You love her. Can you not see how anyone could?"

"Not 'anyone' slept with her. My wife."

He didn't answer for a moment, then he said, "That was a mistake. I make plenty mistakes in my life. But I am not sorry I feel love for Molly, even now, today, I feel this. A piece of my heart is forever broken. But I am very sorry, I have never been more sorry, that I hurt you, my friend, my dear and good friend. I hope some day will come when you no longer feel hate to me."

Then he walked away with his flowers.

I left on the afternoon train for the Tatras, arriving late at night and going back to the Poprad hotel where I stayed while Molly was in the hospital there. Early the next morning I took the mountain train to Starý Smokovec and located a room from a note tacked to a board at the station. It was the end of June, the weather was gorgeous and the mountain villages were filled with hikers, climbers, tourists. I didn't have much to put away, a backpack filled with climbing gear and one duffel bag of clothes. It was a nice room, high ornate ceilings and French doors that opened to a large ground floor balcony, where I could hang clothes to dry. I still live there.

Molly's ashes were buried in a family plot in La Mesa, California. Oddly, somehow it seemed to me that Molly was neither contained by nor exclusive to the jar of ashes under the California earth. Molly was still here, in the mountains where she died, and her plaque in the Mountaineers Symbolic Cemetery was where she rested, where I could be with her.

The equity money I got out of the house would last me in a place like the Tatras, if I only used it for living expenses, probably five or six years, but I needed something to do. My minimal skill in the

Slovak language was a major handicap, but I didn't need much Slovak to wash dishes in a hotel restaurant, which is the job I got the second day after arriving. It was a good job. Because no one in the kitchen spoke much English, I was able to expand my Slovak. I worked nights, from five in the afternoon until the last cleanup was over around midnight. My days were free to go into the mountains.

The summer passed.

I saw Štefan a few times. His main office was in Bratislava, but most of his work was in the mountains. My room was in a large subdivided house less than two kilometers from his office in the Starý Smokovec mountain rescue center building in the center of the village. Once I saw him through the big glass windows that opened into the lobby of the rescue center's A-frame, another time I saw him drinking with friends in the bar of the Hotel Uran, and another time boarding the narrow gauge train that went down the mountain to the depot in Poprad. Maybe I saw him once in the mountains, on the trail to the climbers hut below Rysy, but I can't be sure.

I spent all my free time in the mountains. After three months I had hiked every trail in the Tatras, climbed many of the most interesting solo routes. Not always solo. Sometimes I went with Malý Tomaš and Juraj. I met a young climber named Kazo (much better than I) and he showed me some of the most difficult routes in the Tatras. Kazo liked the big walls, liked climbs that took days, not hours, and I was getting a bit old and tired to keep up with him.

I was happy climbing. Although I did miss Molly's presence. I needed the clink of crampon steel and the snap of karabiners, the strength of the rope and security of the rock. It is so easy to get lost in the rhythm of moving upward on a rock wall. I felt invincible climbing. I could not be hurt. Because it didn't matter.

Being alone changed me. Made me more calm and accepting. Somehow having no one in my life was a new sort of freedom. One of the waitresses, nearly half my age, flirted with me and I liked to joke with her, but we never went out. I never asked her for anything. I think she probably just felt sorry for me. She had a boyfriend anyway.

On the first day of September, 1990, (then) MP Štefan Borák went missing somewhere in the mountains. He had left in the afternoon the day before to hike up to Teryho Chata, a mountaineers cabin in a rugged high valley. Since he wasn't expected, no one knew to miss him. There was a fierce electrical storm, followed by heavy rains that lasted all night. He was supposed to return the following afternoon and catch the train back to Bratislava, and when he didn't appear at the mountain rescue center in Starý Smokovec, a radio call to Teryho discovered that he never arrived there.

It was a horrible day. It had been raining steadily since midnight. The hilly streets in the village were awash. Visibility through the low clouds was hardly 500 meters. I was eating a late lunch at a kiosk across from the mountain rescue center when I saw the activity and knew they were going after someone. I remember thinking what a horrible mess it would be to search in such weather. Kazo pulled into the parking lot in his old Škoda car and I waved to him.

Kazo ran across the road in the pouring rain and asked me if I had heard.

"There's a rescue, it seems."

"Search, not yet rescue. It's Štefan."

"What do you mean it's Štefan?"

"Štefan is missing."

"Missing where?"

"Somewhere on way to Teryho Chata."

"I can't believe it. It's just a hike."

"All the same, he left late in the day yesterday and never got to Teryho last night."

I couldn't believe that Štefan was lost in these mountains, his mountains. Especially not from a hiking trail he must have been on a thousand times. I just shook my head. There had to be something else, maybe something happened in the storm . . .

"I must go now."

"I'm going with you," I said.

"That's good. We need everybody to search in this great weather. Helicopter cannot go."

We grouped into teams and outlined search areas. Kazo and I linked up and took a lower portion where the trail begins. It took us more than an hour to hike up to our area. We searched all afternoon and the rain never let up. They called us all in around sunset.

But I stayed. I didn't work for mountain rescue and I didn't take their orders. Neither did Kazo. He said if I stayed, so would he. Otherwise, he said with a smile, "tomorrow I'll just have to come looking for you, too."

About eight, the rain stopped. By that time we had decided to follow the trail as Štefan would have done, using our helmet lights, walking slowly and listening. We could reach Teryho before midnight if we moved steadily, and sleep there. It would be quicker to join the rescuers who were staying at the hut and begin searching from there in the morning than to come all the way back up from the village.

After a while there were stars, a quarter moon, and the clouds tumbled away like dust balls before a broom. Kazo led. I knew the trail, but he knew it infinitely better. We walked quietly, stopping from time to time just to listen.

We were halfway up, near the place where chains were bolted into the cliff wall to protect along a section of narrow, exposed ledge, when we heard the voice, a woman's voice, calling for help in German. Kazo, who understood quite a bit of German, answered. Her voice became louder, almost hysterical, screaming help and streams of other words. Her voice bounced off the rock walls and reverberated around us, making it impossible to find the direction.

We agreed that she was lower, not higher, and less than 100 meters away.

"What's she saying?" I asked Kazo.

"She is saying she thinks her husband is dead."

"Tell her to keep talking," I said.

"I already did," Kazo answered.

Kazo took the radio and called the rescue center, telling them what we were hearing.

"We have help in two, maybe two and one half, hours," Kazo said. "We have good weather now."

"I think she's back there," I said, pointing out the narrowest passage on the trail, "and down."

"Yes," Kazo agreed. "If we only brought one rope with us . . ."

"What is she saying now? The same thing?"

"She is saying now her leg is broken, and his leg is broken, and he is unconscious, and he is unconscious for a long time."

"I thought he was dead?"

Kazo shrugged. Who knew what was going on. "She has hysteria, I think."

"I can hear that in her voice."

"We are more than two and a half hours to Teryho," Kazo said. "But it is quicker to go down than up. If I go fast, I can meet them coming up and get one rope."

I agreed and told him to be careful moving fast down in the dark. He was out of sight in ten seconds.

"Do you speak English?" I called out.

"Only little. Please, please, you help, okay? Please help fast."

"We have to get a rope. Do you know how far down you are from the trail?"

"Understand, no. Please, help, please."

She repeated that over and over in English, sometimes saying streams of words in German. I moved back down the trail two or three steps at a time, stopping to listen, trying to home in on her voice. It was clearly below and not so far away. I leaned over to shine my helmet light over the edge, but the beam was fading as the battery wore down and penetrated very little distance. I moved farther down the trail, stopping to peer over the side every meter.

About 10 meters back from where we first heard her voice, while peering over the edge, I noticed that a small scrub tree was broken off. Then I noticed a black burn scar along the rocks nearby. There had been a lightning strike. But not the tree. The tree had been snapped off without being burned. I knew this was where she had gone over.

I stood at the edge of the drop-off and took off my helmet. I held it extended as far over the side as I could reach and pointed the light down. "Do you see a light?" I called out.

"I see, I see!" she screamed.

"Okay, I'm coming down. Stay close to the wall and cover your head. Do you understand. I'm coming down."

"I see, I see! Please help, please help."

I could only hope she was smart enough to understand that when I came down I might knock a lot of debris off ahead of me.

Why didn't I wait for Kazo? I don't know. I didn't think about it. I just couldn't stand listening to the terror in her voice, to her pleading for help, and I didn't want her to be alone anymore. And I believed I could do it.

It was not a sheer drop, more a steep slope, littered with scrub trees, deep cracks and boulders. I couldn't see much more than a few meters, but I could see that coming up wouldn't be too difficult, although going down in the dark took all my attention. She kept screaming in German and saying help in English. She said "no light, no light," and I could hear her crying. "I'm still coming down," I called out. Her voice was stronger, closer every minute.

"I see light!" she began screaming over and over. I had come down something like 30 or 40 meters by then. The slope had begun to flatten out; I was more crawling backwards then than down-climbing. If it had not been so wet I could almost have stood and walked down. The angle had softened to less than 45 degrees. I passed another small broken tree.

Sixty meters below the trail, I found them. The battery from my headlamp was almost gone, but I had enough light to see their situation. There was a man still wearing a large rucksack laying on his side wedged between two trees. I could see that he was burned. The woman, who had scrapes, cuts and bruises covering her face and arms, was next to him. She cried hysterically.

I moved over to the man, who was clearly dead, and then tried to calm the woman. I guessed that they were on the trail, probably going to or from Teryho, got caught in the storm, the man was struck by the lightning bolt I saw the evidence of when I went over the side, and the woman probably got hurt going down after him. Judging from their clothes and packs, if they were Germans, they were probably East Germans. I checked her leg and didn't think she had broken it. The index finger of her right hand was broken, though.

"It's all right," I told her as calmly as I could. "Help is coming soon."

She pushed me a little and pointed into the darkness farther down the slope. "Other man," she said. "Other man there."

There was someone else.

I knew before I went down that it was Štefan.

The couple had indeed been on their way to Teryho Chata when the man was struck by lighting and went over the side. His wife fell going after him. About an hour later, during a brief lull in the rain storm, Štefan had heard the woman's screams and went down. He lost his footing on the slippery granite and fell, tumbling past them and another 200 meters down the steepening slope. That's where I found him. Had he tumbled another 10 meters, he would have dropped over a ledge and fallen to certain death.

I stayed with him until first light, when the rescue helicopter took us out. Before that, Kazo and the other climbers reached the German couple. They brought her up first and then recovered her husband's body. By then it was dawn and the helicopter came.

Štefan had a concussion, and had broken his right leg and right arm. The leg was a compound fracture and he lost a lot of blood before it coagulated around the puncture. He went in and out of consciousness all night, and said he only thinks he remembers hearing the German woman's cries for help.

My battery was gone by the time I reached Štefan. There was some light from a bit of moon. At first, the way he was twisted, I thought he was dead. I remember thinking that he had saved my life in the mountains, on Nanga Parbat, and I could not stand to have him die in front of me in the Tatras. But he was alive. I put his head in my lap and held him against the cold and waited for the rescuers.

Abseil: See *rappel.* Term more commonly used in Britain and Europe.

Aid route: Any route up a wall that is too difficult to climb free, so that fixed ropes, ladders, and other devices are required.

Anchor: Borrowed from nautical usage, any location or any device used to secure and protect climbers from a fall.

Arête: A steep ridge line.

Belay anchor: See *belay.* A sling or runner attached to the rock face by a bolt or other means of securing to the rock, to which the belayer is secured to keep from getting pulled off the wall by the force of a climber's fall.

Belay: Borrowed from the nautical usage, essentially means securing a rope to a fixed point. In climbing, it is the action of making safe a climber's upward progress by securing the other end of the rope to which the climber is attached. The word is also used as a noun to indicate the place or location of the belayer.

Belayer: The climber who is responsible for the security of the upward climber, to keep him from falling. This is done by watching the rope to ensure that if a climber falls, he or she won't fall any farther than twice the distance to the last piece of protection.

Bolt: A metal rod with a hook to which a karabiner can be attached. Bolts are secured to the rock by means of drilling a hole and screwing it in.

Boulder problems: See *Yosemite scale.* A rating system devised to rate the difficulty of climbing on boulders, e.g., B1, B2, B3, with the higher number being more difficult.

Bouldering: Name for the sport of climbing on boulders which, being low to the ground, do not require ropes or artificial means of protection.

Cam: A mechanical device which is inserted into a crack and expanded to provide an anchor point.

Chalk: Used to dry the dampness on a climber's hands.

Chimney: A wide, vertical crack, usually wide enough for a climber to get inside.

Cleaning the pitch: The process of the second climber following the leader up and, removing along the way, protection placed by the leader, now no longer necessary as the second is on a top rope.

Crampons: Metal spikes attached to boots to provide more security when climbing or hiking over ice and snow.

Crux: The most technically difficult section of a climb.

Dihedral: A wide-angled, open corner along a rock face.

Figure-eight descender: A metal device named for its shape, with one of its two "eyes" smaller than the other; it is commonly used for descending down a rope (see *rappel, abseil*), and sometimes used as part of a belay system.

Fixed rope: When a rope is secured from above and a climber ascends using the rope for security.

Free climbing: When a climber ascends a wall without dependence on any equipment, except what is necessary to protect during a fall.

French EBS: Name of a particular (and old-fashioned) climbing shoe.

Friction climbing: Using the friction provided by the rubber sole of a climbing shoe against the rock to move upward.

Friend: A spring-loaded cam device that can be inserted into a crack to serve as an anchor point for protection.

Glissade: Essentially, sitting on a snow slope and sliding down.

Hammer: See *piton.* Used to pound pitons into cracks in rock walls.

Hand jams: Making a fist inside a crack and using it as a hold for moving upward.

Harness: A flat, nylon web stitched to fit around a climber's legs and waist, to which the rope is attached for safety. Most harnesses contain loops to which a variety of items may be clipped for handy use.

Heel-kicking: Descending a snow slope by digging one's heels into the snow, making steps.

Hex: An hexagonally shaped machine nut (now manufactured specifically for climbing), which can be wedged into cracks, attached to slings and used for protection.

Karabiners: Metal snap links, usually oval or pear-shaped, used for a variety of purposes, including attaching gear to a harness and clipping the rope to runners.

Leading: When the climber is above the belay anchor, using protection he or she places along the way. The protection is then removed as the second climber comes up via a top rope. See *cleaning the pitch.*

Locking karabiners: Self-locking karabiners to avoid the possibility of a climber forgetting to spin closed the screw-threaded spindle that locks the gate closed.

Mantling: Pushing up with the palms of one's hands to get over a ledge.

Nuts: See *hex.*

Pick: Slang term for an ice axe.

Pitch: A section of a climb, usually designated by the length of rope available; 50 meters is common.

Piton: A metal peg which is used like a bolt, but is hammered into the rock instead of being drilled. (See *hammer.*)

Post-holing: Trudging through deep, unmarked snow, so that the leader's legs leave deep holes.

Protection: Any of a number of devices climbers use to secure themselves against being harmed or killed in a fall; including cams, hexes, nuts.

Rack: See *sling.* An assortment of pieces of protection.

Rappel: Descending from a climb by means of sliding down a fixed, double rope, with the rope then pulled down. Friction to slow the climber's descent is provided by means of a variety of devices, including a figure-eight descender. Often shortened to "rap."

Robbins: Reference to Royal Robbins, a famous American climber from the earliest days of the sport.

Route: The line up a rock wall the climber has chosen to follow, usually picked for its difficulty or interesting elements.

Runners: Nylon or Perlon cords or straps used to protect a climber while climbing. It provides a point of attachment to the rock wall through which the climber's rope is secured with a karabiner.

Slab: A smooth rock face of between 30 and 60 degrees angle.

Sling: See *runners*. A longer runner which a climber can sling over his shoulder from which to hang pieces of protection and karabiners.

Top rope: A more secure method of climbing than leading, due to the belay anchor being above the climber, so the rope's tension is maintained without slack. (See *leading*.)

Wall: A smooth rock face of between 60 and 90 degrees angle.

Yosemite scale: A method of grading the difficulty of climbing routes, ranging from 5.0 to 5.14. After 5.10, route difficulty may be subdivided a, b, c, and d.